The Song of the Quarkbeast

Book Two of The Last Dragonslayer Series

JASPER FFORDE

HODDER

First published in Great Britain in 2011 by Hodder & Stoughton
An Hachette UK company

This paperback edition published 2012

3

Copyright © Jasper Fforde 2011

The right of Jasper Fforde to be identified as the Author
of the Work has been asserted by him in accordance with the
Copyright, Designs and Patents Act 1988.

A CIP catalogue record for this title is available from the British Library

B-format paperback ISBN 978 1 444 70725 0
A-format paperback ISBN 978 1 444 70726 7

Typeset in Bembo by Palimpsest Book Production Limited,
Falkirk, Stirlingshire

Printed and bound by Clays Ltd, St Ives plc

Hodder & Stoughton policy is to use papers that are natural, renewable
and recyclable products and made from wood grown in sustainable
forests. The logging and manufacturing processes are expected to
conform to the environmental regulations of the country of origin.

Hodder & Stoughton Ltd

For Maggy and Stu
With grateful thanks
for kindnesses too numerous to mention

The Song of the Quarkbeast

'For every Quarkbeast there is an equal and opposite Quarkbeast'

Miss Boolean Smith, Sorcerer (Rtd)

Where we are right now

I work in the magic industry. I think you'll agree it's pretty glamorous: a life full of spells, potions and whispered enchantments; of levitation, vanishings and alchemy. Of titanic fights to the death with the powers of darkness, of conjuring up blizzards and quelling storms at sea; of casting lightning bolts from mountains, and bringing statues to life in order to vanquish troublesome foes.

If only.

No, magic these days was simply *useful*. Useful in the same way that cars and dishwashers and can-openers are useful. The days of wild, crowd-pleasing stuff like commanding the oceans, levitating elephants and turning herring into taxi drivers were long gone, and despite the advent of a Big Magic* two months before, the return of unlimited magical powers had not yet happened. After a brief surge that generated weird cloud shapes and rain that tasted of elderflower cordial, the wizidrical power had dropped to nothing before

---

*It's a sort of rekindling of magic that happened two months before the time of this story, and in which Jennifer played a large part.

rising again almost painfully slowly. No one would be doing any ocean-commanding for a while, elephants would remain unlevitated and a herring wouldn't be losing anyone wanting to get to the airport. We had no foes to vanquish except the taxman, and the only time we got to fight the powers of darkness was during one of the Kingdom's frequent power cuts.

So while we at Kazam waited for magic to re-establish itself, it was very much business as usual: hiring out sorcerers to conduct low-level, mundane and very practical magic. You know the sort of thing: plumbing and rewiring, wallpapering and loft conversions. We also lifted cars for the city's clamping unit, conducted Flying Carpet pizza deliveries and could predict weather with 23 per cent more accuracy than SNODD-TV's favourite weather girl, Daisy Fairchild.

But I don't do any of that. I *can't* do any of that. I organise those who can. The job I do is 'Mystical Arts Management', or more simply put, I'm an agent. The person who does the deals, takes the bookings and then gets all the flak when things go wrong – and little of the credit when it goes right. The place I do all this is a company called Kazam, the biggest House of Enchantment in the world. To be honest that's not saying much – there are only two: Kazam and Industrial Magic, over in Stroud. Between us we have the only eight licensed sorcerers on the planet. And if you think that's a responsible job for a sixteen-year-old, you're right – I'm really only *acting* manager until the Great Zambini gets back.

If he does.

So as I said, it was very much business as usual at Kazam, and this morning we were going to try to find something that was lost. Not just 'mislaid-it-whoops' lost, which is easy, but 'never-to-be-found' lost, which is a good deal harder. We didn't much like finding lost stuff as in general lost stuff doesn't like to be found, but when work was slack, we'd do pretty much anything within the law. And that's why Perkins, Tiger and myself were sitting in my parked Volkswagen one damp autumn morning in a roadside rest area not six miles from our home town of Hereford, the capital city of the Kingdom of Snodd.

'Do you think a wizard even knows what a clock is *for*?' I asked, somewhat exasperated, as I had promised our client that we'd start at 9.30 a.m. *sharp*, and it was twenty past already. I'd told the sorcerers to get here at nine for a briefing, but I might as well have been talking to the flowers.

'If you have all the time in the world,' replied Tiger, referring to a sorcerer's often greatly increased life expectancy, 'then I suppose a few minutes either way doesn't matter so much.'

Horton or 'Tiger' Prawns was my assistant and had been with us only for the past two months. He was tall for his twelve years and had close-curled sandy-coloured hair and freckles that danced around a snub nose. Like most foundlings of that age, he wore his oversized hand-me-downs with a certain pride. He was here this morning to learn the peculiar problems associated with a finding – and with good reason. He was to take over from me in two years' time. Once I was eighteen, I was out.

Perkins nodded an agreement.

'Some wizards *do* seem to live a long time,' he observed. This was undoubtedly true, but they were always cagey about how they did it, and changed the subject to mice or onions or something when asked.

The Youthful Perkins was our best and only trainee all wrapped up in one. He had been at Kazam just over a year and was the only person in the company roughly my own age. He was good looking, too, and aside from suffering bouts of overconfidence that sometimes got him into trouble when he spelled more quickly than he thought, he would be good for the company and good for magic in general. I liked him, too, but since his particular field of interest was remote suggestion – the skill of projecting thoughts into people's heads at a distance – I didn't know whether I actually liked him or he was *suggesting* I like him, which was creepy and unethical all at the same time. In fact, the whole remote suggestion or 'seeding' idea was banned once it was discovered to be the key ingredient behind advertising and promoting talentless boy bands, something that had until then been something of a mystery.

I looked at my watch again. The sorcerers* we were waiting for were the Amazing Dennis 'Full' Price and Lady Mawgon. Despite their magical ability, Mystical Arts Practitioners – to give them their official title – could barely get their clothes on in the right order, and often needed to be reminded to have a bath and attend regular mealtimes. Wizards are like that – erratic, petulant, forgetful, passionate, and *hugely* frustrating. But the one thing they weren't was boring, and after a difficult start when I first came to work here, I now regarded them all with a great deal of fondness – even the really insane ones.

'I should really be back at the Towers revising,' fretted the Youthful Perkins, who had his Magic Licence hearing that afternoon and was understandably a bit jumpy.

'Full Price suggested you come along to observe,' I explained. 'Finding lost stuff is all about teamwork.'

'Do sorcerers like teamwork?' asked Tiger, who, after ice cream and waffles, enjoyed questions more than anything else.

---

*After a well-argued plea for gender equality at the World Magic Expo of 1962, 'sorcerers' refers to male or female practitioners. The feminine 'sorceress' is no longer used, except by some of the old duffers who think that a female sorcerer's place is in the home, conjuring up food and cleaning the house by thought power alone.

'The old days of lone wizards mixing weird potions in the top of the North Tower are over,' I said. 'They've got to learn to work together, and it's not just me who says it – the Great Zambini was very keen on rewriting the rulebook.' I looked at my watch. 'I hope they actually *do* turn up,' I added, for as Kazam's acting manager in the Great Zambini's absence, I was the one who did the grovelling apologies to any disgruntled clients – something I did more than I would have liked.

'Even so,' said Perkins, 'I've passed my Finding Module IV, and always found the practice hiding slipper, even when it was hidden under Mysterious X's bed.'

This was true, and while finding something random like a slipper was good practice if you wanted to learn to find stuff, there was more to it than that. In the Mystical Arts, there always is. The only thing you really get to figure out after a lifetime of study is that there's more stuff to figure out. Frustrating and enlightening, all in one.

'The slipper had no issues with being found,' I said in an attempt to explain the unexplainable. 'If something doesn't want to be found, then it's harder. The Mighty Shandar could hide things in plain sight by simply *occluding* them from view. He demonstrated the technique most famously with an unseen elephant in the room during the 1826 World Magic Expo.'

'Is that where the "elephant in the room" expression comes from?'

'Yes; his name was Daniel.'

'You should be taking the Magic Test on my behalf,' remarked Perkins gloomily. 'You know a lot more than I do; there are whole tracts of the *Codex Magicalis*[*] I haven't even read.'

'I've been here three years longer than you,' I pointed out, 'so I'm bound to know more. But having me take your test would be like asking a person with no hands to sit your piano exam.'

No one knew why some people could do magic and others couldn't. I'm not good on the theory behind magic, other than knowing it's a fusion between science and faith, but the practical way of looking at it is this: magic swirls about us like an invisible fog of energy which can be tapped by those gifted enough using a variety of techniques that centre around layered spelling, mumbled incantations and a channelled burst of concentrated thought from the index fingers. The technical name for this energy was 'the variable electro-gravitational mutable subatomic force,' which doesn't mean anything at all – confused scientists just gave it an important-sounding name so as not to lose face. The more usual term was 'wizidrical energy', or, more simply, 'the crackle'.

[*] The so-called 'Book of Magic', which, while full of useful stuff, also has a lot in it that is nonsense. The skill is deciding which is which.

'By the way,' said Perkins in a breezy manner, 'I've got two tickets to see Jimmy 'Daredevil' Nuttjob have himself fired from a cannon through a brick wall.'

Jimmy Nuttjob was the Ununited Kingdom's most celebrated travelling daredevil, and tickets to see his madcap stunts were much in demand. He had eaten a car tyre to live orchestral accompaniment the year before; it had been a great show until he nearly choked on the valve.

'Who are you taking?' I asked, glancing at Tiger. The 'will Perkins gather up the courage to ask me out?' issue had been going on for a while.

Perkins cleared his throat as he built up the courage. 'You, if you want to come.'

I stared at the road for a moment, then said: 'Who, me?'

'Yes, of course you,' said Perkins.

'You might have been talking to Tiger.'

'Why would I ask Tiger to watch a lunatic fire himself through a brick wall?'

'Why *wouldn't* you ask me?' asked Tiger in a mock-aggrieved tone. 'Watching some idiot damage themselves might be just my thing.'

'That's entirely possible,' agreed Perkins, 'but while there's a prettier alternative, you'll always remain ninth or tenth on my list.'

We all fell silent.

8

'Pretty?' I said, swivelling in the driver's seat to face him, 'you want to ask me out because I'm pretty?'

'Is there a problem with asking you out because you're pretty?'

'I think you blew it,' said Tiger with a grin. 'You should be asking her out because she's smart, witty, mature beyond her years and every moment in her company makes you want to be a better person – pretty of face should be at the *bottom* of the list.'

'Oh, blast,' said Perkins despondently. 'It should, shouldn't it?'

'At last!' I muttered as we heard the distinctive *dugadugadugaduga* of Lady Mawgon's motorcycle, and we climbed out of the car as she came to a stop. I caught her eye almost immediately, but wished I hadn't as she was wearing her 'I'm about to harangue Jennifer' sort of look. Of course, being harangued by Lady Mawgon was nothing new; in fact, I was often harangued by her at lunch, dinner and teatime – and at random times in between. She was our most powerful sorcerer, and also the crabbiest. She was so crabby, in fact, that even really crabby people put their crabbiness aside for a few minutes to write gushing yet mildly sarcastic fan letters.

'Lady Mawgon,' I said in a bright voice, bowing low as protocol dictated, 'I trust the day finds you well?'

'An idiotic expression made acceptable only because

it is adrift in a sea of equally idiotic expressions,' she muttered grumpily, stepping from the motorcycle that she rode side-saddle. 'Is that little twerp attempting to hide behind what you jokingly refer to as a car?'

'Good morning,' said Tiger in his best 'gosh, didn't see you there, I wasn't really hiding' voice, 'you are looking *most* well this morning.'

Tiger was lying. Lady Mawgon looked terrible, with lank hair, a complexion like dented bells and a sour, pinched face. Her lips had never seen a smile, and rarely passed an intentional friendly word. She was dressed in a long black bell-shaped crinoline dress that was buttoned up to her throat in one direction, and swept the floor in the other. When she moved it was as if on roller skates; she didn't so much walk as *glide* across the ground in a very disturbing manner. Tiger had bet me half a moolah that she actually did wear roller skates. Trouble was, neither of us could think of a good, safe or respectful method of finding out.

She greeted Perkins more politely as he was, like her, of the wizidrical calling, and talked briefly about his Magic Test and how important it was he passed. She didn't waste a salutation on either of us as Tiger and I were foundlings and thus of little social rank or regard. Despite our low status, our presence aggravated Lady Mawgon badly as Tiger and I were crucial to the smooth running of the company. It was how Kazam's founder the Great Zambini liked it. He always felt that foundlings were better equipped to deal with the somewhat bizarre world of Mystical Arts Management. 'Pampered civilians,' as he put it, 'would panic at the weirdness or think they knew better, or try to improve things, or get greedy and try to cash in.' He was probably right.

'While you're here,' announced Lady Mawgon, breaking into my thoughts, 'I need to run a test spell later this morning.'

'How many Shandars, ma'am?'

The 'Shandar' was the unit of wizidrical power, named after the Mighty Shandar himself, a mage so powerful his footsteps spontaneously caught fire when he walked. The practical use of flaming footprints was questionable and most likely just for dramatic effect – the Mighty Shandar was not only the most powerful wizard who had ever lived, but also something of a showman.

'About ten MegaShandars,'* said Lady Mawgon sullenly, annoyed at having to suffer the ignominy of having to run her test spells past me first.

'That's a considerable amount of crackle,' I said as I wondered what she was up to, and hoped she wouldn't attempt to bring her pet cat Pusskins back to some sort of semi-life, an act not only *seriously* creepy, but highly frowned upon. 'May I enquire as to what you are planning to do?'

---

*One thousand Shandars = one MegaShandar, more usually referred to as a 'Meg' after 'Old Meg McMeddoes', an early proponent of Magical Field Theory.

'I'm going to try and hack into the Dibble Storage Coils. It may help us with the bridge job.'

I breathed a sigh of relief. This changed matters considerably, and she was right. We had agreed to rebuild Hereford's medieval bridge on Friday, and we needed all the help we could get, which was why Perkins was taking his Magic Test today rather than next week. He'd still be a novice, but six sorcerers would be better than five – magic always worked better with the wizards in use divisible by three.[*]

'Let me see,' I said, consulting my pocketbook to check we had no clashes. Two sorcerers spelling at the same time could deplete the crackle, and there is nothing worse than running out of steam when only two-thirds of the way through the spell – a bit like having a power cut just when you get to the good bit in a book.

'At eleven the Price Brothers are moving Snamoo,[†] so any time after eleven fifteen would be good – but I'll double-check with Industrial Magic just in case.'

'Eleven fifteen it is,' replied Lady Mawgon stonily. 'You may observe, if you so choose.'

'I'll be there,' I replied, then added cautiously: 'Lady

[*] No one knows why. The 'Rule of Three' crops up often and is often referred to as 'Mandrake's 3rd Dictum' after the sorcerer who first wrote about it.
[†] Snamoo is the Snodd Seaworld's performing walrus. He can play *Eine Kleine Nachtmusik* on a xylophone, among other tricks. He only liked being moved by the Prices, and it's tricky to argue with 1.4 tons of recalcitrant sea-mammal.

Mawgon, please don't think me insensitive, but any attempt to reanimate Mr Pusskins on the back of the Dibble Storage Coils hacking enchantment might be looked on disfavourably by the other wizards.'

Her eyes narrowed and she gave me one of those stares that seem to hit the back of my skull like a dozen hot needles.

'None of you have any idea what Mr Pusskins meant to me. Now, what are we doing here?'

'Waiting for the Amazing Dennis Price.'

'How I deplore poor timekeeping,' she said, despite being almost half an hour late herself. 'Got any money? I'm starving.'

Perkins gave her a one-moolah coin.

'Most kind. Walk with me, Perkins.'

And she glided silently off towards a roadside snack bar at the other end of the lay-by.

'Do you want anything?' asked Perkins as he made to follow Lady Mawgon.

'Eating out gives foundlings ideas above their station,' came Lady Mawgon's decisive voice, quickly followed by an admonishment to the owner of the snack bar: 'How much for a bacon roll? Scandalous!'

'A running sore has more charm,' said Tiger, leaning against the car, 'and since when was a roadside snack bar eating out? That's like saying listening to the radio out of doors is like going to a live show.'

'She is an astonishing sorceress of considerable

power and commitment, so don't be impertinent. Or at least,' I added, 'not within earshot.'

'Speaking of live shows,' said Tiger in a lowered voice, 'will you go to Jimmy 'Daredevil' Nuttjob's stunt show with Perkins?'

'Probably not,' I said with a sigh, 'it's not a good idea to date someone you work with. If he and I are meant to be, it'll certainly wait the two years until I leave.'

'Good,' said Tiger.

'Why is that good?'

'Because he may give away your ticket, and I'd like to watch someone with more bravery than sense being fired from a cannon into a brick wall.'

'Is there a support act?'

'A brass band, cheerleaders and someone who can juggle with bobcats.'

We turned to see a taxi approaching. It was the Amazing Dennis 'Full' Price, and after I had paid for the taxi, he climbed out and looked around.

'Sorry I'm late,' he said, demonstrating the difference between him and Lady Mawgon almost immediately. 'I got delayed talking to Wizard Moobin. He wants you to witness an experiment he's got cooking.'

'A dangerous one?' I asked with some concern. Wizard Moobin had destroyed more laboratories than I'd had cold and inedible dinners.

'Does he know any other?' he replied. 'Where's Mawgon?'

Jasper Fforde

I nodded in the direction of the roadside snack bar.

'Not with her own money, I'll be bound,' he said, and after giving us a wink, strode off to talk to her.

'Full' Price was another of our licensed operatives. He and his brother David – known as 'Half' – were famous as the most *unidentical* identical twins on record. David was tall and thin and lofty and prone to swaying in a high wind, while Dennis was short and squat like a giant pink pumpkin, only with arms and legs. They hailed from the ramshackle collection of warlord-controlled regions in mid-Wales that were loosely referred to as the 'Cambrian Empire'. Details were sparse, but it seemed the Prices had refused to work with the well-named Cambrian potentate 'Tharv the Insane', and then made their way to the Kingdom of Hereford to escape. They joined up with the Great Zambini soon after, and had been at Kazam for over twenty years.

As Tiger and I stood there smelling the faint aroma of frying bacon on the breeze, a Rolls-Royce whispered to a halt next to us.

In pursuit of lost stuff

The Rolls-Royce was one of the top-of-the-range six-wheeled Phantom Twelves. It was as big as a yacht, twice as luxurious and had paintwork so perfect it looked like a pool of black paint sitting in the air. The chauffeur opened the rear passenger door and a well-dressed girl climbed out. She was not much older than myself, but from a world far removed from the upbringing of a foundling – a world of privilege, cash and a sense of entitlement. I should have hated her, but I didn't.

I envied her.

'Miss Strange?' she said, striding confidently forward, hand outstretched. 'Miss Shard is glad to make your acquaintance.'

'Who's she talking about?' asked Tiger under his breath, looking around.

'Herself, I think,' I said, smiling broadly to welcome her. 'Good morning, Miss Shard, thank you for coming. I'm Jennifer Strange.'

This was our client. She didn't look old enough to have lost something badly enough to call us, but you never knew.

'You must call one Ann,' she said kindly. 'Your recent exploits of a magical variety filled one with a sense of thrilling trepidation.'

She was talking in Longspeak, the formal language of the upper classes, and it seemed that she was not fluent in Shortspeak, the everyday language of the Ununited Kingdoms.

'I'm sorry?'

'It was a singular display of inspired audaciousness,' she replied.

'Is that good?' I asked, still unsure of her meaning.

'Most certainly,' she replied. 'We followed your adventures with great interest.'

'We?'

'Myself and my client. A gentleman of some knowledge, position and bearing.'

She was undoubtedly referring to someone of nobility. By long tradition royals in the Ununited Kingdoms employed others to do almost everything for them; only the very poorest did anything for themselves. It was said that when King Wozzle of Snowdonia tired of eating he employed someone to do it for him. After the inevitable weight loss and death, he was succeeded by his brother.

'I can't understand a word she's saying,' whispered Tiger.

'Tiger,' I said, keen to get rid of him before she took offence, 'why not fetch Dennis and Lady Mawgon, hmm?'

'Were they of a disingenuous countenance?' Miss Shard asked, smiling politely.

'Were who of what?'

'The Dragons,'* she said, 'were they . . . unpleasant?'

'Not really,' I replied in a guarded fashion. Almost everyone wanted to know about the Dragons, and I revealed little. They valued discretion more than anything. I said nothing more, and she got the message.

'I defer to your circumspection on this issue,' she replied, with a slight bow.

'O-kay,' I said, not really getting that either, 'this is the team.'

Tiger had returned with Full Price and Lady Mawgon with Perkins bringing up the rear in his 'observing' capacity. I introduced them all and Miss Shard said something about how it was 'entirely convivial' and 'felicitous' to meet them on 'this auspicious occasion', and in return they shook hands but remained wary. It pays to distance oneself from clients, especially ones who use too many long words.

'What do you want us to find?' asked Lady Mawgon, who was always keen to get straight to the point.

'It's a ring that belonged to the mother of my client,' she said. 'He would be here personally to present his

---

*She was referring to Jennifer's connection with Dragons. Of the only two Dragons on the planet, she knew them both well enough for them to return her calls. Dragons usually don't.

request, but finds himself unavailable owing to a prolonged sabbatical.'

'Has he seen a doctor about it?' asked Tiger.

'About what?'

'His prolonged sabbatical. It sounds very painful.'

She stared at him for a moment.

'It means he's on holiday.'

'Oh.'

'I apologise for the ignorance of the staff,' said Lady Mawgon, glaring at Tiger, 'but Kazam sadly requires foundling labour to function. Staff can be so difficult these days, wanting frivolous little luxuries like food, shoes, wages . . . and human dignity.'

'Please don't worry,' said Miss Shard politely, 'foundlings can be refreshingly direct sometimes.'

'About the ring?' I asked, feeling uncomfortable with all this talk of foundlings.

'Nothing remarkable,' replied Miss Shard, 'gold, plain, large like a thumb-ring. My client is keen to return it to his mother as a seventieth birthday gift.'

'Not a problem,' remarked Full Price. 'Do you have anything that might have been in contact with this ring?'

'Such as your client's mother?' said Tiger in an impish manner.

'There's this,' replied Miss Shard, producing a ring from her pocket. 'This was on her middle finger, and would have clicked against the lost ring. You can observe the marks, look.'

Lady Mawgon took the ring and stared at it intently for a moment before she clenched it in her fist, murmured something and then opened her hand. The ring hovered an inch above her open palm, revolving slowly. She passed it to Full Price, who held it up to the light and then popped it in his mouth, clicked it against his fillings for a moment, then swallowed it.

'Meant to do that,' he said in the tone of someone who didn't.

'Really?' asked Miss Shard dubiously, doubtless wondering how she was going to get it back and in what condition.

'Don't worry,' said Full Price cheerfully, 'amazing how powerful cleaning agents are these days.'

'Why did you ask us to meet you here?' asked Lady Mawgon, thankfully changing the subject.

It was a good question. We were on an unremarkable lay-by and rest area on the Ross–Hereford road near a village called Harewood End.

'This is where she lost it,' replied Miss Shard, 'she had it when she got out of a car here, and when she left she didn't have it any more.'

Lady Mawgon looked at me, then at our client, then at Dennis. She smelled the air, mumbled something and looked thoughtful for a moment.

'It's still around here somewhere,' she said, 'but this

ring does not want to be found. You agree, Mr Price?'

'I do,' he said, rubbing his fingers together as he felt the texture of the air.

'How can you know this?' asked Miss Shard.

'It's been lost for thirty-two years, ten months and nine days,' murmured Lady Mawgon thoughtfully, 'am I correct?'

Miss Shard stared at her for a moment. It appeared this was indeed true, and it was impressive. Mawgon had picked up the lingering memory that human emotion can instil in even the most inert of objects.

'Something that wants to be lost is lost for a good reason,' added Full Price. 'Why doesn't your client give his mother some chocolates instead?'

'Or flowers,' said Lady Mawgon. 'We can't help you. Good day.'

She turned to move away.

'We'll pay you a thousand moolah.'*

Lady Mawgon stopped. A thousand moolah was serious cash.

'A thousand?'

'My client is inclined towards generosity regarding his mother.' Lady Mawgon looked at Full Price, then at me.

'Five thousand,' she said.

*The moolah is the unit of currency in the Kingdom of Snodd. One hundred Herefordian washers = 1 moolah, which is roughly equivalent to the spondoolip, at 2007 exchange rates.

'Five thousand?' echoed our client. 'To find a ring?'

'A ring that doesn't want to be found,' replied Lady Mawgon, 'is a ring that *shouldn't* be found. The price reflects the risks.'

Miss Shard looked at us all in turn.

'I accept,' she said at last, 'and I will wait here for results. But no find, no fee. Not even a call-out charge.'

'We usually charge for an attempt—' I began, but Mawgon cut me short.

'We're agreed,' she said, and made a grimace that I suspect may have been her version of a smile.

Miss Shard shook hands with us again and climbed back into her Rolls-Royce, and a few seconds later the limousine moved off to park opposite the snack bar. Class was no barrier to the allure of a bacon sandwich.

'With the greatest of respect,' I said, turning to Lady Mawgon, 'if it gets around that we've been fleecing clients, Kazam's reputation will plummet. And what's more, I think it's unprofessional.'

'How can civilians hate us any more?' she asked disdainfully and with some truth, as despite our best efforts, the general public still regarded the magic trade with grave suspicion. 'More importantly,' added Lady Mawgon, 'I've seen the accounts. How long do you think we can give our skills away for free? Besides, she's in a Phantom Eight. Loaded with moolah.'

'It's Phantom Twelve,' murmured Tiger, who, being a boy, knew precisely the difference.

'Shall we get a move on?' said Full Price. 'I've got to move a walrus in an hour, and if I'm late David will start without me.'

'The sooner the better,' said Lady Mawgon, dismissing Tiger and me with a sweep of her hand so she and Full could have a meeting. I leaned against the car with Tiger, took several deep breaths and watched them talk.

'I lost my luggage once,' said Tiger thoughtfully, eager to contribute something relevant to the 'losing stuff' conversation. 'On an orphanage trip to the steel mills of Port Talbot.'

'What was it like?' I asked, glad of the distraction and never having been to the industrial heartland of the Ununited Kingdoms myself.

'Red with castors and an internal pocket for toiletries.'

'I meant Port Talbot.'

'Oh. Hot and very noisy.'

'The steam hammers?'

'The steam hammers were fine. It's the *singing*.'

We watched as Perkins circled Mawgon and Price, attempting to hear what was going on.

'Is Perkins going to get his licence, do you think?'

'He'd better. We need him for the bridge job. Fumble that and we'll all look a bit stupid.'

'And on live TV, too.'

'Don't remind me.'

Our concerns about Perkins will become only too apparent when you consider that the person we had to get the licence from was the one person more boneheaded and corrupt than our glorious ruler King Snodd – his Useless Brother, who was the Minister for Infernal Affairs, the less-than-polite term used to describe the office that dealt with all things magical.

'You swallowed it?' we heard Lady Mawgon demand angrily. 'Why in Snorff's name would you do something like that?'

She must have meant the ring, and since there wasn't any real answer to this, Full Price just shrugged in a lame manner. I walked up, ready to mediate if required. Mawgon put out her hand.

'Hand it over, Dennis.'

Full Price looked annoyed, but knew better than to argue. He closed his eyes and took a deep breath, then made a series of odd facial expressions and huffy-exertion noises before rolling up his sleeve. We saw the shape of the ring *beneath* the skin as it moved down his forearm, and as it migrated he sweated and grunted with the effort. I had seen this done several times before, the most recent to expel a bullet lodged perilously close to a patient's spine, the result of a shooting accident.

'Ah!' said Full Price, as the ring-shaped lump moved across the top of his hand. 'Ow, ow, *OW*!'

The ring travelled down the tighter skin of his finger, rotated around his fingertip and, after a lot of swearing, he succeeded in expelling it from under his nail-bed.

'That is *so* gross,' said Tiger.

'I agree,' replied Perkins, 'but it's sort of impossible not to look, don't you think?'

'There,' said Full Price, wiping off the ring and handing it to Mawgon. 'Happy now?'

But Lady Mawgon was already thinking of other things. She took the ring, murmured something around it and handed it back to Dennis, who held it tightly in his fist.

'I don't like the feel of this,' he said. 'Something bad happened.'

'I agree,' replied Mawgon, taking out a small crystal bottle with a silver stopper. We had stepped back to allow them to work, and Perkins, now fully mystified by what was going on, had joined us.

'They'll try to animate the memory,' I said.

'Gold has a memory?'

'Everything has a memory. Gold's memory is quite tedious – got mined, got crushed, went to the smelters, got banged with a hammer – big yawn. No, we're looking for a stronger memory that has been induced in the gold – the recollections of the person wearing it.'

'You can transfer your memories to inanimate objects?'

'Certainly. And the stronger you feel for something, the longer it will stick around. Some people think that objects like jewellery and paintings and vintage cars actually have a *soul*, but as far as we know they don't − just the memories of the people who have been around them. The more something is loved, enjoyed and valued, the stronger the memory, and the more we can read into it.'

'And the crystal bottle?'

'Watch and learn.'

Lady Mawgon placed a single drop on the ring that Full Price was holding, and in an instant the ring had morphed into a small dog that was sitting on the floor wagging its tail happily. It sparkled slightly, indicating that it was not real, and seemed to be made of solid gold.

'Good boy,' said Lady Mawgon, 'find it.'

The small memory-dog* gave a low bark, then scuttled off happily, sniffing the ground this way and that as it tried to remember where the ring might have gone. Lady Mawgon and Full Price followed the terrier away from the road, opened a gate to let it in and then chased the small dog across a field, much to the amusement of several cows. Mawgon and Full

---

*The technical term is a *Canis mnemonicus*, or 'mnemonic hound'. The ability of dogs to find things has a long tradition, and was exploited quite early on by sorcerers.

Price stopped occasionally as the memory-dog paused to think for a while or scratch its ear with a hind leg, then carried on as it chased off in another direction. It would often double back on itself as it tried to catch the memory-scent, all the while with Lady Mawgon's index finger steadily pointed at it. Once, it thought its tail was the quarry and snapped at it, then realised and moved on.

'I wonder what did happen to it?' said Tiger as we followed the sorcerers and the dog across the field, over a stile and a smaller road, then into a small wood.

'Happened to what?'

'My luggage,' replied Tiger, who wasn't yet done on his missing luggage problem. 'Luckily, it didn't have anything in it. I don't have any possessions. In fact, the luggage was my only possession. It was what I was found in.'

Owning very little or even being found in a red suitcase with castors and a separate internal pocket for toiletries was not unusual when you consider Tiger's foundling heritage. He had been abandoned on the steps of the Sisterhood of the Blessed Lady of the Lobster, the same as me, then sold into servitude with Kazam Mystical Arts until he was eighteen. I still had two years to run before I could apply for citizenship; Tiger had six. We didn't complain because this was how things were. There were a lot of orphans owing to the hideously wasteful and annoyingly frequent Troll Wars, and hotels, fast-food joints and laundries needed the cheap labour that foundlings could provide. Of the twenty-three kingdoms, duchies, socialist collectives, public limited companies and ramshackle potentates that made up the Ununited Kingdoms, only three of them had outlawed the trade in foundlings. Unluckily for us, the Kingdom of Snodd was not one of them.

'When we have some surplus crackle we'll retrieve your luggage,' I said, knowing how valuable any connection to parents was to a foundling. I had been left on the front seat of the Volkswagen Beetle that I drove today, and little would part me from my car.

'It's okay,' he said, demonstrating the selflessness and humility with which most foundlings comforted themselves. 'It can wait.'

We followed Mawgon, Full Price and the memory-dog out of the small wood and through a gate into an abandoned farm. Brambles, creeper and hazel saplings had grown over many of the red-brick buildings, and rusty machinery stood in abandoned barns with dilapidated roofs. No one had been here for a while. The memory-dog ran across the yard and stopped at an abandoned water well, where it wagged its tail excitedly. As soon as Lady Mawgon caught up with it she made a flourish and the dog started to chase its tail until it was nothing more than a golden blur, then it changed back to the ring again, which continued spinning on a flagstone with a curious humming noise.

Lady Mawgon picked up the ring and gave it back to me. It was still warm and smelled of puppies. Full Price pulled an old door off the wellhead, and we all gazed down the brick-lined well. Far below in the inky blackness I could see a small circle of sky with the shape of our heads as our reflections stared back up at us.

'It's in there,' she said.

'And there it should stay,' replied Full Price, who still wasn't happy. 'I can feel something wrong.'

'How wrong?' I asked.

'Seventh circle of Wrong. I can sense the lingering aftertaste of an old spell, too.'

There was silence for a moment as everyone took this in, and a coldness seemed to emanate up from the well.

'I can sense something, too,' said Perkins, 'like that feeling you get when someone you don't like is looking over your shoulder.'

'It doesn't want to be found,' said Full Price.

'No,' said Perkins, '*someone* doesn't want it to be found.'

They all looked at one another. Missing objects are one thing, but purposefully hidden objects quite another.

'I can think of five thousand good reasons to find it,' said Lady Mawgon, 'so find it we shall.'

She put her hand above the well in order to draw the ring from the mud below, but instead of the ring rising, her hand was tugged sharply downwards.

'It's been anchored and resists my command,' she said with a voice tinged more with intrigue than concern. 'Mr Price?'

Full joined her and they both attempted to lift the ring from the well. But no sooner had they started the lift than a low rumble seemed to come from the earth beneath our feet and the bricks that made up the low wall started to shift. Tiger and I took a step back but the others simply watched as an old and long-forgotten enchantment moved the bricks into a new configuration, sealing the wellhead tight. Within a few seconds there was only a solid brick cap.

'Fascinating,' said Lady Mawgon, for this was in effect a battle of wits between sorcerers – just separated by thirty years. Whatever enchantment had been left to keep the ring hidden, it was still powerful.

'I vote we walk away now,' said Full Price.

'It's a challenge,' retorted Lady Mawgon excitedly, 'and I like a challenge.'

She was more animated than I had seen her for a while, and within a few minutes had formulated a plan.

'Right, then,' she said, 'listen closely. Mr Price is going to prise open the wellhead using a standard

Magnaflux Reversal. How long can you keep it open, Mr Price?'

Full Price sucked air in through his teeth thoughtfully.

'About thirty seconds – maximum forty.'

'Should be enough. But since the ring is *resisting* a lift we will have to send someone down to get it. I will levitate them head downwards to the bottom of the well, where they will retrieve the ring. You, Mr Perkins, will channel crackle to Mr Price and myself. Can you do that?'

'To the best of my ability, ma'am,' replied Perkins happily. Lady Mawgon had never asked him to assist her before.

'He doesn't have a licence,' I said, 'you know what the penalty could be.'

'Who's going to snitch on him?' she retorted. 'You?'

'I can't allow it,' I said.

'It's Perkins' call,' said Mawgon, looking at me angrily. 'Mr Perkins?'

Perkins looked at me and then Lady Mawgon.

'I'll do it.'

I didn't say anything more as we all knew the consequences of operating without a licence were extremely unpleasant. The relationship between the populace and Mystical Art Practitioners had always been one of suspicion, a relationship not helped by a regrettable episode in the nineteenth century when a wayward sorcerer who called himself 'Blix the Thoroughly Barbarous' thought he could use his powers to achieve world domination. He was eventually defeated, but the damage to magic's reputation had been deep and far reaching. Bureaucracy now dominated the industry with a sea of paperwork and licensing requirements. Reinventing sorcery as a useful and safe commodity akin to electricity had taken two centuries and wasn't done yet. Once lost, trust is a difficult thing to regain. But I said nothing more. I was there to remind them of the rules, not to police them.

'Good,' said Lady Mawgon, 'then let's begin.'

'Wait a minute,' said Tiger, who had just figured out that the 'going down a well head first' plan doubtless included him as he was lightest, 'it's going to be as dark as the belly of a whale down there.'

I passed him a glass globe from my bag, just one of the many useful objects that I liked to have with me on assignment.

'It runs off sarcasm,' I said, handing it to him.

'Great,' he replied, and the globe lit up brightly.*

'You'll also need this,' I told him as I tied a toddler's shoe around his neck. When done, I spoke into the matching shoe I held in my hand.

'Can you hear me?'

---

*The correct term for this is 'sarcoluminescence' and it efficiently converts emotion to power, one of the central pillars of magic. It is one of the first spells to be taught to trainees.

'Yes,' he replied, 'I can hear you. Do I have to go down a well upside down while being sarcastic with a shoe tied around my neck?'

'You could use a conch* to talk,' said Perkins helpfully, before he added less than helpfully: 'only we haven't got any.'

'And you'd look pretty daft with a conch tied to your head,' added Full Price.

'Like I am so not worried about looking a twit,' said Tiger, and the globe went up to full brightness again.

'You're going to have to find the ring within thirty seconds,' announced Lady Mawgon, 'and since it might be tricky to find in the rank, fetid, disease-ridden muddy water, you'll need my help.'

'You're coming down too?'

'Good Lord, no. What do you think I am? An idiot?'

'I'm not sure it would be healthy to answer that question,' replied Tiger carefully.

'Answer it how you want – I'd ignore you anyway. Here.'

She handed him a neat leather glove and told him to put it on while she placed its pair on herself. Like toddlers' shoes and conches, gloves have left-and-right symmetry and can thus be *amicably* linked to one

---

*Conch: the shell of a sea snail that lends itself well to medium-range communication. Giant clams have been used (and still are) for transcontinental message transmission. Toddlers' shoes have a range of about sixty yards, but are a lot lighter to carry than conches, and not as delicate.

another to work together while separated by physical distance. Lady Mawgon clenched and unclenched her fist as Tiger's hand did the same. She revolved her arm around in the air and the paired glove copied her actions perfectly while Tiger stared at his arm and hand. He was, to all intents and purposes, now partly Lady Mawgon. Better still, the gloves were feedback enabled. Lady Mawgon would be able to feel what Tiger was feeling.

'How's that?' asked Lady Mawgon.

'Peculiar,' he replied. 'What if I can't find the blasted ring in thirty seconds?'

'Then the well will close with you inside and it's entirely possible you'll spend the rest of your life at the bottom of a deep well with only bacteria and leeches for company, then utter darkness when your sarcasm runs out.'

'I'm not so sure I want to do this any more.'

'Don't be such a crybaby,' chided Lady Mawgon. 'If our roles were reversed and you were the skilled practitioner and I was the worthless foundling with the silly name, I'd be down that hole like an actor after a free lunch.'

Tiger looked across at me and raised an eyebrow.

'You don't have to do this if you don't want to,' I told him.

'Lady Mawgon is relating a worst-case scenario,' said Full Price in a soothing voice. 'We'll call the fire brigade if we can't reopen the well. The longest you'll be trapped is an hour.'

'Then how could I possibly refuse?' replied Tiger grumpily. 'Let's get on with it.'

Lady Mawgon and Full Price took up their stances, index fingers at the ready. At the count of three Full Price pointed at the wellhead and the bricks opened again, revealing the deep hole in the ground. At the same time, Lady Mawgon pointed at Tiger and my young assistant was lifted from the ground, turned upside down and plunged head first down the well. We peered over to look in. It was all dark until Tiger said 'Gosh, what super fun this is' and the globe lit up to reveal a brick-lined well all the way down. After a few moments Tiger's voice came through the shoe saying that he was at the bottom and that it was wet and muddy and very smelly and all he could see was an old bicycle and a shopping trolley.

'They get everywhere,' I said. 'Let Lady Mawgon have a feel around.'

Mawgon already was. With one hand keeping Tiger floating a few inches above the water level, the other was grasping, feeling and churning above her head, while her other glove on Tiger's hand sixty feet below did the same thing. Tiger kept us informed of what was going on while interspersing his speech with some top-quality sarcasm.

'Fifteen seconds gone,' I said, staring at my watch.

'I can feel something odd,' said Perkins, who was standing to one side, doing little except directing the ambient crackle more efficiently into Mawgon and Price, in the same way as a guttering directs rain into a storm drain.

'Me too,' said Full Price, eyes fixed intently on the wellhead and his index fingers beginning to vibrate with the effort. 'Look at that.'

I looked down the well. Before, only the top course of bricks had closed over to prevent us getting in, but now *other* bricks were starting to pop out from the well sides all the way down. The well was starting to constrict.

'We need Tiger out,' I said to Lady Mawgon, who was still feeling about above her head, eyes closed as she searched the muddy bottom of the well.

'Nearly,' she muttered.

'Twenty-five seconds.'

'What's going on?' came Tiger's voice over the toddler's shoe.

'You'll be out soon, Tiger, I promise.'

The bricks were starting to move inwards with increasing speed, and brick dust, soil and earwigs were tumbling down the well. Full Price was sweating with the effort and shaking badly.

'*I . . . can't . . . hold . . it!*' he managed to mutter between clenched teeth.

'The walls,' came Tiger's tremulous voice, 'they're moving in!'

36

'Lady Mawgon,' I said as calmly as I could. 'It's only a ring. We can leave it be.'

'Almost there,' she said, feeling around with her gloved hand in increased desperation.

'Thirty seconds,' I said as I stared at my watch. 'That's it. Abort.'

She continued, undeterred.

'Mawgon!' yelled Full Price, who was now shaking so hard his index fingers were a blur. 'Get the lad out NOW!'

But Mawgon was unmoved by our entreaties. She was so intent on finding her quarry that nothing mattered – least of all a foundling being crushed to death by an ancient spell sixty feet below ground. The well had shrunk to half its size by now, and Full Price was crying out in pain as he tried to keep the spell at bay. Perkins was shaking with the effort, too, and Lady Mawgon was still wildly looking around with Tiger's arm below when several things happened at once. Lady Mawgon cried out, Perkins fell over and the well shut with a teeth-jarring thump that we felt through the ground. I looked at my watch. Price had kept it open exactly forty-three seconds. Of Tiger there was no sign; the well was now a solid plug of brick, and down below, somewhere, Tiger was part of it.

There was silence. I couldn't think of anything to say. Full Price and Perkins were both on their hands and knees in the dirt coughing after their exertions, but Lady Mawgon was just standing there, her gloved hand half open as if clasped around something. She might have found something, but it didn't matter. The price had been too great.

I felt my head grow hot as anger welled up inside me. I might have boiled over then as I have a terrible temper once riled, but a small voice brought me back from the edge.

'Hey, Jenny,' went the voice from the toddler's shoe, 'I can see Zambini Towers from here.'

It was Tiger's voice. I frowned, and then looked up. High above us was a small figure no bigger than a dot free-falling back towards earth. Lady Mawgon had brought Tiger out of the closing well so rapidly that we hadn't seen him pass, and he had carried on and up, and was now on his way back down. I looked across at Lady Mawgon, who winked at me, and opened her gloved hand wide. She swiftly moved a hayrick twenty feet to the right, where Tiger landed with a thump a few seconds later, and at the same time she caught a muddy object in her gloved hand, which she then passed to me.

'There,' she said with a triumphant grin, 'Mawgon delivers.'

Negative energy

'That was fun in a panicky, exciting, soil-your-underwear kind of way,' said Tiger as he walked up to us covered in a mixture of mud and straw. 'I *didn't*, in case you're interested,' he added. 'The smell is the mud from the bottom of the well.'

Full Price was the first to voice what we all felt.

'Cutting it a bit fine, Daphne?'

'I knew *precisely* how long he had,' she said. 'Master Prawns was never in danger.'

'I don't agree,' I replied, pointing to where a lock of Tiger's hair had been caught in the bricks as they closed upon him as he shot out. 'I'll ask you not to place the staff in danger, Lady Mawgon.'

She stared at me and took a step closer.

'You *admonish* me?' she said slowly and with great deliberation. 'You, who are not worthy to even carry my bag? We'll see where the land lies when the Great Zambini returns, my girl. Prawns was in slight jeopardy, yes, but as an employee of Kazam he must assume the risks as well as the advantages.'

'And what would those advantages be?' asked Tiger,

who clearly thought he could be impertinent, given his recent close shave. 'I'd be very interested in knowing.'

'Isn't it obvious?' she replied. 'Working with the greatest practitioners of the Mystical Arts currently on the earth.'

'*Aside* from that,' replied Tiger, as that was something we could all agree upon.

'What else does there need to be? Clean my glove before you return it to me. I just earned the company five thousand moolah. You should all be mind-numbingly grateful.'

'Why would anyone leave such a spell to keep a ring hidden?' asked Perkins, artfully moving the conversation to where it should be going.

There was silence, as no one had any good answer. I looked at the small mud-covered terracotta pot Lady Mawgon had handed me. It was about the size of a pear and was nothing remarkable – the sort of thing you might use to hold mixed spice. I put my finger in the neck and felt around in the muddy gloop until I felt something and pulled out the gold ring, still shiny and perfect after thirty years down the well. It was a large ring, for a large finger, but was otherwise unremarkable. No inscription or anything, just a simple band of gold. Full Price put his hand near it then hurriedly withdrew it.

'It's suffused with negative wizidrical energy – a

jumble of hateful, hurtful emotions. It remembers violence and betrayal. It's cursed.'

'That would explain all those creepy feelings,' said Perkins with a grimace.

Everyone took a cautious step back. Curses were the viruses of the magical world – mischievous strands of negative emotional energy wrapped up in nastiness and waiting to jump out and ensnare the unwary. They'd attach themselves to anything and anybody and were the devil's own job to remove. It was Lady Mawgon who broke the uneasy silence.

'What are we worrying about?' she said. 'Five thousand moolah is five thousand moolah. Besides, it's none of our business, and what's new about a curse? The country is littered with redundant strands of curse-spells left over from past suffering.'

This was all too true. The sometimes violent history of the Ununited Kingdoms had seeded the ground with spells cast when something terrible had happened. They had an inordinately long life and could be reanimated by something as simple as digging the garden. One moment you're planting the spuds and thinking of dinner and the next you're taking cover from a shower of pitchforks.

'The public can take their chances like the rest of us,' added Lady Mawgon. 'Are you suggesting that all we've been through this morning should be ignored in case we inadvertently pass on the *possibility* of a curse?'

'Odd as it may seem,' said Tiger, feeling where the hair was missing from the top of his head, 'I am in agreement with Lady Mawgon on that count.'

'A rare moment of clarity from someone usually capable only of stupidities,' remarked Lady Mawgon. 'Our work here is done.'

She was right. We returned to the lay-by in silence and Lady Mawgon departed on her motorcycle without another word. I sighed. Earning one's keep by magic was rarely plain sailing. For every simple job there are others, like this one. If the ring had a potential curse, then its return would definitely cause unpleasantness for Miss Shard or anyone associated with it. But then again, five grand would support our key function: the dignity and majesty of the wizidrical arts. But then again, where was the dignity in just finding lost stuff and doing loft conversions? And as Lady Mawgon had said: it's none of our business.

I walked up to where the Rolls-Royce was still parked, the gold ring in the palm of my hand. I tapped on the tinted window, which lowered with a hum.

'Did the finding exercise meet with a modicum of positive fortitude?' asked Miss Shard.

'I'm sorry?'

'Did you find it?'

I paused for a moment, and held the ring tightly in my fist.

'I'm afraid not,' I said, returning the other ring, the

one she had lent us. 'Please offer our apologies to your client. We did all we could.'

'No hints at all as to where it might be?' she asked, mildly surprised.

'None at all,' I replied. 'It's been over thirty years, after all.'

'Well,' said Miss Shard, 'I'm grateful to you nonetheless. Perhaps my client will look for it personally when he returns.'

And after she had bade me good day, the Rolls-Royce purred out of the rest area, rejoined the morning traffic and headed off. I watched the car go with an odd feeling of foreboding. About what, I wasn't sure. I popped the ring back in the pot, and wedged my handkerchief in as a stopper.

As we drove back into town without the five grand, I considered my action over the ring. I had done the right thing. The power we had was power abused if we didn't accept responsibility for any adverse outcomes, and spell-curses damaged our already poor standing. I smiled to myself. I think it's what the Great Zambini would have done.

All in all, it had been quite a morning.

Zambini Towers

I parked the car in the yard at the back of Zambini Towers and after telling Tiger to go and have a shower to remove the stinking well-mud, I made my way through the building. In more glory-scented days Zambini Towers had been the Majestic Hotel, one of only four hotels to ever host the coveted 'Despot of the Decade' award ceremony and was featured in *What Hotel?* as 'the most luxurious hotel to be found in the lesser Kingdoms', where, it noted, 'food poisoning was likely, but by no means a certainty'.

That was then.

Today, the Majestic was a shabby relic far removed from its former glory. The ballroom, where once B-list princes wooed their consorts to the dulcet tones of string quartets, was now a dining room that smelled strongly of burnt toast and damp, and the presidential suite, long ago the playground for an exotic array of noblemen, was these days the dwelling place of the Mysterious X, who was less of a who, and more of a what – with peculiar and borderline disgusting personal habits.

I walked past the lobby, where a mature oak tree had grown, its gnarled boughs wrapped tightly around the furniture and ornate cast-iron railings of what had once been the lobby café. David, the younger of the Price brothers and known to all and sundry as 'Half', had grown it as a first-year student project twenty years ago, but had never got round to ungrowing it.

I walked into the Kazam offices, flicked on the light, dumped my bag on a chair and put the small terracotta pot in my desk drawer. This office was the nerve centre of the company, and a half-century ago, during the days of full-power magic, would have been humming with action as the thirty or so managers fielded calls and scheduled enchantments. The desks were all empty these days, but we kept the tables, chairs and telephones, just to remind us how good it had once been, and if we had our way, would be again.

I sat down at my desk, thought for a moment about the morning's adventure, made a few notes on my pad, then picked up the phone and dialled a number from memory.

'iMagic,' came a snotty voice on the other end, 'better, faster and cheaper than Kazam and home to the All Powerful Blix. Can I help you?'

'That's not helpful, Gladys,' I said. Competition had become fiercer between the two companies since the Big Magic, but at least we at Kazam never stooped to badmouthing the opposition.

'Only speaking the truth, Jennifer,' she sneered. 'I'll get the All Power – I mean, the Amazing Blix, for you.'

I thought for a moment while I was connected. Conrad Blix was not only the Head Wizard over at Industrial Magic, but also general manager, doing what I did here at Kazam. The Great Zambini had disliked Blix intensely, and not just because he was the grandson of the infamous 'Blix the Hideously Barbarous', but because they had never seen eye to eye as regards the direction of the Mystical Arts. Zambini saw them as a tool for social justice and good in general, but Blix saw them as more of a way to make cash, and lots of it.

'Strange by name, Strange by nature,' came a supercilious voice, intentionally to irritate. 'I'm busy, dear girl, so better make it quick.'

Despite the animosity between the two companies, we were compelled to agree on a number of matters to be able to function at all. After all, we all drew our power from the same wizidrical energy source, and any usage above five thousand Shandars was worth a phone call.

'What's with the "iMagic" name change?' I said without preamble.

'Industrial Magic was a bit of a mouthful,' he explained. 'Besides, putting "i" in front of anything makes it more hip and current. Is that why you called?'

'No. We've got a ten–kilo spell cooking at eleven

fifteen this morning and I wanted to make sure we wouldn't clash.'

'We've got nothing big on until half past four this afternoon,' replied Blix suspiciously. 'What are you up to? Ten Meg is a serious chunk of crackle to be using at short notice.'

'You weren't jamming us yesterday, were you?' I asked, ignoring his question and referring to some interference we'd been having at a routine scaffold-build the previous afternoon.

'Jennifer, when you say things like that you really hurt me,' retorted Blix insincerely. 'We are a professional outfit, and accusations of jamming insult our integrity.'

'If a shred of integrity fell into your soul it would die a very lonely death.'

'One day I will make you eat your impertinence, Jennifer – and you won't enjoy it. Anything else?'

'Actually, there is. Since when did your accolade jump from "the Amazing" to "the All Powerful"?'

Accolades were self-conferring, and making yourself seem more astounding than you were was not against any written rules, but bad manners. And sorcerers were big on dignity and honour – or were meant to be, anyway.

'I can't think how that happened,' he replied insincerely. 'I'll speak to Gladys about it.'

'I'm most grateful. And don't forget that we

want a clear hour at two o'clock for Perkins' licence application.'

'Already in the diary, dear girl. In fact, I might even see you there.'

'That would be joyous.'

'You're very disrespectful, Jennifer.'

'Mr Zambini made me promise. *Sandop kale n'baaa*, Amazing Blix.'

'*Sandop kale n'baaa*, Miss Strange.'

And having exchanged the ancient salutation required of us, we both hung up. I thought for a moment. If Blix was attempting to give himself the accolade 'All Powerful', there might be trouble brewing. Wizards on a self-aggrandising kick usually set the alarm bells ringing.

'Do you think Blix will try and sabotage Perkins' application?' asked Tiger, rubbing his damp hair with a towel as he walked in.

'I wouldn't put it past him. Samantha "Pretty-but-dim" Flynt has failed to get her licence for three years running, and Perkins' success would really piss them off.'

'Cadet Flynt couldn't find her foot without tattooed arrows running down her leg,' said Tiger, 'and failed her basic practical skills test. I don't know why they bother.'

'Hopeless she might be,' I said, 'but she's dazzlingly pretty and Blix thinks that a physically attractive sorcerer would be good for business.'

'She'd certainly be unique in that respect,' remarked Tiger. Sorcerers were not known for their good looks.

'In any event, we should be on our guard as regards Blix. I wouldn't trust him farther than Patrick of Ludlow could throw him.'

Patrick, it should be noted, was our 'Heavy Lifter'. His speciality was moving objects, which was mostly used for removing illegally parked cars for the city's clamping unit. He had a heart of gold and was as gentle as a lamb, despite his power and odd-looking appearance.

'I'd like to see Patrick try, though.'

'Me, too. Hello, Hector.'

I was talking to the Transient Moose, who had suddenly materialised in the office over by the water cooler and was now staring into space and thinking grand Moosian thoughts. The Moose was a practical joke perpetrated by a sorcerer in the long distant past. No one knew what the joke had been, who did it, or even whether it was funny or not. The spell that kept him going was skilfully woven and surprisingly resilient. His joke complete, he had very little to do and most of eternity in which to do it, so he consequently looked painfully bored as he appeared and disappeared randomly about Zambini Towers. Despite my speaking to him on many occasions, he had not replied – and since he was a large North American herbivore, I didn't really expect him to.

The Transient Moose stared at us both for a moment, gave a doleful sigh and then faded from view.

'You didn't give that Phantom Twelve girl the ring, did you?' asked Tiger.

He knew me quite well by now. Despite being only twelve, he was pretty switched on. Foundlings generally are.

'No – and I'm sorry you had to risk your neck because of it.'

He shrugged and gave me a smile.

'It was quite fun, actually. Except the bit where I went down the well – and got shot into the air. Do I tell the others we're five grand poorer because of you?'

'Better not.'

I sifted through the mail for anything that looked desperately urgent – bills mainly – and then checked the level of the Background Wizidrical Radiation using a device called a Shandargraph. Unlike the hand-held Shandarmeter which measured local magical energy, the Shandargraph gave one an idea of broad trends of wizidrical energy over time – a bit like measuring atmospheric pressure. You could not only tell when a spell was being cast, but how powerful and where. I looked at the long ribbon of paper that was slowly emerging from the machine and noted that our morning's misadventure was dutifully recorded – fourteen MegaShandars, six miles away to the east. I could even see where it peaked as Full Price tried to

keep the well open. The spells undertaken by iMagic
in Stroud were also apparent. Our workloads seemed
relatively equal, although I knew for a fact Blix would
have the Truly Bizarre Tchango Muttney levitate a
truck somewhere on the other side of town and hold
it there for twenty minutes to make us *think* they had
more work on than they actually did.

iMagic were troublesome, but not a real threat.
With only Blix, Tchango and Dame Corby 'She
Whom the Ants Obey', iMagic had only three
sorcerers to our five. We also had two flying carpeteers* and one decent precog, of which they had
none. But on the upside, they didn't have thirty-six
barely sane ex-sorcerers to feed, and they also had
a secondary income: Dame Corby was the heiress
to the Corby Trouser Press empire, and yearly divi-
dends were apparently still robust, despite the
invention of drip-dry garments.

I picked up one of the two remaining self-cleaning
cups from the draining rack and poured myself tea
from the never-ending teapot, then took some milk
from the perpetually half-empty enchanted milk bottle
in the fridge.

'Hello, Jennifer,' said a voice from the sofa, and a

---

*Since carpets cover the whole floor and rugs only a part of it, a 'flying carpet' is
misnamed. Translated from the Persian – from where all flying rugs originate – as
a 'flying carpet' in the seventeenth century, the term has become so entrenched that
common usage has them now as carpets. A carpeteer is correctly called a Rugeteer,
or, if you're French, a Tapisigator.

very rumpled-looking figure sat up and scratched himself.

'Good morning, Kevin,' I said, handing him a cup of tea and a biscuit from the never-ending supply in the biscuit tin. 'All well?'

Kevin was a lean man whose thirtieth birthday had passed unannounced two decades before. Despite his dishevelled appearance, with tatty clothes that would have been rejected by the most desperate Troll War widow charity shops, he was clean-shaven and his finely cut hair was immaculate. He looked, in fact, like a yuppie in tramp fancy dress.

'As well as ever,' he replied with a yawn.

The reason Kevin always slept fully dressed on the sofa when he had a perfectly good bedroom was because he had foreseen that he would die in his bed, and reasoned that if he stayed away from it he wouldn't die. That might sound daft until you consider that the Remarkable Kevin Zipp was our precognitive, a breed of sorcerer who had turned their attention to shuffling through the millions of potential futures and occasionally picking out a winner. But as with all oracles, his visions could be vague and misleading. The time he foresaw 'killer aliens from Mars', it actually turned out to be about 'millers named Alan in cars', which isn't the same thing at all. And when he predicted the 'reign of a matron named Grace' we actually got a 'rain of meteors from space'. Despite this, his strike rate was a respectable 73 per cent, and since the Big Magic, improving still.

'Anything for us?' I asked, as quite often Kevin had dazzling visions that he never told anyone about as he couldn't see their relevance.

'A few,' he replied, taking a sip of tea. 'Something about Vision Boss, and the price of elevators is set to fall.'

'Fall?'

'Or rise. One of the two. Perhaps both.'

'Vision Boss?' I asked, fetching the Visions Book, in which we logged every vision, notion and fore-sightment our precognitives ever had. 'You mean like the chain of spectacle shops "Should have gone to Vision Boss"?'[*]

'Not sure. It might have referred to the Boss of Visions – the greatest precog ever.'

'Sister Yolanda of Kilpeck[†] has been dead over twelve years,' I said, writing it in the Visions Book anyway. 'Got hit by a tram on the High Road.'

'Yes,' said Kevin sadly, 'didn't see that coming.'

'Why would you be thinking of her?'

'I don't know. Oh, and I had another vision about the Great Zambini.'

---

[*] The first slogan they used was: 'Boss-eyed? You need Vision Boss!' but it was not well received, and hastily withdrawn.

[†] Sister Yolanda's strike rate was the best ever at an astonishing 92 per cent. But then she only made two hundred and twenty-five in her sixty-seven years, which may explain it. Most precogs spew them out by the dozen, daily.

I was suddenly a lot more interested.

'You did?'

'He's going to reappear.'

This was good news indeed. The Great Zambini
had vanished eight months earlier while conducting
a simple dematerialisation during a children's party,
and we had been trying to get him back ever since.
Because Kevin and Zambini knew each other well,
his predictions over Zambini's appearances were *always*
correct – just too late for us to do anything useful
with them.

'When?'

'Tomorrow afternoon at 16.03 and fourteen seconds.'

'Do you know where?'

'Not a clue – but he'll be there for several minutes.'

'That's not so very helpful,' I pointed out. 'There's
an awful lot of "where" in the unUK, and a minute
isn't exactly bags of "when" in which to find him.'

'Precognition is not an exact science,' grumbled
Kevin defensively. 'In fact, I don't think it's a science
at all. But I may know more nearer the time.'

'Can you predict when you might know?' I asked
hopefully.

'No.'

I allocated each vision a unique code – RAD094
to RAD096 – and then asked him to hang around
the office and call me the second he knew more. The
last time this happened, Kevin had us all staking out

a village in the weekends-only Duchy of Cotswold, where Zambini reappeared for a full fifty-seven seconds before vanishing again. Despite fifteen of us dispersed around the village with eyes peeled, we missed Zambini when he turned up in a jam cupboard belonging to a Mrs Bishop. He must have been confused as to where he was, but not so confused that he couldn't manage to consume an entire pot of best loganberry. And that was the problem with Zambini. He was rattling around the Now like a ping-pong ball, doing pretty much the same as the Transient Moose, but on a much broader geography, and with shorter visits. Moobin thought that Zambini must have corrupted his vanishing spell as he disappeared, but we'd not know for sure until we got him back – if we did.

'As soon as you get an *inkling* of a location let me know,' I told him again, and after asking Tiger to fetch Kevin some breakfast and the daily papers, I went and stared at the work schedule for the next few days. Wednesday and Thursday were straightforward, but all of Friday had been kept clear for the bridge job, and the project had been much in our thoughts recently. There was only one interesting bridge to speak of in Hereford, and that was the twelveth-century stone arched bridge. Or rather, that *had* been the most interesting bridge until the structure, weakened by neglect and heavy winter floods, had collapsed three years before. Now it was a pile of damp rubble, with only the remains of piers and abutments to indicate what had once been there.

'We need to rebuild the bridge without any hiccups, don't we?' said Tiger, noticing that I was staring at old photographs of the bridge.

'Yes indeed,' I replied. 'Moving out of home improvements and into civil engineering projects could put Kazam firmly on the map. It'll be a good PR exercise, and we need to increase our standing within the community. I just hope Moobin knows what he's doing. He says he's got the rebuild planned, but I think his definition of "plan" might be more along the lines of "make it up as we go along".'

Tiger snapped his fingers.

'Didn't Full Price say Moobin wanted us to witness an experiment he'd got cooking?' he asked.

'He did. Better go and see when he wants us. When you get back you can fill out the B1-7g forms for this morning's work – but not Perkins' involvement, remember.'

He nodded and trotted out of the door. A few minutes later I heard him yell as he fell up the lift shaft.

There was a knock at the door and I turned to see a small man in a sharp suit holding a briefcase. He looked vaguely familiar.

'My name is Mr Trimble,' announced the man, 'of

Trimble, Trimble, Trimble, Trimble and Trimble, attorneys-at-law.'

He handed me a business card.

'We've met before,' I said coldly, 'when you were representing the Constuff Land Development Agency.'*

'That was one of the *other* Trimbles,' he said helpfully. 'That's me there,' he added, pointing to the second Trimble from the left. 'Donald was disbarred; a most unsavoury episode.'

'I see,' I replied. 'My name is Jennifer Strange, acting general manager of Kazam. Would you like a seat?'

Mr Trimble took the proffered chair, and got straight to the point.

'I have wealthy and influential clients,' he said, 'and they have a proposal for Kazam.'

I didn't like the sound of this, but at least Trimble was being honest – and I had five thousand moolah to earn back.

'Oh, yes?' I replied suspiciously. 'What sort of proposal?'

Mr Trimble took a deep breath.

'My clients would like Kazam to reanimate the mobile telephone network.'

---

*Constuff is a contraction of 'Consolidated Useful Stuff PLC', the Ununited Kingdom's leading purveyor of cheap and shoddy goods. They are so large they actually own a country – Constuffia – which is full of factories where poorly paid labourers toil ceaselessly in order to make the unUK the leading exporter of cheap and shoddy goods. A recent initiative to throw the goods straight into landfill and avoid costly transportation costs has been enthusiastically embraced.

It wasn't the first time we had been asked to switch the network back on, and wouldn't be the last. Mobile phones had been one of the first things to go when the drop in wizidrical power required the slow switch-off of services that ran, essentially, on magic. Mobiles and computers hadn't been possible since 1993, colour televisions since 1999 and GPS navigation since 2001. The last electromagical device to be switched off was the microwave oven in 2004, and that was only because aircraft radar used the same electromagical principle. The only magical technologies of any size still running were north-pointing directional compasses and the spell that kept bicycles from falling over – both of which were so old that no one knew how to switch them off anyway.

'We've been approached by BellShout, N_2O and VodaBunny about this before, I said, 'and our answer is the same: all in good time. The mobile phone network will be active just as soon as we have brought back those electromagical technologies that have priority – medical scanners, and then microwave ovens.'

'Will that take long?'

I shrugged.

'A while. When the electromagical spells were shut down no one made a hard copy of the spell, so much is having to be rewritten – when you consider that a yo-yo has over two hundred lines of spell-text to make it work and a photocopier over ten thousand, you get an idea of the complexity of the task. Besides,' I added, 'the switch-off gave us an opportunity to reconsider the direction magic will take. We'll not make the same mistake we made last time. Licensing the power of magic to individuals and companies placed sorcery in the hands of the unscrupulous. Magic belongs in the hands of all – or none.'

We stared at one another for a few moments. It was a view that the Great Zambini had embraced, and almost everyone at Kazam.

'Well,' said Mr Trimble, 'would you take it to your sorcerers anyway? I'd like to report back to my clients that the refusal was unanimous.'

I agreed I would speak to them, and Mr Trimble rose to fetch his hat, which had automatically made its way to the hatstand, part of a self-tidying spell that ran throughout the building.

'I'm most grateful to you for your time,' he said. 'The executives at BellShout will be very happy to talk if you change your position.'

And after shaking my hand, he left.

I wasn't alone for long. The Prince dropped by with his day's schedule, and I could see he wasn't happy.

'Pizza deliveries *again*?' he said in exasperation. 'When do we do some proper carpeteering?'

'Maybe sooner than you think,' I told him. 'I've got a task for you.'

His Royal Highness Prince Omar Smith Arkwright

Ben Nasil was one of our carpeteers, which might have been a noble and exciting profession were it not for an incident one wintry night when Brother Velobius and his two passengers died when their Turkmen Mk18C 'Bukhara' broke up in mid-air owing to rug fatigue. For safety reasons, the Civil Aviation Authority had introduced strict rules that made it almost impossible to make magic carpet flight profitable. Limited top speed, navigation lights – and worst of all, a ban on passengers. All we could do were deliveries.

'Here's the thing,' I said. 'Kevin has foretold the Great Zambini returning tomorrow afternoon at 16.03 and fourteen seconds.'

'Let me guess,' said the Prince, 'Kevin knows when but not where?'

'That's about the size of it. We need Zambini back, Nasil,[*] so stick to Zipp like a limpet. If he has a vision about where Zambini might show up, I want you to come and find me immediately.'

He said he wouldn't fail me, made some comment about needing to take his carpet off the flightline next month for some remedial patchwork, and we said goodbye.

'Is he really a prince?' asked Tiger, who had just returned.

[*]Despite being of royal stock, the prince insisted he be treated as a civilian. We liked him a lot for it.

'Second in line to the Duchy of Portland,' I told him. 'What's the deal with Moobin?'

'He said come up any time. He said you'd be impressed.'

This worried me as Moobin liked a challenge, and was quite used to risking life and limb on weird experimental stuff that he described as 'important, cutting-edge stuff' but we saw more as 'just being a nuisance'.

'Let's do it.' I sighed. 'It's not like things could get more weird this morning.'

Wizard Moobin

We walked towards the elevators.

'I hope he doesn't blow himself up again,' I said.

'Or make himself attractive to badgers,' added Tiger, reminding us of the time Zambini Towers had been inundated with winsome, lovelorn black-and-white mustelids when a badger-repellent spell had gone badly wrong. Explosions and badger attraction aside, Moobin was easily our favourite sorcerer as he was probably the most normal. He was in his mid-forties but looked a lot younger, and although more powerful than Mawgon, lacked precise control and often surged – the word for a sudden burst of wizidrical energy just when you didn't want it. Just before the Big Magic he had nearly blown us all to pieces when he turned lead into gold, then blew up another laboratory while trying to invent a spell that reversed the effects of laboratories blowing up.

We took the elevator to the third floor, which involved simply saying the floor number and then stepping into the empty lift shaft. You fell to the floor you had requested and had to step smartly out before you fell back down again. Unskilled users had been known to get stuck for some time oscillating back and forth – on one occasion, for three days.

We found Moobin in his room, which was actually three rooms knocked into one. He used it for sleeping and tinkering, which explained the vast amount of apparatus lying about, none of which I understood, but all of which looked dangerously complicated, and hastily mended.

'Jennifer!' he remarked excitedly when he saw me. 'How did the finding job go this morning?'

'It depends on your viewpoint. Did you hear that the Amazing Blix is attempting to accolade himself "the All Powerful"?'

Moobin laughed.

'His arrogance will be his undoing. Right, then,' he continued, clapping his hands together, 'to work. What's the Holy Grail of the Mystical Arts?'

I never saw him so excited as when he was experimenting, and excitement made his wild hair look wilder, and his unkempt manner of dress that much more shabby. He looked less like a person, in fact, and more like an unmade bed with arms and legs.

'Invisibility?' I asked incredulously, for not even the Mighty Shandar had ever achieved that. As far as we knew, no one had, although entire lives had been spent in the attempt.

'Okay,' said Moobin, 'what's the slightly-less-than-Holy Grail?'

'Moving cathedrals?' suggested Tiger.

'Levitation,' sniffed Moobin, 'nothing more.'

'Flying without a carpet or aeroplane under you?' I asked.

'Okay, even-*slightly*-less-than-Holy Grail?'

'Teleportation?' I said.

'*Exactly!*' replied Moobin excitedly. 'The physical shifting from one place to another more or less simultaneously. The current record stands at eighty-five miles.'

'The Great Zambini in his youth,' I said to Tiger, 'over sixty years ago.'

'My personal best,' announced Moobin grandly, 'is thirty-eight feet, and I'm going to try and increase that to . . seventy.'

'I see,' I said, wondering what could possibly go wrong, and thinking of eight possibilities almost immediately, which ranged from the destruction of two city blocks, through several stages of varying destructiveness to nothing more innocuous than liqui-fying the earwax of those in the immediate vicinity – the usual knock-on effect of a teleportation. In fact, the purpose of the original enchantment had been *precisely* that – ear cleaning. Spooky instantaneous transportation was simply found to be a fortuitously useful side effect. The wizard who wrote the original spell in 1698 had been beta-testing it as 'An Improved & Much Sanitary Method of Ear Cleansing' when he found himself inexplicably on the street outside. Much research followed and the range and accuracy greatly increased, but the earwax issue had remained. You could always hear better at the end of a jaunt than at the beginning.

'Not only will I teleport seventy feet,' continued Moobin dramatically, 'but I will also travel through a sheet of three-millimetre plywood on the way.'

Tiger and I looked at one another doubtfully. Moobin's last attempt to pass through solid objects had ended with a broken nose and a bruised knee.

'I've been working with silk, paper and cardboard,' he said, in an attempt to reassure us as he led us into the corridor outside, 'and it's time to move on up.'

'And you're no longer leaving your clothes behind?' I asked, referring to an earlier and mildly embarrassing episode.

'Not at all,' said Moobin, who hadn't been the one embarrassed, 'I had been eating nougat earlier – I should have known better.'

Owing to its status as a former hotel, Zambini Towers was not short on long corridors, and in the one outside his room, Moobin had hung a large sheet of plywood from a light fixture. He drew a cross on the floor about two yards in front of the ply, handed Tiger a pocket Shandometer to measure peak wizidrical output, then gave me a tape measure to hold.

'Call out when I get to seventy feet, will you?'

And he walked off past the sheet of ply and into the darkness while I watched the tape pay out.

'Can't he teleport *around* the ply?' asked Tiger.

'Curved teleporting is not possible.' I told him. 'Magic's effect only works in straight lines. A teleportation around a corner means taking the shortest route *through* whatever the corner is made of. Passing through the rock and soil of the planet on a straight-line journey through the earth from here to Singapore takes a lot of wizidrical energy – it makes carpet travel a lot more crackle-efficient than transcontinental teleportation.'

I thought for a moment.

'There *was* an enchanter over in France who experimented with high-end clear-air teleportation. He started from Paris and reappeared two and a half thousand feet over Toulouse.'

'That must have been unexpected.'

'On the contrary, it was planned – but his parachute failed to open and he fell screaming to his death in a very undignified manner. The power of magic began to wane soon after, and no one tried it again.'

'Isn't that greater than Zambini's record?'

'It's not official if you don't survive it.'

'I can recommend hayricks for soft landings,'

Tiger replied thoughtfully. 'Sorcery isn't really straight-forward at all, is it?'

Tiger had been with Kazam only two months, and he was still trying to get his head around the limiting practicalities of magic. Most people thought you just wave your hands and sim-sallah-bim, but it was a lot more complex than that. Sorcery was not so much doing what you wanted to do, but doing what you *could* do – or ingeniously finding a way around the physical limitations of the craft.

The tape measure continued to pay out, and when it had reached the correct distance I called out and Moobin stopped.

'Okay, here we go, then,' came Moobin's confident voice from the other end of the corridor. 'Seventy feet and through a three-millimetre sheet of plywood.'

I nodded to Tiger, who had lifted the cover from one of the many 'Magiclysm' alarms dotted about the building. In the event that Moobin's spell went squiffy, Tiger would press the red button and the sprinklers would trip, spraying water over the interior of the building and quenching any spells. Wednesday morning was traditionally the spell test day, and many of the residents wore gumboots and raincoats indoors on that day, just in case.

We waited in silence. Magic was odd stuff, and the powers of sorcery are more often found in those who can obsess to a degree that would be considered faintly undesirable in society. You had to focus every synapse in your mind to the exclusion of everything else and fire the magic out of your index fingers. That's why observers remained quiet when spelling was afoot. Break the concentration and whoever was casting the spell would have to start again. It's like interrupting poetry. It just isn't done.

We heard a few grunts from the darkness beyond the sheet of ply, then a pause while nothing happened. There was another pause, more grunts, and then nothing happened again. It was just when nothing was about to happen for the third time that there was a faint 'pop' from the other end of the corridor as the air rushed in to fill the hole in the air where Moobin wasn't, and a half-second later he reappeared in front of us, the air he had displaced hitting us a moment later as a faintly discernible shock-wave.

'Ta-da!' said Moobin, staring at his feet where he had appeared, directly above the white cross. 'Seventy feet, and through a sheet of three-millimetre plywood. Tomorrow I'll try six-millimetre ply, then chipboard.'

'Impressive. I'll mark it up in the records ledger tonight.'

'It's also a new personal best,' continued Moobin excitedly, 'and if those heathen scum over at iMagic aren't also doing teleport work, it makes me the best teleporter on the planet. Why are you both staring at me?'

'You look like you've been glazed,' I said, putting out a hand to touch him, 'like a doughnut.'

Just then, the separate sheets of thin wood veneer that made up the plywood fell neatly into three thin and very flappy pieces.

'Oh dear,' said Moobin, 'I appear to have picked up the glue from the plywood as I passed through. How did that happen?'

He wasn't asking any of us, of course, he was simply confused. But that was what research and development was like. Full of semi-triumphs and perplexing unforeseen consequences, such as the whole violent hiccuping thing when conjuring up fire – or the propensity for fillings to fall out of bystanders' mouths when attempting to tease a rainstorm out of a cloud.

'The Transient Moose can teleport almost without thinking,' muttered Moobin, faintly annoyed, '*and* go around corners.'

'But he's a spell himself,' observed Tiger helpfully, 'and presumably has zero mass, so it must be easier.'

'Probably,' replied Moobin gloomily. 'I wish he'd let me have a closer look.'

The Wizard Moobin had recently become fascinated by the Transient Moose, and had fired a few spell-probes into it to discover just what particular enchantment was keeping it going. The probes had learned little except that the original sorcerer was possibly Greek and the Moose was most likely running Mandrake Sentience Emulation Protocols,* which didn't help, as nearly all spells that made something appear lifelike were run under Mandrake.

It wasn't just curiosity. The Mystical Arts were arcane, secretive and, once a specific spell was discovered, rarely shared. Ancient wizards went to their graves with the really groovy stuff still locked inside their heads. Some wrote it down in big leather-bound books, but most didn't. It would be very valuable indeed to find out not only how the Moose managed to live so long and teleport so effortlessly, but how it could do it on an average crackle consumption of only 172.8 Shandars a day.

'I'm going to have a shower,' said Moobin, 'so long as someone hasn't already swiped the hot water.'

'Oops,' said Tiger.

'What, again?' asked Moobin.

'I was covered in mud.'

'Have you been thinking about the bridge gig?' I asked, changing the subject. I had yet to see a detailed plan or risk assessment.

'I'm working on it,' Moobin said, 'although with the Dibble Coils stuck on standby we'll need all of us if we're to do it in a day.'

---

*A Mandrake Sentience Emulation Protocol is a clever piece of spelling that gives the appearance of life without something actually being alive – ghoulies and ghosties and long-legged beasties all use Mandrake, and if woven well, they are very lifelike.

'Lady Mawgon is going to try to get them back online this morning.'

'The old bat's going to try and hack the Dibble?' replied Moobin with a smile. 'Rather her than me.'

He nodded his head thoughtfully. Hacking into a well-cast spell was not for the faint-hearted. Wizards guarded their work jealously, and would often leave traps for busybodies attempting to copy their work. We watched as Moobin went back into his room, mumbling to himself as his feet made sticky footprints on the oak flooring.

'Right, then,' I said, checking my watch, 'time to see Lady Mawgon – don't mention the fact we took no payment for the finding gig.'

Hacking the Dibble

'What in heck are Dibble Storage Coils?' asked Tiger as we made our way back downstairs. He still had a good decade's worth of learning to do, and only two years in which to do it. I had to teach him most of it, and some of the stuff I needed to impart I hadn't even learned myself.

'It's a spell designed by Charles Dibble the Extraordinary,' I explained. 'In the days when wizidrical power was falling, the Great Zambini looked at several ways to store what crackle there was. Dibble the Extraordinary wasn't so much a practising sorcerer, but one who wrote spells for those who were. He wrote the entire mobile phone network incantation for ElectroMagic, Inc. back in the forties and then committed his energies to wizidrical storage devices. He was long retired when Zambini had him build the coils. Simply put, they transform the building into something akin to a huge rechargeable battery.'

Tiger looked around, as if wondering how he could have missed something so important.

'Where are they?'

I waved my hand in the direction of the building at large.

'The coils are not coils you can see – they are more like a constantly circulating field of negative wizidrical energy that can absorb, store and then discharge vast amounts of crackle on command. The applications are endless, from boring holes in solid rock to making something from nothing. We have the capacity to hold four GigaShandars.'*

'And what could a GigaShandar actually do?' asked Tiger, who was almost permanently inquisitive.

'It's a million Shandars, or if you prefer to use the older imperial measurements, about twenty-six cathedral miles, which is enough crackle to . . .'

'. . . move a cathedral twenty-six miles?'

'You learn fast. Yes, or move twenty-six cathedrals one mile each – or a medium-sized church five hundred miles, or, if you like, take a cricket pavilion all the way to Melbourne.'

'Would there be any point to that?'

'Not really.'

'So a capacity of four GigaShandars is enough to move one cathedral – hang on – one hundred and four miles?'

---

* A thousand MegaShandars is equal to one GigaShandar, and a thousand GigaShandars is one TeraShandar; 28.2 TeraShandars is the estimated total wizidrical power discharged throughout the history of magic – the equivalent of taking Hereford's cathedral to the moon and back, and still having enough left over to take it around the earth ten times.

'Pretty much, although moving cathedrals cross-border by magic would be a bureaucratic nightmare. The paperwork would swamp you before you'd even got as far as Monmouth.'

Tiger went silent for a moment.

'I'm sensing there's a reason why cathedral-moving is not on our rate sheet.'

'You sense right. Dibble died while servicing this enchantment twenty-six years ago and he left it in "standby" mode and passthought protected, so what we have now is a very, very big battery and no charger. It didn't matter when the crackle was negligible because we didn't have a hope of doing any big jobs. But now the power of magic is on the rise, we really need the Dibble back online if we're to do any serious magic, like digging canals or laying railway track or building henges or something.'

'I get that,' said Tiger, 'kind of. But don't you think they should be called "Zargon Coils" or "Znorff Inverters" or something groovy rather than "Dibble"?'

'Isn't "Dibble" groovy?'

'No, not really. It's more . . . *dorky*.'

'I suppose you're right,' I replied, 'but real life isn't like that. Dibble invented them, so Dibble they are.'

We walked across the lobby and into the Palm Court. In the heyday of the Majestic Hotel, this would have been an exotic indoor garden of tropical plants, tall palms and limpid pools with lily pads and koi carp. Scattered around would have been small tables filled with gossiping nobility taking tea, while waited upon by attentive waitresses.

No longer.

The room had not been used for entertaining or growing tropical plants for years, and many of the glass panes in the bell-shaped roof were either cracked or missing. Buckets lay scattered about into which water dripped during rainstorms, and the marble floor was stained and uneven. In the centre of the room was a large and very dry fountain. Standing next to it was Lady Mawgon. She had changed out of her usual black crinolines and into her even blacker ones, which showed she meant business. Her clothes were so black, in fact, that they were simply a dark Lady Mawgon-shaped hole in the world, and it could give one vertigo if you stared too long.

'You never thanked me for putting the hayrick under you, Prawns.'

'I'm most grateful to you for not letting me fall to a painful death,' said Tiger, knowing it was senseless to argue.

'Good manners cost nothing,' she grumbled. 'Did Miss Shard pay up?'

'The matter was concluded satisfactorily,' I replied.

'Hmm. Now, you are here to witness my attempt to hack into the Dibbles. You will not approach me and you will not talk. Do you understand?'

75

Tiger and I weren't sure whether that meant we couldn't answer or not, so we played it safe and nodded vigorously.

'Good. Primarily I will be trying to get into the root directory of the spell's central core to reset the pass-thought.* From there I will attempt to switch the coils back on. You should make notes as I talk my way through it. I shall permit you to wish me good luck.'

'Good luck, ma'am,' I said, taking out my pocketbook and a pencil.

She turned to an empty space in the room and raised her index fingers. After a pause, she drew her hands downwards and out, much like a conductor beginning a symphony. A blue-filled tear appeared in the air, as though a tent flap had been unzipped. She continued to move her hands as if conducting, and as she signalled to an imaginary percussion section, the randomly placed chairs in the room moved away from the tear and the chandeliers tinkled slightly. Lady Mawgon made a few flourishes as one might do to signal in the entire string section, then held one hand in the air as if sustaining a note from the bassoons, and peered closer into the rent. The tear had depth within, and coloured lights flashed to and fro as Lady Mawgon subtly moved her hands between the theoretical harp and kettle drums to probe the

*Very like a password, but infinitely more complex. To share a passthought you really need to have witnessed the event or emotion the passthought was based on.

inner workings of the spell. It was a incantation of great complexity, and Tiger and I stared wide eyed. Spellbound, in fact. I'd worked around spells for years, but never actually *seen* one.

'Hmm,' said Lady Mawgon, speaking over her shoulder while signalling to an imaginary cello section to play pianissimo. 'The enchantment is standard Wa'Seed on a RUNIX core. The secondary spells are off-the-peg Shandar that self-regulate the internal fields, but it seems Dibble added a few gatekeepers to thwart a hack, then set them orbiting the central core in all five directions at once so they couldn't be unwoven.'

'The Great Zambini was always cautious,' I replied, risking her anger by breaking my silence. 'He thought four GigaShandars of raw crackle lying around might tempt a fallen wizard with mischief on their minds.'

'You might be right,' said Lady Mawgon.

There then followed about five minutes of hard spelling which was almost indistinguishable from the gesticulations of a conductor. Indeed, I am told the skills are interchangeable, and the myth about wands may originally have begun with a conductor's baton.

And then, just as Tiger and I were getting bored and thinking of other things to do, our ears popped as something happened.

'Okay,' she said, giving a rare smile, 'I'll just reset the passthought and we're done.'

She made a few more flourishes with her hands to

an illusory woodwind section, and the rent closed.

'There,' she said triumphantly. 'I'm surprised it was so easy. The coils will be full by this time tomorrow and we can run a test spell with them by Friday morning. Prawns, go and fetch Moobin so I can share the passthought.'

Tiger hurried out and I congratulated her on the work.

'I could have done it in my sleep ten years ago,' she replied, 'but I thank you for your praise. Why are you staring at me?'

'You're going grey,' I said.

'I've been grey for years,' she said, 'and I've warned you against impertinence.'

'No, no,' I replied, '*everything* on you is going grey.'

And so she was. Her black crinoline dress was now a charcoal colour, and lightening by the second. Lady Mawgon frowned, looked at her hands and then stared up at me with a wan smile.

'Blast,' she said in a resigned tone, and a few moments later she had turned entirely to stone.

'*Damn,*' I said.

Turned to stone

I'd never seen anyone turned to stone before, and after the initial shock had worn off, I ventured closer. Every single pore of her skin, every wrinkle, every eyelash was perfectly rendered in the finest alabaster I had seen. It felt odd being in such close proximity to Lady Mawgon, even if she was now a four-hundred-pound block of stone, and although getting turned to stone was bad news, it might have been worse. The really serious cases of petrification involved dolorite, marble, or worse, granite.

Moobin laughed as he walked in, closely followed by Tiger.

'Goodness, the old girl will never live this down. Dibble the Extraordinary lived up to his name – a stoning incantation as a gatekeeper. Well, well, never would have thought of it.'

'You can change her back?'

'Child's play. Although to be honest, it *is* a lot quieter with her like this.'

'If I draw a moustache on her,' added Tiger, 'will she still have it on her when she changes back?'

'It's not funny,' I said, even though I, too, had mixed feelings. 'I'd be happier to have her back in one piece as soon as possible.'

'Very well,' said Moobin, and after taking a deep breath, he drew himself into the 'hard spelling' posture, pointed both index fingers at her and let fly.

Nothing happened.

He stood up, relaxed, then tried again.

Still nothing happened.

'That's odd,' he said at last. 'Did she change to stone quickly?'

'About ten seconds.'

'Oh dear. Wait here a moment.'

And he ran out the door.

'She still looks kind of frightening, doesn't she?' said Tiger.

She did, even though her features were not trapped in the more usual Mawgon look of scowling displeasure. Rather she wore the resigned smile she had given when she had realised that the long-dead Dibble had outwitted her.

'Still,' said Tiger, 'it proves what I always thought.'

'What's that?'

'That she does wear roller skates under her dress.'

I looked down, and just peeking out from the soft white folds of her gypsum prison was the shape of a roller-skate wheel pressed against the hem of her dress.

'Holy cow!' said Half Price as he walked in,

accompanied by Full Price and Wizard Moobin. 'I've never seen her looking so *stony* before.'

'She's certainly stuck between a rock and a hard place,' added Full Price with a giggle. 'Did you try the standard Magnaflux Reversal?'

'I tried it twice,' said Moobin, 'not a flicker.'

'Let me try,' said Half, and let fly in a similar manner to Moobin, with similar negative results.

'Hmm,' he said. 'Full?'

His brother tried and failed also, and they all suddenly looked a lot more serious, and went into one of those wizidrical discussions where I generally understood one word in eight. After ten minutes of this, they all let fly together, but all that happened was that the room grew hot and clammy, and our clothes let out a size.

'Did she say anything before she went?' asked Moobin, doing his belt up a notch.

'Only that the coils were taking on power,' I replied, 'and that the spell was written in RUNIX.'

'No one writes in RUNIX any more,' said Full Price. 'It's an archaic spell language that was big in the fourth century before we moved over to ARAMAIC. Half, who's our RUNIX expert?'

'Aside from Lady Mawgon?'

'Yes, obviously.'

'Monty Vanguard always had an interest in old spell languages.'

Moobin told Tiger to fetch Vanguard. He nodded and ran off. The atmosphere, which earlier had all been a bit jokey and silly, was now deathly serious.

'But the Fundamental Spell Reversibility Rule still applies, yes?' I asked.

'Totally,' agreed Moobin, 'there's no spell cast that can't be unravelled if you know precisely how it was written – it just may take a while to figure out.'

'How long?' I asked.

'If we work lunchtimes, about six to seven years.'

'Years?' I echoed in some alarm. 'The bridge gig starts on Friday. We've got less than forty-eight hours!'

'Life is short, magic is long, Jennifer.'

'That's not helpful.'

'Having a spot of bother?' asked a dapper white-haired man in impeccable dress and a thin moustache. This was Monty Vanguard, one of our spellers. Long in retirement, he spent his days putting together the thousands of lines of spell necessary to bring medical scanners back online.

Moobin explained the problem at length, and Monty Vanguard smiled.

'So you young blades have got your fingers burned and need an oldster to help you out, hmm?'

'Something like that.'

Monty opened the rent in the air just as Mawgon had done, and after donning his glasses, looked around inside the enchantment.

'I get it,' he said after a while. 'Do we have the passthought?'

'No.'

'I'll reset it. Are you sure we want Lady Mawgon back? I mean she's—'

He didn't get to finish his sentence as he too was turned to alabaster. But not slowly, like Mawgon, but instantly. It was his bad luck that he had been blinking at the time, and instead of looking elegant and dignified in stone, he had that annoying half-closed-eye look that makes one a bit, well, dopey.

'Okay,' said Full Price after a pause, 'that didn't turn out so well. What now?'

No one had any suggestions so we stood there for a moment, staring at Monty and Lady Mawgon.

'Will it harm her?' I asked. 'Being stone, I mean?'

'Not in the least,' he replied, 'as long as we keep Lady Mawgon away from a sandblaster and no one borrows part of her to mend the front portico of Hereford cathedral, she'll not know even one second has passed.'

And that was when an idea struck me. An idea that might explain something that had been confusing me for a while – how the Great Zambini and Mother Zenobia both managed to live beyond the century with only a small level of decrepitude, in Zenobia's case to well over a hundred and fifty.

'Can I be excused?' I asked. 'I've got an idea.'

'Of course,' replied Moobin, 'but let's keep this top secret. This is something only the five of us need know about.'

'Six,' said Tiger, for the Transient Moose had suddenly appeared, and was staring at Lady Mawgon with a detached interest.

'Six, then. No sense in panicking the residents, hmm?'

I quickly fetched some card and a felt pen from the office and placed a sign outside the entrance of the Palm Court that read: 'Closed for Redecoration'.

'What now?' asked Tiger as we walked through the lobby.

'We're going to visit Mother Zenobia.'

He gave a shudder.

'Do I have to come?'

'Yes.'

'She frightens me.'

'She frightens me, too. Think of it as character-building. Go and find your tie, polish your shoes and fetch the Youthful Perkins. The convent is in the same direction as the castle. We'll take him to his Magic Licence Application afterwards. I'll meet you both outside in ten minutes.'

Quarkbeast & Zenobia

I kept my Volkswagen in the garages beneath Zambini Towers, where it shared a dusty existence with several dilapidated Rolls-Royces and a Bugatti or two, remnants of when the retired sorcerers had money and power. Aside from the Dragonslayermobile,* which was also kept here, mine was the only working car, and since the Kingdom of Snodd granted driving licences not by age but by who was mature enough to be put in charge of half a ton of speeding metal, no male under twenty-six or wizard ever possessed a driving licence. Because of this I was compelled to add 'taxi service' to my long list of jobs.

I pulled around to the front of the building, parked the car and turned off the engine. Lady Mawgon's unfortunate accident dominated my thoughts – especially as this might mean postponing the bridge gig, which I was loath to do – it would make Kazam look weak and useless when we were trying to promote ourselves as strong and confident. Even if Perkins did

*An armoured Rolls-Royce covered in copper spikes that was used by Jennifer when she was the Last Dragonslayer.

get his licence, we would still have only five wizards to rebuild the bridge – and we needed six to be sure.

I sighed and gazed absently across the street. Situated on the opposite side of the road was the Quarkbeast memorial, Kazam's tribute to a loyal friend and ally who gave his life to protect me, and contributed in no small measure to the success of the Big Magic.* I thought about him a lot, and although he often frightened small children and had been known to eat a bunny rabbit or two, he had been a steadfast companion until the end. I frowned. There seemed to be a corner missing out of the oolitic limestone plinth upon which the statue sat. I got out of the car and walked across for a closer look. I was right; something had gnawed a chunk out of the plinth. There was a section of broken tooth stuck in the stone and I tugged until it came free. It was a sharp canine, and was coloured the dull slate grey of tungsten carbide.

'What have you found?' asked Tiger, who had also developed an affection for the Quarkbeast, even though he'd known it only a short time. He had often been dragged around the park on the beast's early morning walks – but in an affectionate, non-malicious, hardly-hurting-you-at-all sort of way.

'Look,' I said, dropping the tooth into his palm. 'It looks like there's another Quarkbeast in town.'

---

*Without the Quarkbeast there to save Jenny's life with the sacrifice of his own, it is unlikely there would be any magic at all.

86

'That'll have the council in a lather – the present Beastcatcher is very pro-Quarkbeast and rarely favours extermination.'

This annoyed the council as they saw the role of the Beastcatcher as very much along the lines of pest control. The previous Beastcatcher had been much more popular, but sadly got himself eaten by a Tralfamosaur who took offence at being poked at with a stick.

'This beast might not be staying,' said Tiger, staring at the tooth. 'Just paying its respects on its way through.'

A Quarkbeast is a small hyena-shaped creature that is covered in leathery scales and often described as: 'One tenth Labrador, six-tenths velociraptor and three-tenths kitchen food blender.' I held a special affinity for these creatures. Not just because I owed my life to one, but because they were one of the Ununited Kingdom's surviving eight species of invented animals, all created by notable wizards in the sixteenth century when enchanted beasts were totally 'the thing'. The Mighty Shandar created the Quarkbeast for a bet in 1783 and apparently won the wager, as nothing more bizarre has ever been created since. That didn't stop them being uniquely dangerous, and a Quarkbeast was regarded with a great deal of suspicion by the authorities – hence the issue with the Beastcatcher. An abiding fondness for metal was one of their many peculiar habits, zinc most of all. In fact, the first obvious sign of a Quarkbeast in the neighbourhood was that all the shiny zinc coatings were licked off the dustbins – the beast equivalent of licking the icing off a cake.

I looked around cautiously, hoping to catch a glimpse of the small creature. There was no sign, so I walked back to the car.

'Do you think the Quarkbeast could have been the pair of yours all the way from Australia?' asked Tiger, doing up his seat belt.

'Quarkbeasts come in pairs?' asked Perkins, who, although quite expert in seeding ideas, was not so hot when it came to magicozoology.

'They don't so much breed as *replicate*,' I explained. 'They divide into two entirely equal and opposite Quarkbeasts. But as soon as they do they have to be separated and sent a long way from each other – the other side of the globe, usually. If a paired positive and negative Quarkbeast meet, they are both annihilated in a flash of pure energy. It was said that Cambrianopolis was half destroyed when a confluence of paired Quarkbeasts came together and exploded with the force of ten thousand tons of Marzex-4.[*] Luckily, Cambrianopolis is such a ruin no one really noticed.'

'I heard it was an earthquake,' said Perkins.

'That's usually the cover story. We can't have people

---

[*] A form of plastic explosive whose principal ingredient is heavily nitrated marzipan mixed with cayenne pepper. Easily shaped, it is manufactured by the Kingdom of Cumbria, which has the largest deposits of natural marzipan in the world.

panicking like idiots as soon as they see a Quarkbeast. The general population is suspicious enough of magic as it is.'

'I suppose not.'

'Why do Quarkbeasts search for their twin?' asked Tiger.

'I don't know,' I replied. 'Boredom?'

'If it's the pair of *your* Quarkbeast,' said Perkins with growing confusion, 'doesn't that mean the new Quarkbeast is unlikely to explode?'

'Exactly. Nothing to fear from this one.'

We drove off in silence, past the cathedral, out of the city walls and headed south into the Golden Valley and past Snodhill Castle with the Dragonlands beyond and down the escarpment to the small town of Clifford. There, on a bend in the river and set about with oak and sweet chestnut, was the place Tiger and I had called home for the first twelve years of our lives. It was as grim as we both remembered it, and Tiger and I glanced at each other as we drew up outside. Perkins took one look at the Sisterhood of the Blessed Lady of the Lobster and announced he would be staying in the car.

'It's not that bad,' said Tiger defensively. 'The foundlings are rarely made to share blankets these days, and gruel no longer has a consistency thinner than water.'

'I wonder how they did that?' I mused, since gruel's

primary ingredient *was* water. 'I've always wanted to know.'

'It must be hard to extract the nourishment out of water,' agreed Tiger, 'but they managed it somehow.'

'I'll leave you both to your trip down memory lane,' said Perkins, staying resolutely on the back seat and hover-orbiting a pair of snooker balls around each other as a 'tuning up' exercise for his Magic Test. 'I'll see you guys later.'

We walked across the car park, up to the great doors, past the slot in the door for after-hours foundling deliveries, and into the quadrangle. I felt Tiger clasp my hand.

'It's okay,' I said, 'no one's taking you back. We're owned by Kazam now. Everything's fine.'

We walked across the quad, where open-air lessons were held in the summer, and from where we used to watch the shells as they were lobbed across the border from King Snodd's artillery battery in the orchard to the Duke of Brecon's small duchy across the river. Although an uneasy peace had once more descended between Brecon and Snodd and the guns were now silent, we had driven past a squadron of landships on our way in. The six-storey-high tracked vehicles had no special significance to me, but they did to Tiger, although he didn't know it – Mother Zenobia had told me Tiger's parents had been a husband-and-wife engineering team on a landship that vanished during the Fourth Troll Wars. Tiger would have been lost, too, had creche facilities not been removed from the land-ships in order to make room for extra munitions, so when his parents never returned he ended up on the steps of the orphanage. Mothers and fathers were a tetchy subject to foundlings, which was why he'd not yet been told what happened. The whole abandonment deal could devour you, so we usually left it until we felt we had the maturity to deal with it. My own parents would doubtless be traceable through my Volkswagen as I had been left on the front seat when abandoned, and although I was arguably mature enough to handle it, life was complicated enough.

'Is that Jennifer?' said Mother Zenobia as we were shown into her office. 'I can smell early Volkswagen upon you. A mix of burned oil, hot mud and six-volt electrics.'

'It is, ma'am.'

'And those footsteps behind you. Guarded and impertinent – yet full of inner strength to be fully realised. Master Prawns?'

'Your servant, ma'am,' said Tiger.

Mother Zenobia was not only old but completely blind, and had been since before most people on the planet had been born. She was sitting in an armchair in front of a fire, her gnarled fingers resting on the top of her cane, and her face so suffused with wrinkles that lost infant tortoises often followed her home. She clapped her hands and a novice entered, took orders for tea or cocoa, bobbed politely and then left again.

'So,' said Mother Zenobia after offering us a seat each, 'is this a social visit, or business?'

'Both,' I said, 'and please excuse my impertinence, Mother Zenobia, but our conversation must be strictly in confidence.'

'May my ears be infested by the floon beetle if I murmur so much as a word, Jennifer. Now, what's up?'

'Lady Mawgon got herself changed to stone.'

A smile crossed Mother Zenobia's features.

'Silly Daphne. What was she trying to do?'

I explained about the storage coils, and what had transpired.

'Not like Mawgon to get caught out by a gatekeeper,' murmured Mother Zenobia when I had finished. 'How is this to do with me? My sorcery days are long over.'

She held up her hands as if we needed proof. They were twisted with arthritis, her valuable index fingers bent and, for a sorcerer, almost useless.

I chose my words carefully. Moobin had said earlier that getting changed to stone was effectively suspended animation.

'I thought perhaps great age in sorcerers might be less to do with spelling away old age than simply pressing the pause button.'

'You are a highly perceptive young lady,' replied Zenobia at length. 'I do indeed change to stone every night in order to delay death's cold embrace. Eight hours' sleep over an eight-year lifetime is about twenty-six years,' She continued. 'Wasted time if you ask me, except for dreaming, which I miss. I've been rock during the winter months for the past seventy-six years as well, and when my last fortnight beckons I will be with you for an hour a year. I may last another century at this rate.'

She thought for moment.

'Self-induced petrification has its drawbacks, though. Changing to limestone at night is no problem, but returning to life in the morning leaves minute traces of calcite in the fine capillaries of the retina.'

Tiger and I looked at one another. The secret of Mother Zenobia's longevity was no more.

'You won't tell anyone, will you?' she added. 'It's all strictly prohibited by the *Codex Magicalis* under "enchantment abuse".'

'Your secret is safe with us,' I assured her. 'So this is how the Great Zambini looks seventy when he is actually one hundred and twelve?'

'Indeed,' replied Mother Zenobia as the novice returned with the tea and cocoa, bobbed politely and then went out again, 'but he could do it better than me. He turns to dolorite and thus has none of the sight difficulties I have with limestone. The really class acts turn themselves to granite, which has no side effects at all.'

'The Mighty Shandar,' I breathed, suddenly realising that he too must change himself to stone on a regular basis. 'That would explain how he has lived for almost five centuries.'

'Right again,' said Zenobia. 'It is said that his dynastic family of agents have instructions only to wake him for the best jobs. They say that the Mighty Shandar won't get out of black granite for less than eight dray-weights of gold a day, and that he has not lived longer than a minute since 1783, the year he finished the Channel Tunnel.'

'He could live almost for ever,' I observed.

'In *theory* you might,' said Mother Zenobia. 'Using petrification to suspend animation indefinitely is less dependent on the spell, and more a case of not letting things drop off. Pity those wizards from Ancient Greece missing either their arms, legs or heads. Come out of a two-millennium sleep missing an arm and you'd bleed to death within five minutes. Still,' she carried on, 'most of them would have been enchanted in RUNIX, and you'd not know how to get them back out anyway.'

'Which brings me back to why we are here,' I said. 'The gatekeeper of which Lady Mawgon fell foul was written in RUNIX, and we wanted to know how you might reverse that, given your expertise in these matters.'

'My spell is written in ARAMAIC-128,' she said, shaking her head, 'which allows for perfectly timed

94

depetrification. You need to find someone who is expert in RUNIX. What about the Great Zambini?'

This suggestion offered at least a possibility. I told Mother Zenobia about Zambini's possible appearance the next day, and she nodded sagely.

'I hope it works out. Bored now. Go away. Drink your cocoa.'

So we did, and drank a little more quickly than was good for us, and it made our eyes water. We left Mother Zenobia soon after, and with our semi-burned tongues, walked back towards the car. I now knew how Zenobia, Shandar and Zambini had lived for so long, but it didn't really help us.

'We *really* need to find the Great Zambini this time,' I said.

'Is it likely?' asked Tiger, who had been on several Zambini searches, and knew the pitfalls.

'If past attempts are anything to go by we have two chances: fat and thin.'

We walked outside and found Perkins peacefully asleep on the back seat, the paintwork of the beetle slowly turning from blue to green to black and then back to blue again. He was ready.

The King's Useless Brother

We partly retraced our route back towards Hereford, but instead of going straight ahead by the grave of the unknown tattooist at Dorstonville, we took the four-lane processional avenue that led towards the King's modest eight-storey palace at Snodhill. The castle covered an area of six square acres, with many of the Kingdom's administrative departments scattered among its two hundred or so rooms. A roof of purple slate topped the stone building, and the eighteen towers were capped with conical towers, each home to a long pennant that fluttered elegantly in the breeze.

After making our way through three sets of draw-bridges, each with their own peculiar brand of point-less and overlong security procedures, we eventually made it to the Inner Bailey, where we parked the car outside the Interior Ministry. I told Tiger to wait for us there, and I walked us to the correct desk, as I came in here quite a lot, usually to submit the endless forms and paperwork that bedevilled modern sorcery.

'Hello, Miss Strange,' said the receptionist, 'here to submit more paperwork?'

'Magic licence,' I replied, nodding towards Perkins. 'We have an appointment to see the King's Useless Brother.'

She stared at us both over her spectacles for a moment, consulted the diary and then pointed us towards the uncomfortable bench to wait. The one with cushions was reserved for those of higher birth, and was today crammed with bewigged aristocracy, who, by their refusal to sit on the citizens' bench, made themselves trebly uncomfortable.

Perkins and I talked through the application process. I was more nervous than I thought I'd be, probably because we were one sorcerer down for the foreseeable future, and Perkins was going to have to prove himself pretty fast if we still wanted to do the bridge gig on Friday.

'How do you think I'm going to do?' he asked.

'You'll pass or my name's not Jennifer Strange.'

'Your name's not Jennifer Strange.'

'What?'

'You're a foundling. You don't know what your name is.'

'It *could* be Jennifer Strange,' I said, unconvincingly, 'as a sort of coincidence.'

'It doesn't seem very likely.'

'Perhaps not. But listen, you're going to pass, right?'

And I took his hand and squeezed it, and smiled at him, and he smiled back.

'Thanks.'

'Miss Strange?' said the secretary again. 'The King's Useless Brother has become bored and will see you early.'

Perkins and I straightened our clothes and followed the secretary into a high-ceilinged room decorated in the 'medieval dreary chic' style that was then very much in fashion. A lot of stone, tapestries on the walls and a stylish cold draught that caught you in the small of the neck like the onset of pneumonia.

Sitting behind a large desk that was full of shiny executive desk toys was the King's Useless Brother: a thin, weedy man with a constantly dripping nose that he dabbed with annoying regularity with a handkerchief.

'Good afternoon, Your Gracious Uselessness,' I said, bowing low. 'I am Jennifer Strange of the Kazam House of Enchantments. I humbly beg to set before you an application for my client Perkins Archibald Perkins to be licensed to commit enchantments in the worthy Kingdom of Snodd.'

'Eh?' he said, so I said the same thing again, only this time much more slowly. When I had finished he thought for a moment and then said:

'You want a magic licence?'

'Yes.'

'Then why didn't you just say so? All that "gracious this" and "humbly beg" makes my head spin. I wish people would say what they want rather than hiding it in long words. Honestly, if we got rid of any word longer than eight letters, life would be a lot more understandable.'

'Except you wouldn't have been able to say "understandable",' pointed out Perkins.

The King's Useless Brother thought carefully and counted on his fingers.

'How right you are!' he announced at length. 'What were we talking about?'

'A magic licence application?'

'Of course. But tell me one thing before we look at the application.'

'Yes?' I asked, expecting to be quizzed about Perkins' fitness to serve, and whether he would uphold the noble calling with every atom of his being, that sort of thing.

'How can you be called Perkins Perkins?'

'My father's name was Perkins, and I'm named after him. It's like Adam Adams or David Davies.'

'Or William Williams,' I added.

'Who's he?'

'Someone I just made up.'

'Oh,' said the Useless Brother, sniffing. 'Right. What happens now?'

I took a deep breath.

'I explain exactly why Mr Perkins should receive a licence, and upon your approval, we turn to appendix F of the Magic Enactments Licensing Act of 1867 and conduct one spell each from Group "A" through to

Group "G". Afterwards, once opposition voices are heard, Mr Perkins performs his Great Feat. You then decide upon the merits of the case and stamp the application into authority . . . or not.'

'Stamp?'

His attention, which had been drifting somewhat, was suddenly renewed.

'I have a number of stamps for all different purposes – look.'

He jumped off his chair and opened a cupboard behind the desk. It was full of rubber stamps. Big ones, small ones, each elegantly made and presumably to enact some sort of legislation for which the Useless Brother had been made responsible.

'This is the one we will use today,' he said, selecting a large and ornately handled rubber stamp that was the size of a grapefruit. 'It carries two colours on a single stamp, which is a remarkable achievement, don't you think? Now, where do I stamp it?'

Perkins and I looked at one another. This was turning out to be much easier than we had thought.

'Don't you want to see Cadet Perkins perform his Great Feat at the very least?' I asked. 'Or even have the adjudicator present?'

'Oh, I'm sure he'll be fine,' said the King's Useless Brother dismissively, staring at the stamp lovingly. I shrugged. The stamp made it all legal, and we'd be fools to pass up such an easy opportunity.

'Just here,' I said, passing the application across the table.

'This is the bit I like,' said the bureaucrat excitedly, 'there's nothing quite like the satisfying thump of a rubber stamp on paper. The sound of freedom, don't you think?'

And so saying, he opened a jewel-encrusted pad, reverentially inked the stamp, brought it up above his head, paused for a moment and—

'One moment, sire.'

Two men had just walked in. The most important of them was Lord Tenbury, one of the King's most trusted advisers, and the Useless Brother's business partner. He was a man dressed in the robes of high office and wore a finely combed grey beard and hair that framed his piercing eyes, also grey. I had met him on a number of occasions and he always left me with the impression that he was an iron fist in a kid-leather glove. Pleasant on the surface, but too smart and savvy for it to be possible to get much past him, and loyal to the Crown through and through – and not averse to making a few sacks of cash on the side.

'My Gracious Lord,' exclaimed Tenbury in an exasperated tone. 'What did we say about stamping things when I'm out of the room?'

'Sorry,' said the Useless Brother, looking bored, 'but she seemed so nice and that person there has the same name as his last name.'

'Perkins,' said Perkins helpfully.

'I see,' said Tenbury, looking at us both suspiciously. 'And why are you here before your allotted time?'

'We were invited in,' I said.

'That's true,' said the Useless Brother. 'It gets very lonely in here sometimes with no stamping to do.'

'You could always look out of the window.'

'Of course I can't, *silly*,' scolded the Useless Brother. 'If I did that all morning I'd have nothing to do in the afternoon.'

'Very well,' said Tenbury with a sigh, 'have we seen the mandatory magic demonstrations or heard opposition statements?'

The Useless Brother frowned.

'Opposition . . . *what*?'

'Have we?' asked Tenbury, looking at me.

'No, sir, although we did ask. His Uselessness waived the normal procedure—'

'Then I must with all haste *reinstate* it,' interrupted Tenbury. 'I am sure you appreciate the importance of protocol and procedure, not to mention the possibility of falling foul of King Snodd's "No Hoodwinking of Simpletons" Law, specifically enacted for his brother?'

'My apologies, sir,' I said bowing low, 'I meant no disrespect.'

Tenbury smiled, and did so with considerable charm. It would be easy to trust him, and that would be one's first and last mistake. Unlike King Snodd and his mediocre dignitaries with their false charm, Tenbury was actually quite good at it. I could imagine him saying 'terribly sorry about this, old boy' as he put someone on the rack.

'But first,' he continued, 'pleasantries. Good afternoon, Miss Strange.'

I bobbed politely.

'Good afternoon, your Grace. May I present Cadet Perkins Perkins, here to apply for a licence to perform magic? Cadet Perkins, this is Lord Tenbury, the King's Chief Adviser.'

'Good afternoon,' said Tenbury with a smile, shaking Perkins' hands, 'so good of you to come. I expect you know this much-respected citizen?'

He indicated the man who had walked in with him. He was dressed all in black. Not the long flowing gowns of old wizidrical tradition, but a sharply tailored suit complete with black shirt, black tie, socks, shoes and, if the rumours were correct, underwear. He was a lean man in his early fifties with greying hair dyed black, a carefully coiffured goatee and upswept eyebrows that he had trained to work independently of one another for increased dramatic effect. He also had the annoying habit of keeping his chin high, so he had the appearance – if you were shorter, which most people were – of someone looking down his nose at you.

It was the Amazing Conrad Blix, chief wizard and managing director of iMagic.

We looked at one another coldly. The disdain wasn't just mine, it was universal. Blix thought it was because his grandfather had been the much-hated Blix the Hideously Barbarous and we were being needlessly prejudiced over his power-mad descendant, but the truth was more prosaic: he just wasn't very likeable.

'Have trouble with a spell this morning?' he asked.

I hoped my consternation didn't show.

'What makes you say that?'

'Several blips on the Shandargraph that were centred on Zambini Towers,' he said, 'One large dip at eleven fifteen that you kindly warned me about, several more ten minutes later, a pause and then a massive drain that almost flatlined the trace. It looked suspiciously like somebody got into trouble, and another tried to reverse it. They failed and then everyone tried together. Yes?'

He was entirely correct.

'Not at all,' I replied, 'we were simply limbering up for the bridge gig on Friday. There'll be some heavy lifting to do, and Patrick of Ludlow can't be expected to shoulder all the work on his own.'

I could see Blix didn't believe me, but I had other things on my mind. Not least, why was Blix buddying up with Lord Tenbury? I smelled a rat, and suspected it would not be long in making an appearance.

'We haven't met,' said Blix to Perkins, so I apologised and introduced them.

'I humble myself in your presence, sire,' said Perkins politely, for irrespective of how you viewed him, Blix was still a skilled practitioner. 'I saw you a few years back levijuggling* thirty-two billiard balls. Each in entirely separate orbits and speeds. It was quite something.'

'Too kind,' replied Blix with a bow.

'That's enough preamble,' said Lord Tenbury, 'and with His Eminence Ruprecht Sawduzt Snodd's approval, we should look at Mr Perkins' application.'

'Who?' asked Blix and I, almost at the same time, and Tenbury pointed at the King's Useless Brother, who was doodling absently on the blotter.

'Oh,' we said, not considering that he even *had* a name.

Lord Tenbury pressed a button on the intercom and asked for Miss Smith to be sent in. I saw Blix stiffen when Tenbury mentioned her name, and I felt my pulse quicken, too. The door opened and an upright woman in early middle age with a shock of white hair walked in. Her eyes were so dark they seemed empty, and an undefinable damp silence of the sort you get in caves moved in with her.

---

*A mixture of levitation and juggling. Although not of any huge practical use, it is a measure of a practitioner's skill. To levitate one or ten objects is easy; to make them all do different things when in the air takes considerable power and concentration. The Mighty Shandar could reputedly also do Blix's trick but with bison. Remarkable to behold, but what the bison thought about it was not recorded. Owing to constraints within the ARAMAIC-128 notation required in the enchantment, thirty-two objects is the maximum anyone can work with.

'Thank you – um – for joining us, Miss Smith,' said Tenbury, shivering as he spoke.

'Right,' she replied, glaring at Blix with her dark eyes so savagely I saw the colour drain from his cheeks.

This was Miss Boolean Smith, once known as 'the Magnificent Boo' and a powerful independent sorceress of considerable talents until kidnapped by anti-magic extremists. She had never practised again following her release, nor revealed why. The only time she did anything related to magic was in her usual job as Beastmaster, and at times like this: she was Infernal Affairs' nominated adjudicator, and would ensure that no trickery influenced Perkins' practical demonstrations. It would be simplicity itself to have another wizard outside doing spells on Perkins' account, or even a disgruntled wizard attempting to thwart Perkins with a jam, and Boo was there to detect any chicanery.

'It is with much pleasure that I meet you again,' I said, since we had spoken occasionally on the subject of Quarkbeasts, on which she was an expert. 'May I present Cadet Perkins?'

The Once Magnificent Boo glared at Cadet Perkins but did not shake his outstretched hand. She never did – not with anyone.

'I am much honoured,' said Perkins, trying to avoid her jet-black eyes.

'Then you honour too easily,' she replied before turning to Blix. 'Still drowning puppies, Conrad?'

'That was never proved,' replied Blix as the temperature in the room lowered another two degrees.

'Pleasantries are over,' said Tenbury nervously, 'The paperwork, if you please, Miss Strange.'

I presented the paperwork to Ruprecht, who stared at it absently for a few seconds before Tenbury checked it and then passed it to Once Magnificent Boo, who grunted her approval.

'You may proceed,' said Tenbury.

'This is my chosen spell from Group "A",' announced Perkins, as the Useless Brother and the chair he was sitting in elevated several feet, rotated once slowly, and then settled back down again.

'Gosh,' said the Useless Brother.

'Accepted,' said Boo.

Over the next twenty minutes, Perkins undertook several other acts of enchantment, which by their variety and scope demonstrated his understanding of the arts. He changed the colour of water in a jug to blue, made a light bulb glow without wires, and took off his own T-shirt without removing his shirt, which, while sounding easy, is actually one of the hardest to do in Group 'C'. In fact, he managed all of the tasks without a problem and to Boo's approval, and after several more assorted enchantments we were ready to hear any arguments opposing his application. This is where I expected Blix to drum up some technicality and block us, perhaps in retaliation for our observation that iMagic's Samantha Flynt was less than perfect when doing her magic feats, and conducting the test in a swimsuit was pointless and demeaning to the profession and women in general. He could have tried to block us, but he didn't.

'We have no objections to Mr Perkins' application.'

This was suspicious – mostly because that's what any reasonable person might have said, and Blix was rarely, if ever, reasonable.

Perkins was now ready to undertake his last act of sorcery, which was to be a Class Six enchantment of one's own invention that 'was to show originality, flair, and must be between one and three thousand Shandars'.

'For my final enchantment,' declared Perkins, 'I will set distant dogs barking.'

'What?' said the Useless Brother. 'That's it? This is *most* unsatisfactory. I was hoping for a shower of mice or conjuring up a marshmallow the size of my head or something.'

'It does sound a bit . . easy,' added Lord Tenbury.

'I concur that it *sounds* lame,' said Perkins, 'but making distant dogs bark is a spell of considerable subtlety that combines distance, canine mind control and pinpoint selectivity.'

'Cadet Perkins is correct,' said Once Magnificent Boo quietly, 'the test is valid.'

'Very well,' said Lord Tenbury. 'Proceed.'

'Yes,' said the Useless Brother. 'Proceed.'

We stepped out on to the ramparts outside the Ministry of Infernal Affairs office, a section of flat lead roof on the high outer wall of the castle. Eight storeys below us was the inner courtyard, and from our lofty perch we could see the Dragonlands, a vast tract of unspoiled land, untrod by humans for over four centuries and now home to the only two Dragons on the planet, Feldspar Axiom Firebreath IV, and Colin.[*]

'Ladies and gentlemen,' began Perkins, 'for this test I will set four distant and very separate dogs barking. But to dispel the notion of chance, you may choose the direction from which the dogs are to bark, and the size of the dog.'

'Can I choose first?' asked the Useless Brother, who was suddenly interested.

'Of course,' said Lord Tenbury, 'you *are* the Minister of Infernal Affairs, after all.'

'I am, aren't I?' Ruprecht said, pleased with himself, looking out over the battlements and waving a finger in the direction of the kitchens. 'I choose a chihuahua, and from over there.'

Perkins concentrated for a moment, and pointed two fingers in the direction Ruprecht had indicated.

[*]Colin is the smaller of the two if you ever meet. At the time of the events surrounding the bridge gig they were spending a fortnight in Washington, DC, reading the entire literary output of mankind at the Library of Congress, in order to better understand the species. They thought it 'in general a charming read, but tending towards monotony'. This is the principal reason they do not feature in this story.

Almost immediately, there came the sharp bark of a small dog, somewhere quite far away, and from the direction he had indicated.

'That's one,' said Boo.

'A Great Dane,' said Blix, 'from there.'

A moment later, there came the unmistakable deep, gruff tones of a large dog. The sound was so distant that if there had not been a breeze to bring it to our ears, we may not have heard it at all. Perkins was doing well, and the bark of a cocker spaniel next up was a similarly expert piece of spelling. If it had been any closer it would not have been distant, and if it had been ten feet farther away, we would not have heard it at all.

'A bull terrier,' I said, for it was my turn to choose the final dog, 'from over there.'

Perkins was relaxed and on a roll. His magic licence was in the bag. Nothing, I thought, could stop us now. He had raised his index fingers to cast his final spell when there was a sharp cough from behind us. We turned to find a footman dressed in full livery with embroidered jacket, tight red breeches, stockings and a wig. He held a staff which he struck twice on the ground, announcing in a shrill voice:

'His Gracious Majesty, King Snodd IV!'

King Snodd IV

Everyone but the Useless Brother and Boo knelt as the King walked out on to the flat roof where we were standing. He was on his own, or more accurately, he had so few courtiers, hangers-on and advisers that he might as well have been alone – I counted an astonishingly low dozen, which was normal when the King was in a solitary frame of mind. Snodd's ridiculously high staffing levels were not unusual within the royalty of the Ununited Kingdoms. He reputedly needed four valets to take a bath, and a minimum of two to go to the loo. One to hold the toilet paper and the other to . . . well, I'm sure you get the picture.

It was Tenbury who spoke first.

'Your Highness,' he said, 'you bless us with your presence.'

'I do rather, don't I?' he replied.

The King was a youthful-looking forty, and was in annoyingly good health for those who thought it might be better for all concerned if he would drop dead and let his wife, the considerably less militaristic and more diplomatic Queen Mimosa, take over. One of the few acts of civil disobedience within the Kingdom in recent years had been a march in support of Queen Mimosa having greater control in government. The King was prepared to use water cannon, riot police and tear gas, until Queen Mimosa stepped in herself and told the marchers to 'return home and be patient', something that they did, much to the King's astonishment and annoyance – he'd not used his riot police for a while and thought they needed some practice.

'I heard my good friend Jennifer Strange was in the castle,' said the King, 'and I just – why is that woman not grovelling or averting her eyes in my presence?'

Everyone looked up from where they were kneeling.

'This is the Once Magnificent Boolean Smith, Your Majesty, the magic test adjudicator and recently appointed Beastmaster.'

'What happened to Hugo?'

'He came off worse in an argument with a Tralfamosaur.'

He stared at Boo again and took two steps forward to remonstrate with her.

'Now listen here, good lady, I am the . . .'

His voice trailed off as he fell into the inky blackness of her eyes.

'Lumme,' he said, 'I have the queerest feeling that I'm drowning.'

'Not yet,' replied Once Magnificent Boo in an ominous tone, 'but you shall, and in mud, deserted by those you thought were friends.'

There was a difficult pause as the King and his courtiers took this in. The fact that there *was* a pause rather than an instant contradiction seemed to suggest not only that the King thought this a feasible demise, but his attendants did too.

'Now listen here—'

'Your Majesty should forgive a respected ex-enchantress her eccentricities,' said Tenbury in a soothing tone, and whispered something in the King's ear.

'Indeed,' said the King, 'all may rise, since we are friends together.'

We got to our feet, the King cleared his throat and, ignoring Boo, began again.

'I heard my good friend Jennifer was in the castle and I popped by to say "wotcha".'

I was immediately suspicious. The King never 'popped' by anywhere, rarely said 'wotcha' and was *definitely* not a friend.

'Come here, child,' said the King, and I approached cautiously. The last time we had met he had me put in jail for daring to meddle in his plans to invade the Duchy of Brecon. Thankfully, 'averting a war with pacifist aforethought' couldn't be found anywhere on the statute books so I was released after two weeks of half-rations and a single sheet to sleep under in a damp cell without natural light. To anyone else it might have been unbearable, but after being brought up by the Blessed Ladies of the Lobster, it was really quite relaxing. I'd not slept so well for months.

'Good afternoon, Your Majesty,' I said, curtsying. 'How best can I serve you?'

When I was a Dragonslayer I could do more or less what I wanted, but now I was simply an agent at Kazam and a loyalish subject of the King I had to be more careful. With despots it was always best to flatter and say 'yes' as often as possible. The King smiled, revealing a set of ridiculously white teeth. He wore a monocle and was thought of as handsome for a member of the royalty, and slightly like a weasel if he'd been anyone else. He had a silly habit of always wearing a crown, and lots of scarlet and ermine.

'I have decided that I should take this Mystical Arts nonsense with more seriousness than I have in the past,' he announced, 'and now the power of your old-fangled "magic" is arising once more, I must have a dedicated wizard at court in order to see how best the nation's newest asset can be efficiently exploited.'

He thought for a moment.

'I mean, 'how magic can best be used to serve the people'. What do you think?'

'I think that the Mystical Arts are best independent,' I replied. 'They should serve no one in particular, and be beholden to no—'

'You are but a child,' he said patronisingly, 'simplistic and unversed in the way of the world. What do you say, All Powerful Blix?'

I thought of mentioning that he was simply 'the Amazing Blix' but then this whole thing seemed to have a certain degree of stage management about it. There had been negotiations behind my back, and right now I was not guiding events, but their passenger.

'I think that is a fine idea, sire,' said Blix obsequiously. 'Your Gracious Majesty has a responsibility to better promote this new power for the betterment of the Ununited Kingdoms.'

'I could not have put it better myself and did,' said the King, turning back to me. 'You are appointed to the post, Mr Blix. Miss Strange, can I rely upon Kazam to afford all help that Court Mystician All Powerful Blix requires?'

I stared at him for a moment. A Court Mystician was a big jump for Blix and a worrying one. By ancient decree from the days when wizards were more powerful than they are now it made him eighth in line to the throne, after the royal family and Lord Tenbury. At times like this, I simply did what the Great Zambini would have done. He had expressly told me that Blix was not to be trusted in any way, shape or form. I chose my words carefully.

'I'm afraid to say that we would have to rigorously

examine any requests from Blix and consider each very carefully on its individual merits.'

The King raised an eyebrow.

'Is that a yes?'

'No.'

The King smiled at me.

'You are so very, very predictable, Miss Strange. I could force your houses to join, and even enact legislation to have Kazam outlawed. But those are the acts of a despot, not those of a fair, just and much-loved leader. Me,' he added, in case I was wondering who he was referring to. 'No, I suggest that a new company be formed from Kazam and iMagic which will be called "Snodd Magic PLC" and from these fine beginnings great things will be achieved. What do you say?'

I didn't have to choose my words so carefully this time.

'I believe I speak for all Kazam's members when I say that I must reluctantly decline your Majesty's generous offer. We will not support the Amazing Blix in any form whatsoever, and would strongly resist any attempt at a merger.'

'Is that a no?'

'Yes.'

'Oh dear.' The King sighed. 'An impasse. What do we do when we reach an impasse, Useless Brother?'

'A what?'

'I'll tell you,' continued the King, 'we should have

a contest to decide the matter. Magical contests are always enjoyed by the unwashed and the destitute – and *especially* by the unwashed destitute. I understand it is a traditional way to resolve matters between those versed in the Mystical Arts. Is that not so, Court Mystician?'

'Most definitely,' said Blix, turning to me. 'From the head of one House of Enchantment to another, I challenge Kazam to a contest. Winner takes control of the other's company.'

I couldn't really back out even if I'd wanted to. The Sorcerer's Protocol was obscure, ancient, mostly illogical and cemented into law by long implementation. To refuse a challenge was unthinkable, but then to *issue* a challenge was also unthinkable – it was something only ill-mannered dopes without any manners would do. Wizards like Blix, in fact.

'I reluctantly accept,' I replied, annoyed by the inflexibility of the Protocol, but not too worried. We could easily outconjure iMagic in any test they chose. 'What shall the contest be?'

'Why not Hereford's old bridge?' suggested Tenbury. 'Kazam were planning on rebuilding it on Friday, and we can instead have a contest. Kazam can build from the north bank, and iMagic from the south. First one to get their keystones fitted in the centre of the middle arch wins the contest. Royal Magic Adjudicator, is that fair?'

'As fair as you'll see in this kingdom,' said the Once Magnificent Boo, which I *think* meant she agreed.

'I agree the terms,' said Blix with a smile I didn't much care for. 'Jennifer?'

'I too agree,' I said, 'with the proviso that if Kazam wins, the position of Court Mystician is taken up by someone of our choosing.'

'Very well,' said the King. 'Blix, you agree to this?'

'I agree.'

'What's a keystone?'[*] asked the King's Useless Brother.

'Well, there it is, then,' said the King, ignoring him entirely, 'carry on,' and he swept from the roof with his entourage. A contest was always stressful, but we weren't in much trouble. Even with Lady Mawgon as alabaster we still had five sorcerers to their three. Besides, dealing with Blix and the rest of the rabble over at iMagic once and for all might actually help matters.

'Well,' said Blix, 'may the best side win.'

'We plan to,' I replied.

'Can we finish the application?' asked the Useless Brother. 'I'm keen to use that stamp.'

'A bull terrier,' I said after a brief pause, 'from Dorstonville.'

---

[*]It's the stone at the top of an arch that holds it all together. Oddly enough, an arch is held up by the very force that should make it collapse – gravity.

Unfazed, Perkins gesticulated with his fingers and, far away, a bull terrier barked.

'The test is complete to my satisfaction,' announced Boo. She signed the form awkwardly with her gloved hands and left without a word to any of us.

The form was duly countersigned by the Useless Brother and the heavy rubber stamp descended.

We stayed for a few minutes in the outer office while the paperwork was processed, and twenty minutes later we were back outside, where Tiger was waiting for us in the Volkswagen.

'How did it go?' he asked.

Perkins showed him the certificate, and Tiger congratulated him. We all talked about the contest on the journey back to Zambini Towers.

'I've never seen a wizidrical contest before,' said Tiger.

'Few have,' I replied, 'and although an unwelcome distraction, they never cease to be anything but dramatic.'

'The most spectacular contest was chronicled in the seventeenth century by Dude the Obscure,' said Perkins, who was more up on this sort of stuff, 'and was between the Mighty Shandar and the Truly Awesome Spontini. Shandar won three forests to a seven-headed dog in the first round, but lost nine castles to a geyser of lemonade in the second. It has been calculated that the deciding round used in excess of half a GigaShandar an hour, and involved some deft transformations, several vanishings, an exciting and wholly unrepeatable global teleport chase and an ice storm in summer. It was said the crackle was depleted so completely that no useful magic was done anywhere in the world for over six months.'

'Who won?' asked Tiger.

'The Mighty Shandar,' replied Perkins, 'who else?'

'Spectacular perhaps,' I said, 'but the most *nail-biting* was reputedly a low-level contest between two spell-managers of middle ranking who simply had an armchair hover-off in 1911. First one to touch the ground in their armchair lost. The tension had been considerable, apparently, and the contest was won after seventy-six hours of eye-popping concentration by Lady Chumpkin of Spode, who apparently lost three stone in weight with the effort.'

'Will we win the bridge contest?' asked Tiger.

'Without a doubt,' I said, with not quite as much certainty as I could have wished.

Zambini Towers

We'd had lunch, congratulated Perkins and were now gathered in the Palm Court. The only member of the 'inner sanctum' of licensed sorcerers absent was Patrick of Ludlow, who was busy moving an oak for a wealthy client eager to alphabetise his arboretum.[*]

Lady Mawgon and Monty Vanguard were still there, exactly the same as when we left. It would take ten or twenty years before a thin coating of lichen would make them look any different, although they might need a dusting by Tuesday week.

'Goodness,' said Perkins, who'd not seen a spell gone so badly wrong before. 'Have we attempted a Magnaflux Reversal?'

'Several times.'

'Has anyone asked the Mysterious X?' suggested Half Price. 'Since he's less of a who and more a what, he might have a different take on the problem.'

This was entirely true. Because of Mysterious X's

---

[*]Arboretum: it's a sort of tree garden. Putting the trees in alphabetical order is quite pointless. A better use of his money would be supporting the Troll War widows' fund.

nebulous state of semi-existence, we often gave him small jobs to do, such as retrieving cats stuck up trees, and it could persuade pianos into tune by glaring at them. The fact that he didn't have a licence didn't bother us, as there was little tangible evidence to say X even existed at all.

'I could speak to it,' volunteered Tiger. 'I think it quite likes me – I'm the only one who can give X its weekly degauss[*] without it causing trouble.'

'Go on, then,' said Wizard Moobin, and as Tiger hurried off, he passed the Transient Moose, who had just reappeared in the doorway, and watched us all in his usual laconic manner.

'Let's talk about the bridge contest,' I announced. 'Let's suppose we can't get Lady Mawgon back or use the Dibbles to help us – what problems do you think we might have?'

'We're still five to their three,' said Moobin. 'Blix is about on a par with me and a powerful levitator, but both Tchango and Dame Corby are less powerful than the Price brothers. Patrick is a solid plodder and can be trusted to get any heavy stone into position. We can keep Perkins in reserve and still beat them comfortably.'

They then talked about crackle allocations and

---

[*]Put simply, it means *demagnetising*, a problem to which the Mysterious X is prone given his strange, semi-charged particle existence. A good degaussing for X is like delousing for a dog – they don't like it much, but it's good for them in the long run.

technical stuff like that, and although half my attention was on the meeting, my mind always tends to wander a bit during technical discussions, which are, to be frank, boring. Wizards in general don't make good conversation. They are always reluctant to talk about how fantastic the conjured thunderstorm actually was – the size of the tempest and the bright flashes of lightning, the fearsome and towering storm-clouds and suchlike – but go into almost excruciating detail about the strands of spell that went into it. It would be like meeting Rembrandt only for him to talk about nothing but the wood of his brush handles.

As I looked around the room in a bored manner my gaze fell upon the Transient Moose. I narrowed my eyes. For as long as anyone could remember the Moose had simply stood around doing not very much at all. As I watched he faded from view, but not to another part of the hotel as he usually did, but to where Lady Mawgon was rooted to the spot in her calcite splendour. The Moose stared at the alabaster, shook his antlers and then vanished.

'Did you see that?'

'See what?' asked Moobin, who had just launched into a long and tedious discussion about Zorff's 6th Axiom.

'The Moose. He was examining Lady Mawgon as though he were . . . *aware*.'

'The Moose was written with Mandrake Sentience

Emulation Protocols,'* said Full Price, 'and like a Quarkbeast it shows considerable *evidence* of consciousness. But as to whether they are *really* alive or designed to make us think they are, we'll never really know.'

I opened my mouth to answer, but then noticed Tiger waving at me from the door of the Palm Court. I excused myself and hurried over, glad of a distraction.

'Problems?'

'Could be,' he said. 'Patrick of Ludlow just phoned. He said he's run into oversurge issues moving the oak in the arboretum and wanted a wizard to go down and help sort things out.'

'If it's an oversurge issue why not take Perkins?' said Moobin when I asked him whether he could help. 'He should know what it's like to absorb crackle rather than use it.'

Perkins agreed wholeheartedly as he was keen to begin his new career as a sorcerer, so a few minutes later myself, Perkins and Tiger were walking out the door towards my parked car. Tiger was carrying a partially inflated bin-liner as this was the way Mysterious X travelled when outside Zambini Towers. When you

---

*Lucy 'The Honourable' Mandrake, 1642–1734 was one of the 'Four greats,' and it is thanks to her work on MSEPs that magicians are able to make something *appear* to be alive. Up until this point, wizards could only create inanimate objects. Mandrake's unveiling of her groundbreaking Protocols at the 1732 World Magic Expo came with a demonstration of a shower of toads, each one of them apparently alive, but not. The 'Shower of Toads' spell is still regarded as a watershed of wizidrical knowledge and understanding – and despite its utter pointlessness, often copied.

are nothing more than an inexplicable energy field of unknown origin, even a light breeze has a dispersing effect which can be quite unsettling.

'Can you drop us off at the zoo?' asked Tiger. 'I kind of get the idea that Mysterious X *might* be able to help with the whole RUNIX deal, but wants to see the new Buzonji cub first.'

That was how the Mysterious X communicated. Not by words, but by ideas that popped into your head. Perkins had spent many hours consulting with him on the powers of suggestion – or, if you didn't believe in Mysterious X, Perkins had been sitting in a room, mumbling to himself.

'I never thought X was big on zoos,' I said as we climbed into my car, 'but then again, the Buzonji cub is *very* cute. All gangly legs and a pink nose.'

Shifting oaks

I dropped Tiger and the Mysterious X at Hereford Zoo. While disappointingly having neither elephants nor penguins, it was saved from ignominy by possessing several animals that were not created by evolution, but by magic. Back in the days of almost unbridled power, Super Grand Master Sorcerers would attempt to outdo one another in their creation of weird and wonderful beasts. Of the seventeen known 'non-evolutionary' creatures, only eight were still represented by live specimens. Of those, Hereford Zoo had an unprecedented four. They had the only captive breeding pair of Buzonji, which is a sort of six-legged okapi; two species of Shridloo, a desert and dessert – one being the edible variety. The only captive Tralfamosaur also had its home here, and was now in a more secure compound after it ate the last Beastcatcher. A Frazzle named Devlin completed the small collection – it was not just the only specimen living outside its natural habitat in the wetlands of Norfolk, but also the only one glad to be doing so. They used to have a Quarkbeast, but it kept on frightening people, so was removed from display.

'Here's some money for a taxi home,' I said, 'and remember to get a receipt – and don't let the cabby charge you extra for X.'

Tiger assured me that he wouldn't and asked for a sixpence for an ice cream. I bid him goodbye and then took the main road towards Colonel Bloch-Draine's country estate at Holme Lacy.

'So what's an oversurge?' asked Perkins as we drove out of Hereford.

'The art of magic is all about channelling the wizidrical energy that swirls invisibly around us. It usually takes skill and concentration to gather and focus the required power, but in some instances the opposite can happen, and the wizidrical energy comes in too thick and fast to be used safely.'

'Like an overflowing bath where you can't switch off the taps or take the plug out?'

'Something like that. It's unpredictable so pretty useless, like the wasted heat in a steam engine, so what you have to do is redirect the crackle elsewhere, like a safety valve. It can be quite fun, apparently – spelling anything just to use up the power. Showers of toads, levitation – whatever takes your fancy.'

'A sort of magic free lunch?'

'Kind of, except you still have to fill out Form B1–7G. If the paperwork isn't in order, the penalties are severe. The rules against illegal sorcery are quite fourteenth-century.'

'They don't think much of us, do they? Civilians, I mean.'

'Let's just say the relationship between the public and sorcerers has been strained ever since the whole Blix the Hideously Barbarous "world domination" episode. It was over two hundred years ago but memories are long when it comes to having one's will drained away and made into an empty husk, suited only to mindlessly follow the bidding of your new master.'

'I can see how that might not go down too well,' he conceded, 'but don't worry: I won't let you or Kazam down.'

There was quiet for a moment as we motored down the road.

'Jenny?'

'Yes?'

'Have you considered my offer to go and see the Jimmy Nuttjob Stunt Show?'

I looked across at him.

'Is this a date?'

'Might be,' he said, staring at his feet.

I said the first thing that came into my head.

'I'm only sixteen. I'm too young for you.'

'There's only two years between us. And let's be honest, you don't act much like a sixteen-year-old, what with the responsibility and dealing with Blix and matters of ethics and whatnot.'

'It's a foundling thing,' I told him. 'You grow up

quick when you have to fight every night with forty other girls for the only handkerchief in the orphanage.'

'To blow your nose?'

'To use as a pillow. I'm sorry to have to mention this but you're going to have to be careful with . . . personal relationships. Rejected partners can some-times get sniffy and wonder what they saw in you, and this can lead to accusations of *beguiling*. It's not a custodial offence as it's not provable, but the negative publicity is harmful, and there always remains the faint possibility of being hunted down by a crowd of angry and ignorant villagers, all holding torches aloft and eventually imprisoning you in a disused windmill which they set on fire.'

'Worst-case scenario?'

'Yes.'

'Do you think I'm beguiling you?'

I looked across at him and smiled.

'If you are, you're not that good at it.'

'Ah,' he said, and lapsed into silence.

Holme Lacy was less than ten miles away, and we pulled into the imposing front entrance of the colonel's residence a quarter of an hour later. Perkins looked nervously out of the window. It was his first gig. Up until now it had just been practice spells at Zambini Towers and a lot of classroom theory, and none of it to deal with surges.

I parked the car outside the colonel's imposing

eighteen-room mansionette. Lieutenant Colonel Sir Reginald George Stamford Bloch-Draine had been one of King Snodd's most faithful military leaders, and had personally led a squadron of landships during the Fourth Troll Wars twelve years before.

The point of the Fourth War had been pretty much the same as in the first three: to push the Trolls back into the far north and teach them a lesson 'once and for all'. To this end, the Ununited Kingdoms had put aside their differences and assembled one hundred and forty-seven landships and sent them on a frontal assault to 'soften up' the Trolls before the infantry invaded the following week. The landships had breached the first Troll wall at Stirling and arrived at the second Troll wall eighteen hours later. They reportedly opened the Troll gates, and then – nothing. All the radios went dead. Faced with uncertainty and the possible loss of the landships, the generals decided to instigate the ever popular 'let's panic' plan and ordered the infantry to attack.

Of the quarter of a million men and women who were lost or eaten during the twenty-six-minute war that followed, there had been only nine survivors. Colonel Bloch-Draine was one of them, saved by an unavoidable dentists' appointment that had him away from his landship at the crucial moment of advance. He retired soon after to devote his time to killing and mounting rare creatures before they went extinct. He had recently started collecting trees and saw no reason why it shouldn't be exactly the same as collecting stuffed animals: lots of swapping and putting them in alphabetical groups. Clearly, moving trees around his estate was not something he could do on his own, and that was the reason Kazam had been employed.

Patrick of Ludlow was waiting for us outside the colonel's mansionette.

'Apologies for calling you out, Miss Strange,' he said, wringing his hands nervously as we got out of the car, 'but things aren't as they should be.'

'No problem,' I said soothingly, 'you and me and Perkins will sort it out.'

Patrick was our Heavy Lifter. He could levitate up to seven tons when humidity was low and he was feeling good, which was more often these days as his six-ounce-a-day marzipan habit was now well behind him. He was a simple soul, but kindly and gentle despite his large size and misshapen appearance. Like most Heavy Lifters he had muscles where he shouldn't – grouped around his ankles, wrists, toes, fingers and the back of his head. His hand looked like a boiled ham with fingertips stuck on randomly, and the muscles on the back of his head gave him a fearful apearance. He generally stayed hidden when not working in case he was mistaken for an infant Troll.

'So, what's the problem, Pat?' I asked.

'Problem?' came a voice behind us. 'Problem? I expect no problems, only solutions!'

We turned to find the colonel, who, despite being retired, still wore a military uniform, with his chest an impressive array of brightly coloured ribbons, each representing a military campaign he had somehow missed owing to some unforeseen prior engagement.

'Gadzooks!' he said when he saw me. 'A girlie. Bit young for this sort of work eh?'

I ignored his comment and stared at his florid features. He had a large moustache, and his eyes were wide and very blue. Oddly, they seemed to have no real life to them – looking into them was like staring at a creepily lifelike waxwork.

'Mr Perkins and I are here to ensure the oak-moving goes as planned. It goes without saying that this is all within the price we quoted.'

'Oh,' he said, 'right. Do you take tea?'

I thanked him and said that we did, to which he replied that he was only asking me, and after persuading him that tea for all of us would get the job completed that much more quickly, he trotted off indoors.

'So,' I said, turning back to Patrick, 'what's the problem?'

Patrick beckoned me across to the colonel's arboretum, a small spinney of trees surrounding a lake. He indicated two large circular holes in the ground fifty yards apart. One presumably from where the oak had been, and another where it was meant to end up.

'Everything was going as planned,' said Patrick, indicating the half-done job, 'but just as I'd got the oak halfway from one place to the other, I had a surge and . . . well, can you see over there?'

He pointed to the far shore of the lake. Sitting on the lakeside was the oak tree, roots and all.

'That's about half a mile away,' said Perkins.

'I surged,' said Patrick simply, 'and then every time I tried to move the oak closer, the power just leapt and I dumped it even farther away.'

'Okay,' I said, 'this is what we'll do: Patrick, I want you to walk around the lake, lift the oak and bring it back. If you get another oversurge, I want Perkins to channel the excess into anything he wants. Questions?'

'What should I channel the oversurge into?'

'See how many fish you can lift out of the lake.'

Perkins looked at the lake, then at his fingers. Levitation was something he could do. There were no more questions and they began to walk off around the lake. I stood and watched them for a moment, then heard a noise on the wind. Something odd and familiar that I couldn't quite place. I walked across the lawn and towards a rusty battle tank that the colonel had transformed into a tasteless garden feature by the addition of several pot plants and a Virginia creeper on the gun barrel.

'Who's there?' I asked, and heard a rustling.

I pushed aside the azaleas and walked behind the armoured vehicle, where I found a pile of grass clippings and a compost heap. Nothing looked even remotely unusual, but as I was leaving I noticed that one of the tank's heavy tracks had been chewed, and recently. I peered closer at the toothmarks on the torn section of track, then searched the soft earth near my feet. I soon found what I was looking for: several dullish metal ball bearings of varying size. I picked them up and moved farther into the scrubby woodland, but after searching for five minutes and finding nothing more, I returned to wait for Patrick and Perkins to bring the oak back, which they did without any problems at all. The oak fitted snugly in its new hole, and the earth was soon moved in.

'Easy as winking,' said Patrick, 'without any surging at all. I guess you guys had a wasted journey.'

'Never a waste, Patrick,' I said thoughtfully. 'Call us any time.'

'Sorry for the delay,' said the colonel as he returned with the tea things. 'I made some scones. Good show with the oak. Have you time to move the silver birch twelve feet to its left?'

'You'll have to rebook, sir, we have quite a full—'

'Where did you get those?'

The colonel was staring at the ball bearings I had found behind the tank. I knew what they were, but

I hadn't expected him to as well. They were cadmium-coated cupro-nickel spheres with a zinc core.

'Quarkbeast droppings!' exclaimed the colonel. 'I've been after a Quark for years. I must fetch my dart gun.'

And he was off, running surprisingly fast for a seventy-year-old.

'A Quarkbeast?' said Perkins. 'The same one that was nibbling the plinth outside the Towers?'

I shrugged and told him I had no idea, then suggested they return to Kazam and lend their minds to the depetrification of Lady Mawgon.

'Where's the odd-looking fella and the young one with the sticky-out ears?' asked the colonel when he had returned with his gun.

'The next job,' I replied, but the colonel wasn't listening. With his hunting instincts all a-quiver, he had already reached the tank, examined the gnaw marks, and loaded the weapon with two large tranquilliser darts.

'Tipped with carbide steel,' explained the colonel, 'to penetrate their hide.'

'While I applaud your efforts to *not* kill it,' I said, 'might I ask what you are thinking of doing with an unconscious Quarkbeast?'

'Do you know how much people will pay to hunt for Quarks?' he said with a grin. 'The King's deer park over at Moccas would be an admirable base from which to run hunting trips.'

'They'll be hard to catch,' I said.

'I'm counting on it.' The colonel grinned. 'I might get ten or more hunts out of it before the blighter is finally bagged. Now listen, girlie,' he continued, 'I need to know all about Quarkbeasts. What they like, what they dislike. Best way to sneak up on one, favourite colour, that kind of stuff.'

'Why don't you speak to Once Magnificent Boo?' I replied. 'She runs a Quarkbeast rescue centre in the west of town.'

'I tried, but Miss Smith is somewhat . . . angry,' admitted the colonel. 'I thought I might get more sense out of you. And don't pretend you know nothing about them. Your affection for the little beasts is well documented. There's a bronze statue outside Zambini Towers, for goodness' sake, raised by you and your wizardy chums.'

I could have told him many things. About how they like to chew on scrap metal and aren't particularly fussy – except about lead, which gets stuck between their teeth, and cobalt, which gives them the runs. I could have told him how they change colour when they get emotional, or how they need linseed oil to keep their scales shiny, or how they like a walk twice daily. I might have told him that they were loyal, rarely ate cats and, despite appearances, were warm and faithful companions that it would be an honour to walk alongside. I could have said all that, but I didn't. I said this:

Jasper Fforde

'They can chew their way through a double-decker bus lengthwise in under eight seconds, and know when they are being tracked. If threatened, they will launch a pre-emptive attack with a degree of savagery that would make a Berserker faint. You don't want to be hunting Quarkbeast, Colonel.'

'Yes, yes, whatever you say. Now be quiet. I don't want to lose it.'

And so saying, he began to track the Quarkbeast, and I with him. If there was a chance to put him off his aim or alert the beast, I would take it. The tracking was quite easy, as beasts can rarely pass any metal without a quick bite to see whether it would make a good snack or not. In this manner we passed a sheet of nibbled corrugated iron, a bitten wire fence and an abandoned car with the chrome licked off the bumpers. The colonel dropped to one knee and peered around carefully.

'Reminds me of the time I was hunting Frazzle in East Anglia,' he whispered. 'Vicious blighters. Tracked a male for almost nine hours, you know.'

'Impressive,' I said sarcastically, 'given the Frazzle's agility, great speed and ability to outwit predators.'

He looked up at me and narrowed his eyes.

'Do you mock me, girlie?'

I certainly did. A Frazzle is a cross between an armadillo and an elephant seal. Hugely ungainly, and well armoured. If he'd been tracking it for nine hours, he must have done it riding a tricycle.

'What's that noise?' said the colonel, looking up.

'I didn't hear anything.'

Actually, I did. I leaned across and peered in the open window of the abandoned car and found the intelligent mauve eyes of a Quarkbeast staring back at me. The leathery scales that covered its back were partially raised in defence, and acidic drops of saliva hissed where they splashed upon the corroded metal. I placed my finger to my lips and it wagged its tail twice to say that it understood. This was bad news as Quarkbeasts have weighted tails, and it thumped against the old car like a drum.

In an instant the colonel had spotted the Quarkbeast and raised the gun to his shoulder. He didn't get to fire. Instead, there was a bright flash of green and a deep *whoompa* noise – and in an instant, myself and the colonel were rolling end over end in the long grass.

I sat up and looked around. The Quarkbeast had vanished, but that wasn't all that had changed. The remains of the abandoned car – every last mangled part of it – were now perfectly transformed into caramelised sugar, and the grass within the immediate vicinity was bright blue. I looked at the colonel, who now had his string vest and boxer shorts on the *outside* of his uniform. I was grateful that this had not happened to me, but noted that I had not been totally spared: my clothes were now on back to front, which is uncomfortable and disconcerting all at once.

'What was that?' asked the colonel, who seemed unconcerned that I now knew he had pictures of dancing hippos on his underwear.

'I have no idea at all,' I told him as I picked myself up. 'Nope, none. None at all. Nothing whatever. Zip.'

'Hmm,' said the colonel, 'think the Quarkbeast has gone?'

'Long gone.'

I walked with him back to the house and borrowed the downstairs loo to put my clothes back on the right way – and was mildly perturbed to find that my clothes had been untouched and *I* had been turned back to front. I was now right handed and the small mole on my left cheek was now on my right. I'd have to ask Moobin if there might be any long-term health issues.

I drove back to Zambini Towers deep in thought, mostly about the Quarkbeast. I had lied when I told the colonel I didn't know what we'd just witnessed. The beast had escaped in a short burst of wizidrical energy that had caused randomised passive spelling, hence the caramelised steel, clothing manipulation and my mirroring. Quite why it might suddenly do this I had no idea.

Quarkbeasts were weird, but up until then I had no idea *how* weird.

The King's address

I wandered into the Palm Court as soon as I got home to see whether anyone had managed to unravel Lady Mawgon or unlock the passthought, but they hadn't. Full Price was there among a pile of old books attempting to figure out a solution, and just to add more frustration to the mix, the Dibble Storage Coils were now at 60 per cent capacity and still rising. They'd vent crackle when they were full, and start to make cloud shapes* over Zambini Towers.

'Any idea what caused the surge?' said Full Price.

'No,' I replied. 'It had gone by the time we got there.'

'You look different.'

'I got blown back to front by a sudden burst of wizidrical power.'

'From what?'

'A Quarkbeast escaping in a panic. Did you know they could do that?'

---

*Unusual and realistic cloud shapes were the usual method by which bursts of wizidrical energy could be detected. The cloud shape above the experimental forty-megaton wizidrical detonations in the Cambrian Empire was a staggeringly realistic rendition of an *Amanita phalloides*, coincidentally one of the major ingredients of the potion that built the device.

'No – but then there's much we don't know about them,' said Full, returning to his work.

'Is it dangerous?' I asked

'Is what dangerous?' he asked, without looking up.

'Being reversed.'

'Not at all. We could try and change you back, but as with all complex procedures, there are risks. Unless you're unhappy, I'd stay as you are.'

I told Full Price I'd see how it felt being right handed and let him know, then went to the Kazam offices, where I found Kevin Zipp staring into space.

'Anything?' I asked.

'I'm afraid not,' replied Kevin. 'A possible winner at the three twenty at Haydock Park, something about a friend hidden behind a green door and that warning about Vision Boss again.'

'But nothing about the Great Zambini?'

He shook his head so I jotted what he'd seen in the Visions Book under codes RAD097 to RAD099.

I was doing paperwork and dealing with messages when Tiger reappeared.

'How did the Mysterious X like the zoo?' I asked.

'So-so,' he replied, 'but then it seemed to be saying that the cinema might also help clear its mind, so I took it to see *Rupert the Foundling Conquers the Universe*.'

'Hmm,' I mused, wondering whether perhaps Mysterious X was simply milking the situation to get a day out, or had decided to take Tiger out on the sort of day *he* wanted. Unsurprisingly, the Mysterious X often worked in mysterious ways.

'Is X any closer to helping us?'

'I don't think so.'

'It was worth a try. You'd better put it back in its room.'

'Okay, then,' said Tiger, and walked off, inflated bin-liner in hand. Perkins and Patrick wandered in a little later, and presented their B1-7G forms to be processed. All spells had to be logged, listed and presented to the Minister for Infernal Affairs. It was as boring as dusting, but like dusting, necessary.

'Your first form,' I said to Perkins, stamping and countersigning the B1-7G, 'congratulations. You can get your mother to stick it on the fridge.'

Supper was always early, and once the jam roly-poly had been left uneaten for the sixty-eighth consecutive day – a new record – Moobin had all those involved in the bridge gig convene in the Palm Court. Both Full and Half were there, Patrick, Perkins, myself and Tiger – oh, and Lady Mawgon and Monty Vanguard, but strictly in a non-speaking capacity. We were there partly to have a meeting, and partly to watch a repeat of the King's early evening Television Address to the People.

He usually used the address to tell citizens to consume less water, buy more shares in Snodd

Industries or simply to announce another tedious milestone in Princess Shazza's very public upbringing. Today's big news, however, was that Conrad Blix was Court Mystician. Blix was there on the telly next to him, trying to appear dignified and stately but actually looking smug and odious.

'It was to be expected,' I said, reviewing the footage sadly. 'The King likes to publicise almost everything he does.'

'I know,' said Moobin, 'but look carefully in the background.'

We craned closer as he ran the six-minute address again. As was usual, the address was filmed wherever the King happened to be, and he was surrounded by whoever he happened to be with. On this occasion he was naming a new landship and there, standing suspiciously close at hand, was the King's Useless Brother, Lord Tenbury – and Mr Trimble.

'Looks like BellShout Communications are covering all bases,' murmured Half Price.

Mr Trimble had been sounding me out earlier for Kazam's feelings on reactivating the mobile phone network, and I had foolishly given him a straight answer: that attempting to apply such a fundamental force would be like trying to tax gravity or own the stars. It confirmed what we all suspected – the King was attempting to control the administration of magic for financial ends, and with the help of Blix and Lord

Tenbury. They could name their own price to Mr Trimble and BellShout Communications. And that would just be the beginning. Magic for sale to the highest bidder.

'We *really* need to win the contest on Friday, don't we?' said Perkins.

'Definitely,' replied Moobin as he switched off the TV. 'There's a lot riding on it. It's not just about the ownership of Kazam, but of magic itself.'

We fell silent then, thinking about what the magic industry would be like run by the King and Blix. It wasn't a happy scenario, no matter how upbeat you tried to be. Quite the opposite, in fact – it would be a disaster.

'We'll win easily so long as we keep our heads,' said Moobin breezily, pointing at two pictures of the bridge. One as it should look, all nice and neat, and another of how it looked now – several hundred tons of damp slippery rubble.

'It'll be a standard lift and fix, with two teams working in pairs. One to raise the stones from the river bed, and the other to hold them in position while the first speed-sets the mortar. I suggest Perkins and Full in one team and Half and Patrick in the other. I'll be on hand to offer assistance wherever it is needed and to direct the operation. We shouldn't have any problems, but we should all practise tomorrow, and try to get Mawgon back – despite being a monumental

J>

pain in the backside, she is actually a first-class sorcerer. Jennifer has some ideas on this. Jenny?'

I stood up and cleared my throat.

'Kevin Zipp has prophesied that the Great Zambini will return tomorrow at 16.03 for a few minutes. I've got the Prince shadowing Zipp, and as soon as we have a location for his reappearance, I'll get straight over there. My primary job will be to find a way of unlocking Lady Mawgon and the Dibble Storage Coils, and after that, to try and help Zambini.'

'Good,' said Moobin, 'any questions?'

'Yes,' said Tiger, 'why do "inflammable" and "flammable" mean the same thing?'

'Sorry, I should rephrase that: any questions relating to the job in hand?'

There weren't.

'Well,' said Moobin with finality, 'there it is, then. Rest well.'

The perfidy begins

Sleep was difficult and both fitful and restless, and I was reduced to staring at the fireflies that flickered about the window, feeding off the gentle buzz of wizidrical energy that leaked out of the building.

Once a reasonable hour had arrived, I had a bath and came downstairs. I found the Youthful Perkins and Patrick of Ludlow in the lobby, busily at practice building an arch out of some cobbles. It was a tricky act, and one that required not only good co-ordination, but teamwork. The trick was to hold them all in a semicircle until the final cobble – the keystone – was placed at the apex, at which point they could both relax and the arch would stay up on its own.

Trouble was, it didn't seem to want to. On the few occasions they managed to get a complete arch made, it tumbled down as soon as they relaxed.

'It will be easier with bigger stones and the abutments to take the outward forces,' said Perkins, and Patrick grunted an agreement.

I had some breakfast and went to the office to check on Kevin Zipp. He was still asleep. Owen of

Rhayder was standing by on Kevin-watch for a few hours while Prince Nasil ran some errands. Owen was our second carpeteer and, through no fault of his own, the lesser of the two. Whereas the Prince's carpet was a frayed and moth-bitten artefact that would make the inside of a skip look untidy, Owen's was eight times worse. A carpet's design life was twenty thousand hours or three centuries before remanufacture, and Owen's was well beyond both.

'Did Kevin say anything in his sleep?' I asked.

'Not much,' replied Owen, 'just mumblings about index fingers, the Tralfamosaur, important people being blown to bits and how ice cream will be on the menu more than once a month from this time next year.'

'I like the sound of that,' said Tiger, who had just wandered in.

'I hope you're referring to the ice cream and not the blowing to bits. Put the visions in the book, will you? I think we're at RAD099. I'm going to have a look at the contest preparations.'

I stepped out of the hotel into Snodd Lane and walked to where it widened out into Snodd Street before turning left into Snodd Boulevard. I picked up a copy of the *Hereford Daily Eyestrain* from the seller on the corner and noted without much surprise that the competition was headline news.

TWO HOUSES BATTLE FOR TOP WIZ SLOT

The article was more or less correct, but heavily skewed in favour of Blix, who the state-controlled paper described as 'Newly appointed Court Mystician,' and also repeated the incorrect 'All Powerful' accolade. Farther down they referred to him as 'a *very* distant relative of Blix the Hideously Barbarous' and then quoted him as saying that 'the forces of good must be properly managed for the benefit of the people'. I went and gave the newspaper back to the seller and skilfully negotiated a partial refund, and then made my way to the wrecked bridge.

There had been many attempts to shame King Snodd into footing the bill for repairs following the bridge's collapse. The most persuasive argument was that without the bridge there was nowhere to dangle the corpses of the recently executed, as local city health ordinances forbade it within the city precincts. To be honest, no one had been executed for almost two decades as it was considered unfashionable these days, and it was for perhaps this reason that the King hadn't ordered a rebuild.

I stood at the abutment on the north end and looked at the large heap of rubble that stretched all the way to the opposite bank. There had been four piers, and although they still projected about a yard above the waterline, most of the stone was now on the river bed. Working in water was always difficult as it was a poor conductor of wizidrical energy. Moving a block of masonry a yard in water would take as much energy as moving one fifty yards out of it.

Snoddscaffolding, Inc. had already constructed a footbridge across the river to enable the sorcerers to better survey the rubble, and were now hastily erecting the tiered seating and royal box. I went and found the Minister for Glee, who was dicussing with his staff how best to accommodate the maximum number of people, how much they could charge them for seats, popcorn and hot dogs, and what concessions to give to the unwashed and destitute – if any.

After introductions I explained that owing to health and safety considerations all observers would have to be at least fifty yards away to guard against secondary enchantments that split off the main weave.

'Fifty yards?' repeated the minister. 'That's not really a close-up view of anything. The King himself insisted that he had a ringside seat to watch the action at close quarters.'

'It's your call,' I said, 'but I'm not going to be the one who has to explain why His Gracious Majesty and his family will be spending the next two weeks with donkey's heads.'

There was a pause.

'Donkey's heads?'

'Or two noses. Perhaps worse.'

'Fifty yards, you say?'

'Fifty yards.'

There was little to be gained from hanging around here so I walked back to Kazam, stopping on the way to buy some liquorice for no other reason than I liked liquorice. The sweetie shop was next to Vision Boss and, mindful of Kevin's prediction, I went into the shop and looked around. It was a popular chain of opticians with a huge array of frames to choose from. Everything seemed normal enough, and after digging out my Shandarmeter and testing for any wizidrical hot spots and finding none, I wandered out again. That was the problem with precogs. You rarely knew the meaning of their visions until it was too late. Sometimes it was better not to know at all.

'Ah!' said a familiar voice as soon as I had stepped outside. 'Good to see you again, girlie.' It was Colonel Bloch-Draine. He was dressed for hunting this time, and was carrying his dart gun.

'You're very patronising,' I pointed out.

'Very clever of you to notice, girlie. Have a look at this.'

He produced an official-looking certificate that told me he had been engaged by Court Mystician Blix as a 'licensed agent' to personally oversee the capture of any 'rogue' or 'feral' magicozoological beasts that were 'terrorising' the city or causing 'public unease'.

'So you and Blix aim to start Quarkbeast hunting tours?' I asked, putting two and two together.

'The tourism sector is an underexploited resource in

this Kingdom,' he said. 'The Cambrian Empire earns over eight million moolah in Tralfamosaur hunts alone.'

'And those same hunters get eaten on a regular basis, I've heard.'

'We will insist on payment in advance,' replied the Colonel, who was clearly of a practical, if callous, frame of mind. 'Now, where would I find a Quarkbeast?'

'I can't help you, Colonel.'

'You *can* help me,' he replied, 'and will. Failure to assist a royal agent in the execution of their lawful duties is an offence punishable by two years in prison with hard labour.'

I stared at him for a moment and decided to call his bluff.

'Then you will have to have me arrested, Colonel.'

He looked at me and a faint smile crossed his lined features.

'You have spirit,' he said at last, 'and I respect that. Are you yet lined up for a husband? My third son is still without a wife.'

It wasn't an unusual question; in the Kingdom of Snodd 95 per cent of marriages were by arrangement. The only benefit of being a orphan was that you were entitled to arrange your own.

'Three possibles with five in reserve,' I said, lying through my teeth. I'd had offers, of course, but nothing serious.

'Can I put my son down as sixth reserve?' he asked.

'No.'

'He has six acres and a steady job in waste disposal – *and* all his own teeth.'

'How tempting,' I replied, 'but still no.'

'Tarquin will be disappointed.'

'I dare say I can live with that.'

The colonel thought for a moment.

'Are you sure you won't help me find the Quarkbeast?'

'I would sooner sunbathe in the Tralfamosaur enclosure draped in bacon.'

'I don't need your help anyway,' he said at last. 'I have what information I need from the All Powerful Blix. Good day, Miss Strange. You'll regret not considering Tarquin.'

And he hurried off in the direction of the bridge.

'It's "the *Amazing* Blix",' I called out after him, but to no avail. I shrugged, and turned for home.

As soon as I stepped into Zambini Towers I knew something was wrong. Wizard Moobin was sitting on a chair in the lobby looking worried.

'Problems?' I asked.

'Full and Half Price have been arrested pending extradition to face charges in the Cambrian Empire,'[*]

---

[*]Despite the grand title, the mid-Wales-located Cambrian Empire is a ramshackle collection of warlords nominally controlled by the Cambrian potentate Tharv the Bountiful. The empire has almost no economy or government, but despite its lawless nature, visitors are shockingly well-treated, and the crime figures of the nation are the lowest in the unUK.

replied Moobin sadly. 'It is alleged they were key figures in Cambria's illegal thermowizidrical explosive device programme in the eighties, as banned by the Genevieve Convention of 1922.'

'Is that serious?'

'It's a Crime against Harmony – the worst sort. It carries a double death with added death penalty.'

'That's insane,' I replied. 'The Prices wouldn't hurt a fly. This is all totally trumped up, right?'

Moobin didn't say anything. He just stood there and bit his lip.

'Blast,' I said under my breath, knowing from his look that this was *precisely* what the Prices had been fleeing when they arrived here twenty years before. The Great Zambini gave shelter to all those versed in the Mystical Arts, irrespective of past histories. I shuddered as I tried to think who else we might have in the building, and what they might have done.

'We can still win the contest,' said Moobin. 'Me, Patrick and Perkins against Blix, Corby and Tchango. Look at it this way: three against three is a fair fight.'

'With the greatest of respect,' I replied, 'Blix is not after a fair fight. He won't stop until it's his three against our one – or less.'

We sat in silence in the empty lobby, the only sounds the clock, the rustling of oak leaves and the occasional 'pop' as the Transient Moose moved in and out.

'I'm sorry,' I said at last.

'What for?'

'For agreeing to this contest.'

'You didn't have any option,' said Moobin, placing his hand on my arm. 'A challenge is a challenge. The real fault lies with Blix. How long do you think it will be before they arrest the next one of us?'

'Any minute now, I should imagine.'

Just as I spoke Detective Norton and Sergeant Villiers walked into the lobby. If there was work to be done of a dubious nature that needed a veneer of legality, these two would be doing it.

'Miss Strange,' said Detective Norton. 'How delightful to meet you again.'

I didn't have time for this.

'Where are the Prices?' I demanded.

Norton and Villiers gave me their well-practised triumphant grins.

'Under lock and key until the hearing on Monday,' said Sergeant Villiers, who was the physical opposite of Norton – heavily built in body and face compared to Villiers' almost painful thinness. We often joked that they were the 'Before and After' in a weight-gain advert. I'd crossed swords with them in the past, and didn't like them.

'Monday? Conveniently two days *after* the bridge gig?'

'These are serious charges, Miss Strange. But we're not here for idle chit-chat.'

'No?'

I thought they had come about my refusing to help hunt the Quarkbeast, but they hadn't. Maybe the colonel wanted to keep me sweet for the Tarquin option.

'Wizard Gareth Archibald Moobin?' asked Norton in that way police do when they already know the answer is 'yes'.

'You know I am.'

'You're under arrest for committing an illegal act of magic; for failing to declare said act of magic; for not submitting the relevant paperwork; for plotting to hide said act of magic from the authorities.'

I noticed Villiers take Moobin's arm. They knew he could teleport and weren't going to risk losing him.

'And what act was this?' I asked, knowing full well that in the four years I had been at Kazam not a single act of sorcery had gone unrecorded.

'It's about a bunch of roses produced "from thin air" as a gift for a certain Miss Bancroft,' said Villiers, 'on or around 23 October 1988.'

'Jessica,' said Moobin in a quiet voice.

'Yes,' said Norton, 'Jessica.'

He looked at me and shrugged while they slipped on the lead-lined index finger cuffs to stop him spelling.

'Bet you regret trying to impress her now, eh?' sneered Norton.

'Oddly, no,' he admitted with a fond smile. 'She was

quite something. What we call a "refuzic" — possessed of magical powers, but convinced she had none. Get this: she could lick a man's bald head and tell what he had for breakfast. Don't tell me that's not magic. What's she doing these days?'

'She's Mrs Norton,' said Norton, 'and if you go spreading the bald head thing about it won't be just the King and Blix playing "jail the wizard".'

'Hey, plod,' said Tiger, who had just walked in, 'I can make a bacon roll vanish — and then make it reappear the following morning in a completely different form. You going to arrest me for illegal wizardry too?'

Norton and Villiers glared at Tiger, appalled at his gross impertinence. If they'd not been busy they would have arrested him too.

'Bloody foundlings,' said Norton, 'a waste of space the lot of you. One more thing: if you're looking for Patrick of Ludlow, don't. We just picked him up, too — on charges relating to marzipan abuse. So long, Jenny.'

And a moment later the doors were swinging shut behind them.

'This is all my fault,' I said, sitting down and putting my face in my hands. It was now Perkins up against the powers of Blix and his cronies. One of ours against three of theirs.

'It's not your fault and it could be worse,' said Tiger in a soothing voice.

'How could it possibly be worse?'

'It could be Friday. It isn't. It's only Thursday morning. Lots can happen. So we're down to only one sorcerer. Big deal. There must be others we can use.'

'No one else has a licence.'

'What about sorcerers who had licences from the old days? Ones who never had them taken away?'

'If they were sane enough to work, they would be.'

Tiger nodded his head towards the front door.

'I wasn't thinking of in here. I was thinking of . . . out there.'

I sat up. Hope had not yet fully departed.

'You're right. There are two I could try. I'll start with Mother Zenobia.'

'Would she help us?'

'Almost certainly not – but it's worth a shot. And listen, if Blix wants to play dirty, so should we.'

'Meaning?'

'Meaning we should find out something about him. Something we can use against him. Past misdemeanours, dirt, unpaid parking tickets – I don't know. You do some snooping, and I'll try and rustle up some sorcerers.'

I walked out of the front entrance, suddenly remembered I'd forgotten my keys, pushed open the door to Zambini Towers, stepped inside – only to find myself stepping out of the back entrance of the hotel. I held the door wide open and, impossibly, *the front entrance led straight to the back*. It was as if the old hotel wasn't there at all. I closed the door again and pressed the doorbell.

The door was answered by Perkins, and, oddly, he was in the hotel – behind him I could see the lobby.

'Forget your keys?'

'Look at this.'

He stepped out and I closed the door, then told him to reopen it. He did so, and stared not at the lobby, but at the alleyway on the far side of the building.

'Where's the hotel gone?'

'I was hoping you'd tell me.'

'You think I did this? No way. I have trouble making dogs bark at a distance.'

'Then who?'

He shrugged.

'I don't know. Listen, you must have a word with Tiger. He was trying to fool me into thinking that Patrick, Moobin and the Prices have all been arrested, and he really shouldn't joke about such things.'

I raised an eyebrow and stared at him.

'Crumbs. You mean he wasn't kidding?'

'I wish he was.'

I pressed the doorbell again and a few minutes later Tiger answered. I explained what had happened, and after checking the other entrances and the windows – but with one of us keeping the door open so we could get back in – we found that all access points led to an instant exit on the other side of the building.

We couldn't agree who might have done it, but did agree that it was an excellent defence – something that was tested twenty minutes later when Norton and Villiers returned to 'interview' Lady Mawgon. I shouted through the door that she would be surrendering herself to the authorities on Monday, and after a brief exchange of discourtesies, they left.

'Right,' I said once I'd found my car keys, 'I'm off to get help.'

'What can I do?' asked Perkins.

'Help Tiger find out what you can about Blix. There must be something we can use to our advantage. Oh, and congratulations. You're doing the bridge gig on your own tomorrow.'

He stared at me with a look of horror.

'If I'm going to fail I guess I should do it in a spectacular fashion.'

I told him it wasn't over until it was over, picked up my car and was soon heading out of town.

Mother Zenobia

As I drove to Clifford to see Mother Zenobia, I wasn't very hopeful that I would have much luck recruiting her to our cause. She was old, tired and for almost 75 per cent of the day a form of limestone. What wizidrical powers she had available to her were most likely limited, and I knew for a fact that she hadn't been out of the convent for years. But I wasn't the only person who wanted to see Mother Zenobia that afternoon, and their presence was neither welcome, nor, as I considered it later, surprising.

It was none other than Conrad Blix, and I met him walking out of the Sisterhood of the Blessed Lady of the Lobster as I was walking in.

'Jennifer!' he said with a mockingly pleasant demeanour. 'How is the team bearing up?'

'You know well enough,' I replied coldly. 'What are you doing here?'

He leaned closer.

'Dealing with a few flies in this particular ointment, Miss Strange. This morning Norton and Villiers were merely assuring our victory. Just now I was guaranteeing it.'

I didn't like the sound of this.

'What have you done to her?'

He smiled.

'I will get so much satisfaction watching you work for me as a parlourmaid for the next two years. And for your complete and utter humiliation, I will *insist* you wear the uniform.'

'You're a coward to use such underhand means to win the most noble of contests, Blix.'

He narrowed his eyes.

'And you're very impertinent considering you're nothing but a foundling who lucked out in your work allocation.'

'On the contrary,' I replied evenly, 'foundlings are *always* impertinent – it's because we've nothing to lose. I'm actually one of the politer ones.'

'You'll regret your words, Jennifer.'

'And you your actions,' I replied, 'and even if you do win, none of us will ever work for you.'

'I wouldn't expect you to,' he said. 'All I need is control of Kazam and with it a monopoly on magic – surely that's obvious?'

'To reanimate the mobile phone network?'

He grinned.

'That's just for starters. You have no idea how much

a wise investor can make by exploiting the crackle. The licensing deals on electromagical devices will make a fortune – millions alone for something as simple as a pocket calculator. And all that work you're doing to reanimate medical scanners for *free* – deluded. How much do you think people will *pay* to detect an early tumour?'

I clenched and unclenched my fists.

'Magic is not for the one,' I said through gritted teeth, 'it's for the many.'

'I agree wholeheartedly. But in this particular instance, "many" means only myself, Lord Tenbury, the King and his Useless Brother. Oh, and good move with Zambini Towers and the "infinite thinness" enchantment. Lady Mawgon, was it?'

He didn't know she was stone, which was a small plus in our favour.

'She's very talented, if a little severe. We'll defeat you tomorrow, have no fear of that.'

He laughed.

'With who? A cranky washed-up old has-been and a winsome newbie who can barely levitate a brick? No. You'll be thrashed. Why don't you concede now and save the magic industry a lot of embarrassment?'

'The future of magic is not negotiable.'

'You're wrong, and what's more, it's not your decision to make. Here's the deal for you to take back to Kazam: concede before midnight tonight, and I will ensure that all those hopeless ex-sorcerers at Zambini – I mean, "all those venerable past masters" – are looked after in a five-star nursing home until they croak. I will offer every licensed practitioner a job under my leadership or, failing that, two million moolah cash in return for surrendering their magic licences. What's more, you and Tiger will be paid to do nothing until your indentured servitude is finished, at which point you will be granted full citizenship. Do we have a deal?'

'Go to hell.'

'Almost certainly,' he replied with a smile, 'but I'll go there wealthy. I'll expect an answer by midnight, yes?'

He smiled at me in a smug and triumphant manner, but something didn't quite ring true.

'That's a very generous offer,' I said, 'for someone so utterly sure they will win. If you can thrash us as you claim, you can take what you want from the wreckage without spending a bean. Do we *worry* you, Blix?'

He smiled again, but not with quite so much confidence. He was scared of us.

'Let's just say,' he added, recovering his composure, 'that the magic industry has enough bad PR at present without petty infighting. If we're to start selling magic as a benevolent force for good – as essential to daily life as the water in the tap and electricity in the plug – then we need to show we are responsible and upright citizens. Take the offer, Strange.'

I had no intention of accepting his offer.

'We'll see you at the bridge site tomorrow morning for the contest. Nine on the dot, wasn't it?'

'Nine it is. *Sandop kale n'baaa*, Miss Strange.'

'*Sandop kale n'baaa*, Amazing Blix.'

And after staring at me for a moment, he turned on his heel and left. I walked into the convent and soon found what Blix had been up to. Mother Zenobia was sitting in her chair, stony features looking straight ahead. She had changed to stone for her afternoon nap, and Blix, presumably, had blocked her return. I was too late. Blix had won this round, too. I took a deep breath and prepared to leave.

'Is there anything I can do?' asked a tearful Sister Agrippa, who was Mother Zenobia's attendant.

'Put a sheet over her and give her the once-over with a feather duster every fortnight. Don't use a vacuum cleaner in case you knock something off – she'd never forgive you when we get her back.'

I walked out of the convent with the saddening realisation that we were pretty much stuffed. With one potential sorcerer crossed from my list, my last hope was a woman who won an unprecedented six golds in the sorcery events at the 1974 Olympics. She was a sorcerer of undisputed skills, but also secretive, obstinate and prickly beyond measure. She was the Once Magnificent Boo.

Boo and the Quarkbeasts

You couldn't work in the magic industry without knowing something about the Once Magnificent Boo. Indeed, when one considers the strange practitioners associated with the industry, it is often hard not to talk about anything else. Miss Boolean Champernowne Waseed Mitford Smith, to give her her full name, was an infant magic prodigy. At the age of five she was writing her own spells, was deemed 'amazing' by her tenth birthday, 'incredible' by her fifteenth, and 'magnificent' by the time she turned twenty. Her theory on 'spell entanglement' for multitasking was one of her most brilliant contributions, allowing for several enchantments to be done at the same time, a problem unsolved since the twelfth century. In short, she was doing stuff in her teens that the Mighty Shandar couldn't perform until he was in his thirties, and she was tipped to become the Next Great Thing – a sorcerer of astonishing powers of the sort that crops up only every half millennia or so, and change the craft in new and exciting ways.

She never fulfilled that early promise, and not

through her own fault. She was kidnapped in 1974 by anti-magic extremists and hadn't done any magic since her release, and rarely socialised with those who did. No one knew quite why, nor were ever greeted with anything but a damp stony silence when asked. But she hadn't totally forgotten her roots, and by way of the respect accorded to her, still carried the 'Once Magnificent' accolade.

Thirty-three years after her kidnapping she was still in Hereford, working as a magic licence adjudicator, and Beastmaster to the Crown. More importantly to me, she was also running the only rescue centre for Quarkbeasts in the northern hemisphere. This was in Yarsop, a small village just off the Great West Road that led to the border with the Duchy of Brecon, and that's where I ended up a short drive later.

Once Magnificent Boo's house was unremarkable, and indeed, I had to recheck the address as past experience with sorcerers suggested that they usually lived in eccentrically built thatched hovels, full of junk and with owls and stuff hanging around outside. Not this house, which was one of a pair sitting at the end of a gravel drive with weeping willows and flower beds all neatly laid out in a way that was a picture of unmystical normality. I opened the gate and crunched down the drive.

I pressed the doorbell and Once Magnificent Boo answered. Her white hair was tied back and more neat, but her eyes were still as dark as pitch, and I shivered as a cold rush of air escaped from the house. She took one look at me, snorted, and shut the door in my face.

I didn't leave. She knew I was there so it didn't make any sense to ring again, so I simply waited. Eight minutes ticked past and eventually the door reopened.

'There's no business for you here, Miss Strange.'

I took a deep breath.

'A Quarkbeast once chose me for companionship.'

'Yes; and your reckless custodianship led to its death.'

This was true, and something that had preyed on my conscience these past two months. It had been a risky time in my life, and I'd made no effort to stop the Quarkbeast following me into danger.

'For which I will never cease to be ashamed,' I said softly. 'I miss him greatly. Did you hear that a wild Quarkbeast was wandering around Hereford at present?'

'The colonel was here,' she said shortly, 'asking questions on how to trap one.'

I told her about his plans for Quarkbeast-hunting holiday breaks for people with a lot more money than sense – and Blix's involvement.

'They have no idea what they're meddling with,' said Boo.

'Is there a way to stop him?' I asked.

She narrowed her eyes, thought for a moment and then opened the door wide.

'Come in but be warned: ask me to help you by doing some M-word and I'll punch you in the eye. Understand?'

'Yes.'

I stepped in and was immediately struck by the ordinariness of the interior. Of her past life as potentially one of the all-time greatest sorcerers ever, there was hardly any evidence at all. From the interior I could discern only that she was obsessed with Quarkbeasts to a degree that was probably unhealthy, played croquet for the county, and liked to cross-stitch cushions.

'Nice place you have,' I said.

'Adequate for my needs,' she replied, seemingly less unfriendly now we were in her house. 'Which Quarkbeast was yours?'

I took a picture from my shoulder bag and showed her.

'The photographer was trembling with fear when he took it,' I explained, 'so it's a bit blurred.'

'Hmm,' said Once Magnificent Boo as she took the picture to a desk, where she opened a book full of Quarkbeast illustrations. It wasn't just a rescue centre – she was studying them. She pulled out a picture and showed it to me.

'Was that yours?'

I stared carefully at the picture.

'No.'

She turned to the large Florentine mirror above the mantelpiece and held up the picture so I could see the same picture *but in mirror image*, and I felt a tear spring to my eye with the sudden recognition.

'That's him.'

'Not him, *it*,' corrected Once Magnificent Boo, scribbling in a notepad. 'Quarkbeasts are genderless. You had Q27. Is this the beast you saw in town?'

She showed me the photograph I had given her of my Quarkbeast, but reflected in the mirror.

'Yes, that's him.'

'Then we've got the pair of your Quarkbeast sniffing around – Q28. It took him two months to get here from Australia, which was to be expected. Quarkbeasts aren't strong swimmers.'

'It swam twelve thousand miles?'

'Don't be ridiculous. It only swam *eight* thousand miles – the rest would have been overland at a fast trot.'

'That's quite a migration.'

'Quarks are remarkable beasts. Do you want to see some?'

'Yes, please.'

We walked out of the back door, which I noted had been broken recently and hastily repaired, and into a paddock at the back, where four Quarkbeasts were happily sunning themselves.

'Quark,' said the one closest.

'Quark,' said another.

'Quark,' said the third.

'Quark,' came the muffled call of one that was inside the pen.

It was quite an emotional moment, and although their calls were subtly different and none of them looked like mine, they all looked as if they *might* be, which is a bit odd and unnerving.

'That's Q3,' said Boo, pointing to a mangy-looking specimen who was missing most of its back-plates. 'I rescued it from a Quarkbaiting ring. A very cruel sport. Over there is Q11, which got run over on the M50 and was dragged for six miles. You can still see the eight grooves its claws made in the road all the way to the Newent exit from the Premier Inn. Q35 is the one in the iron filings wallow. It was captured alive in the jam and biscuit section of the Holmer Road Co-op. The beast with the missing teeth is Q23. I got it from the zoo after they thought it was frightening the public too much. I had them all registered as dangerous pets. Legally, no one can touch them – not even the colonel.'

She looked at me for a moment, then opened a cardboard box that contained tins of dog food. She picked them up with her gloved hand and tossed them toward the Quarkbeasts, which crunched them up eagerly, tin and all.

'What do the neighbours think about having them here?' I asked, since the four of them looked so intimidating that only those well acquainted with the species would be relaxed in their company.

'They're okay about it – they think it keeps burglars at bay. It doesn't.'

She indicated the broken back door.

'Last Tuesday night. Did the beasts let out a single Quark? Not a bit of it.'

'Take much, did they?' I asked, stalling as I tried to figure out a way to raise the 'can you help us?' issue without getting punched in the eye.

'Money, jewellery, that kind of stuff. I thought of leaving a Quarkbeast in the house at night, but, well, there are some things you baulk at doing, even to burglars.'

She was right. No one deserves a savaging by a Quarkbeast – or even being surprised by one when you're off doing a spot of innocent villainy.

'Do they like it here?'

'They *seem* happy, but since they're running on Mandrake Sentience Emulation Protocols to make us think they're real, we can't ever know for sure.'

'So what is Q28 doing in town?' I asked. 'If its twin is dead, it can't be looking for him, surely?'

The Once Magnificent Boo stared at me intently.

'Are you ready to be confused?'

'It's how I spend most of my days at Zambini Towers.'

'Then here it is: Quarkbeasts breed by creating an

exact mirror copy of themselves – and since the Mighty Shandar created only one Quarkbeast, every Quarkbeast is a copy of every other Quarkbeast, only opposite.'

'I was blown back to front yesterday,' I said. 'Is that the same thing?'

'No, and if I were you, I should stay that way. It will save your life.'

'Right. But wait a minute,' I said, looking at the picture of Q26, the one that paired to give mine, 'if Q27 is the mirror of Q26 and Q28 is the mirror of Q27, then why don't Q26 and Q28 look the same? Alternate generations must be identical, yes?'

'No. It's more complicated than that. They create identical copies of themselves in six different flavours: *Up, Down, Charm, Strange, Top* and *Bottom.* All are opposite and equal, but all uniquely different and alike at the same time.'

'I don't understand any of this,' I said, feeling increasingly lost.

'I still have problems with it after twenty years,' confessed Boo. 'The complexities of the Quarkbeast are fundamentally unknowable. But here's the point: there can only ever be thirty-six completely unique yet identical Quarkbeasts, and as soon as the combinations are fulfilled, they will come together and merge into a single Quota of fully Quorumed Quarkbeasts.'

'What will happen then?'

'Something *wonderful.* All the great unanswered

questions of the world will be answered. Who are we? What are we here for? Where will we end up? And most important of all: can mankind actually get any stupider? The Quarkbeast is more then an animal, it's an *oracle* to assist in mankind's illusive search for meaning, truth and fulfilment.'

'Really?'

'Don't take my word for it – it was foreseen by Sister Yolanda of Kilpeck.'

Yolanda was a good precog. If she said enlightenment would be attained when there was a full thirty-six Quarkbeast Quota, there was a good chance it would.

'When will this quota happen?'

'Good question. The last near-Quota was two months ago. For eight minutes there were thirty-four Quarkbeasts in existence. When yours died it dropped to thirty-three. By the end of the week there were twenty-nine. We're down to fifteen at the moment. The colonel needs to be stopped. Quarkbeasts shouldn't be messed around with, and never held against their will. Can I rely on you to do what you can to ensure it remains free?'

'Of course.'

I suddenly had an idea.

'They use magic to copy themselves, don't they?'

'You learn fast,' she replied. 'They do, but since they require a whopping 1.2 GigaShandars for a successful separation they can't do it alone. They need a sorcerer of considerable power to channel the energy. They can store power, too, just like fireflies – only unlike fireflies, which transmit it out as light immediately, Quarks can store it for a day or two.'

'Patrick surged yesterday. There was a Quarkbeast close by.'

'Pat's a sweet man, but he doesn't have the skill to channel that amount of power. Since Zambini vanished, no one has. Quark division is unlikely, but if it happens, we have plans in hand. See that vehicle over there?'

She pointed to a riveted titanium box about the size of small garden shed that was mounted on the back of a rusty E-type Jaguar fitted with blue lights and sirens.

'Yes?'

'Quarkbeasts have to be separated within a thousand seconds of dividing or they may merge again with devastating results,' said Boo. 'I'm the Kingdom's Beastcatcher, so I have full emergency vehicle status. If you think a pair are about to conjoin, call 999 and yell "Quarkbeast" in a panicked, half-strangled cry of terror. They'll put you straight through.'

I took a deep breath. It was now or never. I looked behind me to make sure there were no sharp objects close by.

'What are you doing?' asked Boo.

'I'm going to ask you something, and you're going to punch me in the eye, and I wanted to make sure

I didn't hurt myself on the way down.'

She glared at me with her inky-black eyes, and a coldness suddenly washed around me as though someone had opened a tomb. I closed my eyes.

'I need help,' I said. 'Magic is in dire straits.'

I winced, expecting the blow to fall, but it didn't. After a few seconds I opened my eyes to find that Once Magnificent Boo had walked away and was dropping a truck gearbox into the beasts' compound, where they would gnaw off the soft aluminium casing and use the harder cogs for nesting.

'Magic is *always* in dire straits,' said Boo, 'it's the nature of magic. But that part of my life has finished. I can do nothing for you. I haven't cast a single spell since the anti-magic extremists dumped me in that roadside rest area thirty-three years ago.'

'But Blix wants to control Kazam and commercialise magic,' I pleaded. 'We can't let it happen.'

She took several steps closer in a menacing fashion and I backed away until I had my back pressed against a water butt. She looked at me with her empty eyes and spoke in a low voice that seemed to reverberate inside my head.

'And who's better qualified to decide what's best for Magic? Blix or Zambini?'

'Zambini.'

'Are you sure? The right way, the wrong way – it's all regulation. Maybe magic shouldn't be regulated at all. Maybe it should take its own path, like the Quarkbeast, unfettered by our meddling. Perhaps magic needs to be used for evil before it can take the right course for good, and if so, Zambini's need to control it is as damaging as Blix's. The only thing that separates the pair of them is their viewpoint and dress sense.'

This was true; Zambini was a shabby dresser, and Blix was always well turned out.

'With respect, you're wrong,' I said. 'Zambini's nothing like Blix. He's kind and good and honest and—'

'Missing?'

'Okay, yes, but Blix is no friend to the right and true direction of magic, and I need help to defeat him.'

She took another step towards me and was now so close that I could feel her breath on my face and see every detail of her face. From the fine capillaries in her eyes to the broken blood vessels on the side of her nose. Her eyes were very black – it looked as if she had just massive pupils and no iris at all.

'I can't help you. I can't help *anyone* any more.'

'Is there nothing I can do or say to persuade you to help us?'

'*Nothing.*'

The Once Magnificent Boo turned back to the Quarkbeasts and continued to feed them, so I thanked her, said goodbye and returned to my car.

I drove back into town in a despondent mood. I was disappointed but not surprised that Boo had rejected my request, and with it had ended any realistic hope of winning the contest. I would have to think very carefully about either taking Blix's offer to concede the contest, or come up with another plan, and quickly.

And that was when a large black Daimler 4x4 with tinted windows pulled in front of me. I stamped heavily on the brakes and skidded to a halt.

The High North Tower

I slammed the Volkswagen into reverse as another
Daimler screeched to a halt behind me. I opened the
car door and tried to jump out, but in my hurry I'd
forgotten to unlatch my seat belt, and was still struggling to extricate myself when four huge bodyguards
dragged me out of the car, put a hood over my head
and cuffs on my wrists and threw me into the back
of their car.

'Don't hurt me,' I said from the floor as the car
sped off.

'Then be a good girl and don't struggle,' came a
patronising voice.

'It's not for my benefit,' I told them, 'it's for yours.
If I lose my temper, those of you still conscious in
five minutes will be picking up the teeth of those
who aren't.'

There was a pause and I was then picked up and
placed on a seat.

'Comfy?' came the same voice, this time tinged
with a little more respect. It seemed they had been
briefed not to underestimate me.

'Yes, thank you.'

'Cuffs not too tight?'

'No, they're fine.'

'Sure?'

'Yes, really,' I said in a sweet voice, just to unnerve him, 'you're most kind.'

The journey was not long, and from the sounds of creaking drawbridges and tyres on cobbles it didn't take a genius to figure out where I was being taken. After a short time the car stopped and I was carried bodily up a long flight of steps. I was then laid on a soft bed and heard some hurried footsteps, a door slam, a lock turn, and then hurried steps down a stone staircase followed by another door, another lock turning, and then the whole thing repeated itself until I could no longer hear them.

After a few seconds my bonds and hood melted away into nothing. Proof, if any were needed, of Blix's involvement.

As expected, I was in the High North Tower of the King's castle at Snodd Hill. It was comfortable if a bit austere in the 'medieval dreary chic' style, similar to the Useless Brother's office, and the large pile of provisions and bottled water clearly meant that I was to be here for some time – or at the very least, until after the contest. I tried the door to find it firmly locked, then looked out of the window. The High North Tower had been well if unimaginatively named, being a tower, to the north and, most pertinent to me, high. The room was circular and barely twenty feet across, and it sat precariously atop a long and mildly off-kilter column of crumbling stonework.

I wasn't going to escape from here without a lot of help.

After a wait of almost two hours, the phone rang.

'Pinocchio's Pizzas?' I replied, picking it up.

'Oh, sorry, wrong number,' came Blix's voice before the phone went dead.

I smiled to myself as I replaced the receiver, then waited a couple of seconds before it rang again.

'Hello, Blix,' I said before he could say anything, 'adding kidnapping to your long list of felonies?'

'We prefer to think of it as "holidaying at the specific invitation of His Majesty",' replied Blix. 'Open the top drawer of the bureau.'

I did so, and found an agreement for Kazam to concede the competition, and all the details that Blix had already outlined. The document had been prepared by a firm of solicitors in Financia and lodged with the Ununited Kingdoms' Supreme Court, so even if King Snodd had wanted to rescind the deal, he couldn't.

'It's all there,' said Blix. 'I knew my or the King's word would not be good enough, so I made it official. Sign it and your holiday in the North Tower is over.'

'And if I don't?'

'Then you'll stay there until six Mondays from now, and we'll have Kazam for nothing.'

'Blix?'

'Yes?'

'Are you in the castle watching the top of the North Tower at the moment?'

'I might be.'

I ripped the phone from the wall, and tossed it out of the open window. It took almost five seconds to hit the ground.

I went and sat on the bed, glad of a quiet time to think. Oddly enough, the one thing that gave me any confidence that we'd win the contest was the fact that Blix was still nervous enough to want to do deals. I went over the events of the past few days as I attempted to find something I had missed that might help us. The answer *had* to be there.

I was stirred from my thoughts by the wail of an air-raid siren and the unmistakable *crack* of an artillery piece close by. I looked out of the window as the massed anti-aircraft defences of Snodd Hill Castle opened up as one, a cacophony of noise so loud I had to put my hands over my ears, and with the shells bursting so close that I could hear the shrapnel striking the tower. One piece of red-hot steel flew in the window and landed on the bed, where it began to smoulder; I used my handkerchief to pick it up and dumped it in the sink.

I ventured another look out and amid the din, smell

of cordite and black bursts of flak that were drifting past my window, I saw something shoot past, the flak-bursts following it. The notion of the Kingdom being under attack was unlikely as the king currently had no enemies interested enough to attack him, and it was only when my name was called that I realised what was going on.

'Jenny!' came Prince Nasil's familiar voice, as he whipped past on his carpet. 'Can't stop!' he added as he went back past in the opposite direction, then yelled 'Jump!' as he tore past the third time, with two anti-aircraft shells exploding so close the tower shook and plaster fell from the ceiling.

I needed no further bidding. I shoved Blix's concession agreement into my bag, waited until the Prince turned to make another pass, and then jumped out of the window.

I'd never fallen from a high tower before and would not hope to do so again, but after the initial sense of fear and rapid acceleration, the only thing I could feel was the air rushing past me. I could see the top of the tower move swiftly away from me as I fell, and didn't see the Prince at all until he gently scooped me out of the air. With a flick of the carpet we were out of the range of the artillery, which stopped as quickly as it had begun.

'Thanks for the rescue,' I said, 'but it might have been easier and safer to extract me at night.'

'At night?' echoed the Prince. 'If we'd left it until then there would be no chance of seeing Zambini.'

The penny dropped.

'Kevin knows where the Great Zambini is going to reappear?'

'Not *precisely* – but close enough. Somewhere near the Troll Wall.'

My heart fell.

'The Troll Wall is almost fifty miles long!'

'If we head up there now, we can home in when Kevin has a more accurate fix.'

This was undoubtedly true, as Kevin's predictions of Zambini's return had been uncannily accurate – just too late to be of any real use. I looked at my watch. We had less than an hour to go before Zambini was due back.

'We'll never make it,' I said as we flew through the ballroom windows and slid to a halt on the shiny floor.

'We have a plan,' said the Prince, and I looked up. Perkins, Owen of Rhayder, Kevin Zipp and Tiger were all staring at me.

'I'm all ears,' I said as Tiger handed me two jumpers, some thermal leggings, a heavy leather flying jacket and then a flying helmet.

'It's a straight-line flight of two hundred and eighty miles to the Troll Gates at Stirling,' said Owen, referring to a blackboard upon which a diagram had been hastily drawn, 'and if we leave in five minutes we have only thirty-two minutes to get there. That's an average speed requirement of five hundred and twenty-five miles per hour.'

I saw the problem immediately.

'Even by moving at the carpet's top design speed of five hundred miles per hour,' I murmured, 'we would still be . . . two and a half minutes too late.'

But Owen and the Prince were already ahead of the curve.

'*Precisely*,' said the Prince, 'that's why we need to push the carpets up to over seven hundred and sixty miles per hour during the flight to give us any hope of getting there in time.'

I looked at them both in turn.

'You intend to go . . . *supersonic?*'

'Trust us,' said Owen with a smile, 'it's faintly possible that we know what we're doing. Get prepared. We'll be rugging off in two minutes.'

Owen and the Prince went to rewrite a few lines of the carpet's source spell-code, and I turned back to Tiger and Perkins, who handed me a large pink seashell.

'You'll be out of range with a toddler's shoe so we're going to conch.'

He held a pair of left- and right-handed conches together for a moment, whispered a spell and then gave one to me.

'Can you hear me?' he said, and his voice echoed out of the shell, clear as a bell. In fact, I heard him slightly *before* he spoke, which created an odd reverse echo.

'How did it go with Once Magnificent Boo?' asked Tiger.

'Not well. She's doesn't want to help us, and I got the feeling she'd hit me quite hard if I asked why she stopped doing any magic. But it sounded like something pretty unpleasant.'

'It figures that she knew Zambini and Blix well,' said Tiger as he showed me a photograph, 'they were all on the unUK Olympic sorcery team in 1974.'

The photo showed the three of them when much younger, all posing after winning gold for the prestigious '400 Meters Turning into a Mouse Relay' event. Boo was in the middle of the photo and grinning broadly while Blix and Zambini were standing on either side. Unlike Boo's smile, theirs looked somewhat strained.

'They were the best of friends,' said Tiger, 'and inseparable until Boo was kidnapped. Zambini was away when it happened so Blix negotiated the ransom. Blix and Zambini fell out big time, and have been at each other's throats ever since. That's about it.'

'Past history of petty infighting doesn't help us,' I said with a sigh. 'Did you discover the source of the thinness enchantment?'

'Not yet, but the spell's holding up well. Blix's sorcerers have been out there attempting to get in all afternoon, but however much power they use to attempt to break the enchantment, the spell uses even more to stop them.'

'Let's hope it stays that way,' I said, digging Blix's concession document from my bag and handing it to Perkins.

'As acting senior wizard you can sign this without my consent,' I told him, explaining exactly what it was. 'You should ask the retired sorcerers, too. I can't make this decision alone, and what's more, shouldn't have to. We've got until midnight tonight. Nothing on Lady Mawgon or the passthought, I presume?'

'Nothing,' said Perkins, 'except the Dibbles are at full capacity and occasionally venting into the atmosphere.'

'I saw the cloud shapes as we flew over.'

Perkins' eyes opened wide as he read the document.

'Two million moolah if I agree never to spell again?'

'All that moolah must be worth a fortune,' remarked Tiger.

I looked at the Prince, who nodded that they were ready. This was it.

'If I don't make it back,' I said to Perkins, 'you're to take over as acting manager in my place.'

Tiger gave me a hug, and Perkins looked as though he wanted to.

'Break a leg,' he said.

I walked over to where Owen and the Prince were making last-minute adjustments to the hemp backing of Owen's carpet.

'You're sure about this?' I asked.

'Not at all,' said Owen as he handed the Prince and me parachutes while he strapped one on himself, 'but we need the Great Zambini back, and this is the best chance we've had so far.'

'Then what are we waiting for?' I asked, giving them both a nervous smile.

I put on the heavy woollen flying jacket and then the parachute with Tiger's help, then stepped on to the front of the carpet, sat cross-legged and pulled the goggles down over my eyes. The Prince jumped on the back, raised the carpet into the hover, turned it around and then sped out of the open windows with Owen in close formation behind. I just caught a glimpse of the many assorted police cars and military vehicles that had surrounded Zambini Towers before we were off and away, heading for Trollvania.

Mach 1.02

As we headed off to the north-west I had an opportunity to examine more closely the state of Nasil's carpet: old and threadbare and long in need of replacement. It needed a complete overhaul, but since the chief component necessary for flight was angels' feathers and these were as rare as hen's teeth – coincidentally *also* one of the components – replacing his or Owen's carpet any time soon was just shy of impossible. There was little to do except fly them sparingly until they could fly no more.

I can't say I ever really felt at ease travelling by carpet. Partly because of the ropy state of the rug, and partly because one felt so very exposed. It wasn't possible to fall off owing to the 'RugStuck' enchantment that clamped passengers and operators to the weave, but the rush of air was highly disconcerting, which was why carpets rarely went above twice the Speed of Horse. It was just too cold. Besides, if you wanted to do pizza deliveries it cooled them down too fast and everyone complained.

We climbed to our higher-than-normal operating

height of five thousand feet, with Owen of Rhayder keeping station less than ten feet away. Pretty soon we were over the verdant countryside of the Kingdom of Shropshire, and once clear of built-up areas, we prepared for the jump to supersonic. The Prince told me to lie flat, and he joined me as the front of the carpet folded up in a curve with the ragged hem now level with our shoulders. It would keep the worst of the wind from us, make the carpet more aerodynamic and, crucially, act as a safety measure. Striking a bee at transonic speeds could take out an eye – and ruin a bee's day, too.

Owen then manoeuvred in behind us as we zipped along, and the hem on the front of his carpet intertwined with the rear of ours, making us into one long carpet. After they had given each other the thumbs-up, they hunkered down in a crouched position to reduce drag and both carpets started to accelerate rapidly.

I have been on wild rides before and since, but nothing could quite compare with that flight up to the Troll Wall. It was, in fact, a world speed record had we cared to have it ratified, but those thoughts weren't really on our mind.

'We have to use Owen's carpet to accelerate us up to six hundred and fifty,' shouted the Prince as the wispy clouds whipped past faster and faster, 'after that, we're on our own.'

I have to admit that I was scared. As the Prince

yelled 'Four hundred' the rug began to vibrate in a most disturbing manner, but this was nothing compared to the bucking and twisting that occurred at five hundred, and by six hundred we were shaking so much it was hard to focus on the lakes, rivers, trees and houses that shot past beneath us.

'Six hundred!' yelled the Prince, and I twisted around to look at Owen, who was lying flat on his carpet, waiting for the signal. His carpet was the older and more worn of the two, and as it exceeded its design speed, the weave and weft started to separate with the strain, and at just under six hundred and twenty a hole opened up. In an instant the air caught it and the carpet was suddenly gone in a burst of tattered wool and cotton. Owen, his part of the job complete, was tossed into the void. We watched him fall away, his body splayed out to allow him to decelerate enough to safely deploy his parachute. We breathed a sigh of relief when we saw his canopy blossom open somewhere over Midlandia, and I felt the Prince's body tense as he urged his carpet on.

The carpet was still vibrating badly, and I saw small holes appear in areas where the carpet was already badly worn. I had just moved my hand to grasp the 'D' ring of the parachute when there was a muffled concussion somewhere in the far distance.* The vibration suddenly

---

*Jennifer must have imagined this; it's not possible to hear the sonic boom from within the craft making it.

stopped and everything became smooth. I opened my eyes and looked out. Either side of us were two trailing shock waves barely a yard wide that travelled back from the front edges of the carpet. I turned to the Prince but he was concentrating hard, and we continued as this pace for several minutes while, with every passing second, more wear showed up on the carpet.

I had my eyes tight shut as soon as the vibrations began again, and I had just resigned myself to my second free-fall that day when I realised that we weren't breaking up, but *decelerating*, and a few minutes later we were flying slowly along the First Troll Wall. The relief was extraordinary and I wanted to hug the Prince, but royal protocol disallowed it, so I simply smiled and congratulated him.

'Do you think Owen's okay?' I asked.

'I saw his parachute open.'

'Me too. What about your carpet?'

He looked around at the even shabbier rug. Large sections had peeled off and were flapping in the breeze.* He shook his head sadly.

'We'll take longer to get home, Jennifer, my friend, and she'll not be flying until a rebuild.'

'Then let's hope Zambini's close by.'

The Troll Wall was a vast stone-built edifice over

---

*Flying carpet wear is measured in footfall-hours, and it was later calculated that the transonic jump was the equivalent of being walked on continually for eight years in the lobby of a busy hotel.

three hundred feet high and topped with rusty spikes. A second Troll wall was located about ten miles farther north, the result of a foolish misunderstanding three centuries previously over which particular wizard was allocated the building contract. It hadn't made much difference. One wall or two, the Trolls still made meat patties of anyone who crossed over. The two walls stretched from the Clyde to Loch Lomond in the west, used the loch as defence, then rose once more and curved off in a westerly direction towards Stirling in the east.

We approached and then circled the City of Stirling, where the Troll Gates were located – a pair of oak doors seventy feet high strengthened with steel bands. The last Troll War had been twelve years before, and after repairs and a change of lock on the Troll Gates just in case, everything had pretty much returned to normal, except that human settlers in the zone between the first and second walls had been moved out 'just in case'.

'Jennifer?' came Tiger's voice over the conch.

I told Tiger we were at Stirling, and looked at my watch. We had three minutes before Zambini was due to reappear.

'Okay,' said Tiger, 'Kevin's not sure, but he thinks you're to head to an abandoned village called Kippen, about eight miles west of the main gates and four miles north of the First Troll Wall.'

Jasper Fforde

I relayed the information to the Prince, who whirled his carpet round, and we shot off in that direction, skimming along the top of the wall as fast as the tattered state of the carpet would allow.

'See any Trolls?' asked the Prince as we crossed the First Troll Wall and went into what was now termed 'unfriendly' territory.

'What does one look like?' I asked, as few had seen one and survived.

'Large, and usually covered in tattoos and warpaint. Clubs and axes are optional.'

'We'll know when we see one, I guess,' I said, but even looking hard I could see no sign of life – just an empty landscape that, while devoid of recent human habitation, showed much evidence that people had once lived here. We saw a few abandoned landships encrusted with ivy as we headed west, their rusty flanks suggesting they'd burned first.

After another few minutes the remains of a long-abandoned town hove into sight, and a quick look at the road sign on the outskirts told us we were indeed at Kippen. The Prince started to orbit slowly as I checked my watch. It was 16.02 and fourteen seconds. We had made it with a minute to spare.

Trollvania

'That will be my LZ,'[*] said the Prince, pointing at an open area of scrubby land behind the church. 'I'll drop you off and then orbit until you signal me in for EVAC.'

'Don't come and get me until I call you,' I said, 'no matter what. If I'm longer than half an hour, I'm not returning, and tell Tiger he can have my Matt Grifflon record collection and the Volkswagen. Understand?'

'I understand. Good luck.'

'Thank you.'

I looked around nervously as we approached low across a heavily overgrown housing estate, half expecting a Troll to jump out at any moment, as they are noted for two things: their ability to hide motionless and undetected in a damp river bed or pile of dead wood for months if necessary, and a lack of any sense of moderation when it came to the use of violence. An arm pulled from the socket was generally

---

[*]LZ: landing zone. The Prince served in the Portland Light Rug for six years, and although he rarely mentioned his military service, he often used military terminology. 'EVAC' means 'evacuation'.

for starters, and it got more unpleasant from there on in.

The Prince stopped the carpet a few feet from the ground and I jumped off. In an instant he was off again and I was suddenly quite alone. I stood there for a moment, looking around. After the noisy rush of air that had accompanied our journey north, all was now deathly quiet. Around me were the remains of houses partially reclaimed by a healthy growth of trees, brambles and moss. I could see a church near by with a damaged tower, the clock stuck permanently at ten to four. To my right there was a rusty landship, apparently now a home only to ravens. There was no sign of Zambini, Trolls or indeed any life at all, so I released my parachute, pulled off my flying helmet and bulky jacket and dumped them on the grass. I put a Fireball* in my pocket and placed the conch close to my lips.

'Tiger?' I whispered as I climbed over the wall at the back of the church. 'Are you there?'

'I'm here,' he said. 'Kevin's gone into a trance and mumbling. Is that good news?'

'Usually.'

'Good. Hang on, he's saying something.' There was a pause. 'Okay, here it is: *The monument at Four Roads.* Make any sense?'

---

*Fireball – a sort of marker flare that glows deep black in the daylight and bright white at night.

'Not yet,' I replied, 'but knowing Kevin, it soon will.'

As my ears gradually stopped ringing from the flight I could hear rustles and creaks from the abandoned village, which made me more apprehensive, not less. I walked up the road, which now had weeds growing out of large cracks, and passed a rusty bicycle and scattered bricks and broken tiles. There was evidence of fierce fighting, too. Lying in among the dirt was the occasional corroded weapon, sections of body armour and human bones, some of which looked as if they had been cracked to extract the marrow.

'Okay,' I said to Tiger, 'I'm at the top of Fore Street where there is a crossroads and the remains of a stone monument.'

'I think you're there,' he replied over the conch.

I looked around at the empty, shattered town. Towering above the crossroads was the abandoned landship I had seen from behind the church. It had halted atop the rubble of some houses opposite the monument, its twenty-foot-wide tracks sitting atop a rusty ice-cream van. It was 16.03 and fourteen seconds precisely and the Great Zambini was nowhere to be seen. I yelled his name as loud as I could and regretted it almost immediately. The sound echoed around the still village, and from somewhere in the distance I heard the breaking of roof tiles. Something had moved. Something big.

'I need some more help,' I said into the conch, 'anything at all.'

I hid behind the heavy tracks of the landship and then peered cautiously out. Farther up the road I saw a large tree sway as it was pushed aside. There was another distant crash and the sound of breaking glass, and I caught a glimpse of something move between two houses. Then, from the direction of the church, I heard a low guttural cry of interest and I froze. There were two of them, and one had just found my flying jacket and parachute.

I felt myself break out into a sweat and pressed myself harder against the rusty tracks of the landship. I dug the Fireball out of my pocket in readiness. If I broke it on the ground a small burst of energy would fly to a hundred feet before exploding like a flare, and the Prince would come in and pick me up – but it would also give my position away to the Trolls. I'd have to hope he could move faster than they.

I heard another crash and looked up the road to where I could see a cloud of dust roll into the street. A few seconds later a Troll stepped into the roadway. I like to think not much frightened me, but Trolls certainly did. It was a muscular male of perhaps twenty-five feet in height and it carried a large club fashioned from the bough of an oak. It was dressed in a leather loincloth made of cowhides stitched together, and aside from a pair of sandals and a small leather skullcap into which was stuck a juniper bush and a dried goat, it was otherwise naked. It seemed to have no body hair, and its face was smooth with just two holes for nostrils, no chin to speak of, a large mouth with two tusks jutting up against its cheeks and small eyes set deep into the skull. But what was wholly remarkable about the Troll was the adornment of its body, which was covered in a swirling pattern of fine tattoos that made it look both utterly fearsome and somehow curiously elegant.

The Troll sniffed the air and then called to its partner in a voice that sounded like the deepest of organ pipes. Its partner answered and soon joined the first, absently removing a brick chimney on its way past and scrunching the bricks to powder in its massive fist.

'Is this from a human?' asked the second Troll, holding out my flying jacket between finger and thumb in the same way you might hold a week-old dead mouse. The jacket, while big and bulky on me, looked like an article of doll's clothing in the Troll's massive hand.

'Regretfully so,' replied the first as he unclipped a bugle he wore at his waist. 'I'll call pest control.'

'Do we have to?' said the second Troll, laying his hand on the first Troll's forearm. 'I know vermin have to be kept down, but one's not going to cause any trouble, surely?'

The first Troll looked at his colleague reproachfully. 'Don't get all sentimental, Hadridd. They're dirty, spread diseases and breed *endlessly*. Did you know that a colony can outgrow the capacity of its environment in as little as twelve centuries? I know they look cute and can do tricks and make that funny squeaking noise when you stare at them close up, but honestly, culling is really for their own good.'

'We could keep it as a pet,' said the second Troll in a hopeful sort of voice. 'Hagridd has two and says they're delightful.'

'I've always thought keeping humans as pets a bit disgusting,' said the first with a shudder, 'and if you let the children play with them they inevitably get thrown around the garden, and that's just cruel. No, better to just snap their necks and be done with it.'

'I suppose so,' said the second Troll, then added: 'Shouldn't we make sure there's an infestation *before* we call pest control? You know what a strop they get into over false alarms.'

'You're right,' said the first, and they sniffed at my jacket again, and began to walk in my direction.

'Not what you expect, are they?' came a familiar voice. I turned, and there was the Great Zambini. He was tall and handsome and was smiling in that fatherly manner that I had found so calming when I was new at Kazam. It was all I could do to stop myself crying and flinging my arms around him.

'Thank heavens,' I managed to say, swallowing down my emotions. 'We haven't much time—'

'Then we won't waste it here, young lady,' he said, ushering me through a rusty ground-level escape hatch in the landship, just as the Trolls rounded the corner.

'This way,' he said, leading me past some machinery and up a steel staircase in the semi-gloom. As we reached the lower storage deck of the fighting vehicle, we heard the Trolls talking outside.

'We'll *never* get it now,' said one of them.

'I've an idea,' said the other.

We heard them walk off, then some low murmurs as they talked to one another.

'We're safe for the moment,' said Zambini, leading me past the main engine room and up towards 'B' Deck, where the crew quarters were located. 'Their knowledge of humans is fairly rudimentary.'

This particular landship had not been set on fire, and all the crew's provisions and equipment were still where they had been abandoned – food, water and racks of weapons – all with the *Snodd Heavy Industries* logo on them. Zambini sat on a crew couch and stared at me.

'How long have I been gone?' he asked.

'Eight months.'

He opened his eyes wide and shook his head sadly.

'That long? This is my sixteenth return, and each runs into the next – it's like casting oneself into stone but without the splitting headaches on waking. We've got about six minutes, by the way – I can't stop myself vanishing again, but I can delay it. However did you find me, and what's been going on?'

I told him about Kevin, and how we had to trash both the carpets to get up here in time, then about the Big Magic, how we have two more Dragons, the wizidrical power on the rise, then how King Snodd made Blix the Court Mystician.

'Theoretically that makes Conrad eighth in line to the throne,' said Zambini incredulously.

'It sounds as if the King and Tenbury are hell-bent on commercialising magic,' I told him, 'and they want to take control of Kazam. We've got a contest to decide the matter tomorrow.'

'Kazam will win hands down,' observed Zambini. 'Blix and his cronies are useless.'

'I'm not so sure. Lady Mawgon got changed to stone while trying to hack the Dibble Storage Coils and all the others are in prison on trumped-up charges – which leaves only Perkins. We haven't a chance, unless you can tell us how to unlock the Dibbles. We've got four GigaShandars of power sitting there doing nothing.'

'Without a passthought, you can't, and the only people who know RUNIX well enough to crack it are myself, Mawgon, Monty Vanguard and Blix.'

'Monty is stone too, and I'm not keen on asking Blix for help.'

Zambini smiled.

'Conrad as stone might solve a lot of problems.'

'But what if he succeeds? I'm not sure handing him four Gig of raw crackle is a good idea.'

'I think I agree with you on that score.'

And that was when we heard the Trolls again.

'Here, person person person,' came a deep voice from near the rear cargo door, 'I've got some lovely yummy honey for you. Here, person person person.'

There was a pause.

'Do you think it's gone?' said the same Troll.

'No. Leave the honey there and we'll S-Q-U-A-S-H it when it comes to get it.'

'Right,' said the other Troll, and it all went quiet again.

'Anything else?' asked Zambini, getting to his feet and pacing around the crew quarters.

'Anything else?' I echoed. 'Does there need to be anything else? The future of magic is in the balance!'

'The thing about magic,' said Zambini in a soft voice, 'is that it often seems to have an intelligence. It moves in the direction it wants to. It may decide to let iMagic win as part of some big mysterious plan to which we are not yet party. Or, if it thinks Kazam should win tomorrow, it will find a way to ensure that we do.'

'I'm not sure how,' I replied somewhat dubiously. 'I even asked Once Magnificent Boo to help us.'

Zambini looked up at me, genuine concern on his face.

'How is she?'

'She lives alone with a lot of Quarkbeasts. A bit batty, if you ask me, and horribly selfish – she refused to help us.'

'Do you know why?' asked Zambini.

'Why what?'

'Why she hasn't undertaken a single spell since her kidnapping?'

I shook my head. Zambini thought for a moment and took a deep breath.

'Ever wondered why she never shakes hands? Why she always wears gloves?'

I stared at him, and an awful realisation welled up inside me.

'Yes,' he said, holding up his own index fingers – the conduit of a sorcerer's power, without which they would be powerless, 'she wasn't returned unharmed. *The kidnappers removed her index fingers.*'

I didn't speak for several moments. She could have been one of the all-time greats, and now she was studying Quarkbeasts and going slowly nuts. She had lived with her loss every day, knowing that a life of wonder and fulfilment in the Mystical Arts had been cruelly taken from her. I couldn't imagine what it might be like. Greatness had slipped from her grasp.

'Who did it?'

'Two of the gang were found dead a week later, apparently over a squabble. There might have been others, but no trace was ever found. I was away in Italy talking to Fabio Spontini about his work on Magical Field Theory, and by the time I got back they'd already taken her fingers. She blamed me for not being there, and Blix for messing up the negotiations.'

'Did he?'

'I don't know, but I don't think he would have. We both loved her dearly and the three of us could have done great things together – stuff that would have made the Mighty Shandar look like a Saturday afternoon hobbyist. But then Boo lost her fingers, Blix and I fell out over the direction of magic, and that was it. She's not talked to either of us since.'

He sighed and looked at his watch.

'Two minutes left. I need to give you something.'

He reached into his pocket and pulled out an envelope covered with tiny writing.

'This is a list of notes I've been making while I've been jumping around. I thought it was an accident for a while – that I'd mispelled while vanishing – but now you've told me about the failure of Shandar to destroy the Dragons, I'm beginning to think it might have been the Mighty Shandar himself who wanted me out of the picture during the Big Magic, and now he has unfinished business he'll keep me trapped out here for as long as he wants, rattling around the here and now like a pea in a whistle.'

'What sort of unfinished business?'

'This: he was paid eighteen dray-weights of gold to rid the Ununited Kingdoms of Dragons. He failed, and the Mighty Shandar doesn't do refunds. He'll want to return and deal with the Dragons once and for all. He'll also want to take his revenge on the person who helped the Dragons foil his plan in the first place. Who was that, by the way?'

'Me.'

'Oh dear.'

He paced for a moment as he thought. I remember him doing this when he was back at the Towers, and I think it was then that I missed him more than ever. I wanted him to be back. To take the decisions, to be the one in charge, to sometimes make the *wrong* decisions, and ignore the criticism.

'You must be vigilant,' he said at last. 'The job of Shandar's agent has been filled by the D'Argento family for four centuries. They report to him when he comes out of granite for a minute every month. He'll leave the donkey work up to them and only appear himself for the seriously big spelling stuff, so you should know what to be wary of. His agent will be well spoken, well dressed, ride around in a midnight-black top-of-the-line Rolls-Royce, and have an anagrammatic name. A bit corny, I know, but it's traditional, apparently.'

I covered my face with my hands. The young lady in the Phantom Twelve. I was a fool not to have realised.

'Someone named "Ann Shard"?' I asked.

'Yes, exactly like that. You must remain—'

He stopped talking as he saw my look of consternation.

'You've met her?'

'Two days ago. She wanted us to find a gold ring. She had some story about her client's mother or something. I didn't give her the ring because it didn't want to be found and was sticky with negative emotional energy. I didn't want anyone to get hurt.'

He frowned and paced some more.

'I don't get it. A ring? No ring ever had any power, least of all a curse. It's just one of those dumb stories that get around, like pointy hats and wands and broomsticks and stuff. Hang on a minute. Yes, I've got it. If Shandar was going to get rid of me then he must have been worried about—'

He didn't get to finish his sentence. Zambini's six minutes were up; he had melted into non-existence until the next time – if there was a next time.

I sniffed the air and noticed that there was smoke coming up through the hatch from 'C' Deck. The Trolls were trying to smoke me out. Without wasting any time I ran up the stairs that led to the command deck at the top of the landship. I didn't stop here, and instead pulled the lever to blow the emergency roof-access hatch. The door vanished with a explosive concussion and I climbed out on to the riveted top of the landship. The Trolls were nowhere in sight, so I took the Fireball from my pocket and threw it on to the steel plates. There was a sharp crack and in an instant the marker flare burst high above my head.

'Ha, smoked you out!' came a rumbling voice from behind me, and I found myself staring into the small green eyes of one of the Trolls, who had climbed up the outside of the landship. I picked up a branch to defend myself, and rather than waiting for the Troll to make the first move, I ran towards him and swung the branch as hard as I could at his head. It was a futile gesture, of course. The Troll merely smiled cruelly and thrust out a hand to grab me. He would have done so, too, had the emergency hatch I had blown out not returned to earth at that precise moment and landed right on the Troll's head. He yelled in pain, lost his footing and fell off the landship.

I looked over the edge to where he was being helped by his comrade.

'What happened?' asked the second Troll.

'That one may look small,' said the first, rubbing his head tenderly, 'but she can sure pack a punch.'

'Jenny!'

It was the Prince. He had come in for my EVAC as promised. I needed no second bidding, jumped on the carpet and we were soon flying back across the Troll Wall to safety.

'That was cutting it a bit fine,' said Nasil as he

expertly held the carpet together on the short journey to Stirling railway station. 'Did you see him?'

'And how.'

Back at Zambini Towers

We took the train back to the Kingdom of Hereford. After the afternoon's action, the carpet was in no fit state to be used for anything – not even as a carpet. The Prince had no money, so swapped two first-class travel permits for a minor dukedom back in his home kingdom of Portland, and we caught the first train out of Stirling station. As a foundling I was not permitted to sit anywhere but third class, but when the ticket inspector questioned my presence in first, the Prince said that I was his personal organ donor, and travelled everywhere with him, just in case. The inspector congratulated the Prince on such a novel usage for a foundling and told me I was lucky to have such a kind benefactor.

We made Hereford by 10.30 that evening and we walked to Kazam by a back route to avoid being seen. Tiger and Perkins were waiting at a window on the ground floor just next to the rubbish bins to let us in, as the 'infinite thinness' spell was still very much in force. We dropped in to the Palm Court, where

Mawgon and Monty Vanguard were much as I had seen them last — stone.

'No change here, then.'

'None at all.'

'Moobin and the others?'

'Still in jail,' replied Perkins as we walked across the lobby. 'I tried to contact Judge Bunty Patel to overturn the King's illegal edict and got as far as the judge's secretary's secretary's secretary. She laughed and asked if I was insane, then hung up. How did it go up north?'

We sat on the sofa in the Kazam offices next to the sleeping form of Kevin Zipp and I related pretty much everything that Zambini had told me — from the so-called 'Ann Shard' being the Mighty Shandar's agent, to the worthlessness of rings as a conduit of power, to Blix being one of the few people able to work in RUNIX, to Once Magnificent Boo's disfigurement.

'Ouch,' said Perkins, looking at his own fingers.

I then told them that Zambini thought magic might have an intelligence and would 'find a way' to let us win if it had a mind to.

'That's like saying electricity has free will,' said Perkins, 'or gravity.'

'Gravy has free will?' said Tiger, who hadn't been listening properly. 'That explains a lot. I *knew* it didn't like me.'

'Not gravy, *gravity*.'

'I'm not sure I buy that.'

'Me neither,' I replied, 'but he's the Great Zambini, so we can't reject the idea totally out of hand. He wasn't out of ideas about his own predicament, either. Here.'

I handed him the old envelope covered in Zambini's handwritten notes.

'He thinks these observations may help us crack the spell.'

'And he said the Mighty Shandar cast it?'

I nodded.

'Not good,' said Perkins after studying the notes for a while. 'It seems Zambini is locked into a spell with a passthought on auto-evolve: one that changes randomly every two minutes. One moment it's all about swans on a lake at sunset, the next about spoon-bills in the Orinoco delta, and the very act of entering the passthought changes the passthought. We can't crack Mawgon's and it's static, so what hope with one that changes?'

We were all silent for a while.

'Did you see any Trolls?' asked Tiger.

'Two of them. They think we're vermin.'

'We don't like them much, either.'

'No, they *really* think we're vermin – a pest that needs eradicating. They're entirely indifferent to humans. We're to them as rabbits are to us – only more destructive and less cuddly.'

'Oh,' said Tiger, who, being a Troll War orphan, had an interest in Trolls. 'Then the invasions are even *more* of a waste of life, cash, time and resources then we had suspected?'

'It looks that way.'

I took a deep breath and looked at my watch. It was quarter past eleven. Blix's concession offer ran out at midnight.

'Did you talk to the residents about taking Blix's offer?'

Perkins reached into his top pocket and pulled out a notebook.

'They may be a bit odd, but they're quite forthright in their views.'

He consulted his notes.

'I could only speak to twenty-eight of them. Monty Vanguard is stone, Mysterious X and the Funny Smell in Room 632 are nebulous at best, the Thing in 346 made a nasty noise when I knocked on the door, and the Lizard Wizard just stared at me and ate insects.'

'He does that,' I said.

'I'm not totally convinced the Thing in Room 346 is a sorcerer at all,' remarked Tiger, 'nor the Funny Smell.'

'Who's going to go and find out? You?'

'On reflection,' mused Tiger, 'let's just assume they are, for argument's sake.'

'So anyway,' continued Perkins, 'the residents have without exception poured scorn on Blix's offer and announced they would sooner descend into confused old age and die in their beds while subsisting on a diet of rotten cabbage, weak custard and dripping.'

'Isn't that what they're doing already?' asked Tiger.

'Which shows their commitment to things continuing as they are,' I said.

'Right,' agreed Perkins, 'but nearly all of them said they would also trust in the judgement of Kazam's manager.'

'That's not good,' I said, 'Zambini is still missing.'

'They didn't mean Zambini,' said Perkins, 'and even though half of them don't know your name and refer to you as "the sensible-looking girl with the ponytail" they're all behind you.'

There were over two thousand years of combined experience in the building, and that wealth of knowledge had approved of what I did. All of a sudden, I felt stronger and more confident thanks to their trust. But it didn't solve our immediate problems.

'What about you?' I said to Perkins. 'Are you going to take the two million moolah?'

Perkins looked at me with a frown.

'And miss all this craziness? Not for anything. I'm astonished you even had to ask.'

'Thank you.'

We said nothing for several moments.

'We found out where the "infinite thinness" enchantment was coming from,' said Tiger, 'though not who might have cast it.'

He rose and went across to my desk and passed a pocket Shandarmeter across the small terracotta pot. The needle on the gauge showed a peak reading of two thousand Shandars. We didn't know how the enchantment that protected the old building worked nor who was casting it, but this was the source.

I picked the ring out of the pot. It was utterly plain and unremarkable – just large. I had a thought and picked up the phone.

'Are you calling Blix?' asked Perkins.

'No – the Mighty Shandar's agent. We need to find out more.'

I dialled the number the so-called 'Ann Shard' had given me, and after two rings it was answered.

'Miss D'Argento?' I said. 'It's Jennifer Strange.'

'I can see my impertinent yet wholly necessary subterfuge took a modicum of cerebral activity to divine,' she announced in her odd Longspeak, 'but in this pursuit you were proved correct.'

'I'm sorry?'

'It took you a few days to figure out I wasn't Ann Shard.'

'Oh,' I said. 'Yes.'

There was a pause before she carried on.

'Is this communication to impart knowledge about the geographical whereabouts regarding my client's mother's ring?'

'We haven't got it, if that's what you mean, but yes,

it is about the ring: what's so special about it and why did the Mighty Shandar want it found?'

'There is nothing special about it,' she said simply, 'you have my word on that.'

'And Shandar's reason for wanting it found?'

'We have many clients,' said Miss D'Argento in a mildly annoyed tone, 'and we never betray their confidence.'

Zambini was right; it *had* been Shandar. If there wasn't at least some truth in it, she would have simply laughed or dismissed it out of hand.

'Is there anything else?' asked Shandar's agent. 'Miss D'Argento is really most frightfully busy.'

She was talking about herself again.

'Yes,' I said. 'The next time Shandar wakes from granite, tell him that we'll be after him once Zambini is freed – and he will be, mark my words.'

'Goodbye, Miss Strange. We'll meet again, I'm sure.'

And the phone went dead. I relayed what she had said to the others, but none of it seemed to help much, except to perhaps confirm what we suspected – that the Mighty Shandar was keeping a watchful eye on events here in the Kingdom of Snodd, and that if Shandar was behind Zambini's disappearance, then it was going to be trebly tough getting Zambini back.

'Hullo, Jennifer,' said a voice from the sofa, 'did my vision work out?'

'It did, thank you, Kevin.'

It was Zipp, our precog. He looked tired and drawn. He usually did when trying extra specially hard to see more clearly into the foggy murk of the yet-to-be.

'Do I get a ten?'

'On both counts.'

Tiger dutifully fetched the Visions Book so I could rate Kevin's powers. I turned to the correct page, and noted that his last vision, the one by which we found Zambini, was coded RAD105. I gave him a ten for this, countersigned it and then gave him ten also for RAD095. It took his Correct Vision Strike Average up to 76 per cent – just out of 'Remarkable' and into 'Exceptional', but not yet beyond the 90 per cent mark and the highest accolade of all, 'Blistering'.

'Jenny?' said Tiger, who had been staring at the entries in the Visions Book. 'What does that look like to you?'

'RAD105?'

'No, I mean, what if the 5 was an S? What would you think then?'

'RADIOS?'

I stared at Tiger and he stared back. The kid was a genius.

'Kevin,' I said excitedly, 'are you still getting the "Vision Boss" prediction?'

'I had it again just now. Why?'

'It could mean 'Vision BO55'. You may have just had a vision . . . about a vision.'

'That's a first,' said Kevin, unfazed by it all, as usual.

Tiger dashed off to the library to fetch the relevant volume of the Precognitives' *Gazetteer of Visions.*

'It must have been made some time in the mid-seventies to be numbered so low,'* observed Perkins.

'We'll soon find out.'

Tiger returned with a dusty volume and laid it down in front of me. I soon found the entry.

'Vision BO55, 10 October 1974,' I read, 'was seen by Sister Yolanda of Kilpeck.'

'Yolanda? Cool. What was it about?'

'Doesn't say. It was a private consultation – contents undisclosed.'

'If it was Sister Yolanda it probably will or did come true,' said Kevin. 'She didn't make many, but her strike rate was always good. Who was the recipient?'

I read the name and suddenly felt cold all over.

'Mr Conrad Blix of Blix Grange, Blix Street, Hereford.'

We all looked at one another. Blix was involved in a strong prophecy from Sister Yolanda, and Kevin had been hinting at it all week, just without knowing it. We'd be fools not to pick up on a lead like this.

'I think we need to find the contents of that vision – and quickly,' said Tiger.

---

*Visions were not allocated code numbers until late 1973, something that had been long overdue. The main reason was to enable precogs to calculate an official strike rating, and thus a logical scale of payment.

'Easier said than done,' I replied. 'It was a private consultation. Only Blix would have the details.'

'We need someone at iMagic,' observed Tiger, 'someone on the inside.'

'Who?' asked Perkins. 'Corby, Muttney and Samantha are all loyal to a fault.'

I thought for a moment.

'Perkins,' I said, 'you've just betrayed us.'

'I have?'

'Like the worst kind of leaving-the-sinking-ship rat. I want you to accept Blix's offer for two million moolah, get into Blix Grange, go to where Blix keeps his records and find out what Vision BO55 relates to.'

'How am I going to do that?'

'I don't know. Guile and ingenuity?'

But Perkins was still reluctant.

'Blix will never believe me. He'll think it's a trick of some sort.'

'You're right,' I said, 'he'll need convincing.'

Reader, I punched him. Right in the eye, a real corker – a punch such as I'd never inflicted on anyone, except that time back at the orphanage when Tamara Glickstein was bullying the smaller kids.

'YOW!' yelled Perkins. 'What was that for?'

'He'll believe you now. Tell him I went apeshit when you betrayed us. Tell him I've gone a bit loopy.'

'No need to lie, then,' remarked Perkins grumpily,

nursing his eye, which was already beginning to go purple.

'Better get going,' I said, glancing at the clock and then giving him my warmest hug. I even kissed him on the cheek as an apology for the punch. Tiger offered to hug and kiss him too, but Perkins said 'no thanks' and went off to make the phone call. It was three minutes to midnight, and Perkins was gone by five past. Gone too with midnight was Kazam's chance to cut a deal with Blix. The die was cast. The contest would go ahead.

And as likely as not, we'd lose.

Before the contest

I lay in bed staring at the water-stained ceiling of my room on the second floor of Zambini Towers, a room I had chosen for the fact that it faced east, and the sun woke me every morning. The sun didn't wake me this morning as I had yet to get to sleep. Magic contests rarely ended happily, and through the years had resulted in recrimination and despair, bruised egos and lifelong feuds. There were always winners and losers, but this was the first time in wizidrical contest history that the defending team were *unable to field a single sorcerer of any sort.*

I had tried to fool myself that Zambini's 'trust in providence' approach was actually sensible and worthwhile, but could not. We were, without a shadow of a doubt, stuffed.

'What are you thinking about?' asked Tiger, who occasionally slept on my floor as he was not yet used to sleeping on his own, and missed the cosy dormitory companionship of eighty other foundlings, all coughing, grunting and crying.

'I was thinking about how everything would be fine.'

'Me too.'

'Actually I wasn't.'

'No,' said Tiger, 'neither was I.'

I went downstairs after my bath and wandered into the office. I made myself a cup of tea and sat down, deep in thought.

'You seem sad,' came a low voice with a sing-song Scandinavian lilt to it, 'is everything okay?'

I turned to find the Transient Moose staring at me.

'You can talk?'

'Three languages,' replied the Moose, 'Swedish, English and a smattering of Persian.'

'Why haven't you spoken before?'

The Moose gave a toss of its antlers that I took to be a moosian shrug.

'No one here really shares any of my interests, so there's not much to say.'

'What are your interests?'

'Snow . . . female moose . . . grazing . . . getting enough sodium and potassium in my diet . . . snow . . . avoiding being run over . . . snow . . . female moose . . . snow.'

'You're not likely to be run over in here,' I said, 'or find snow or a female moose – and you don't need sodium, since you're a spell.'

'As I said,' said the Moose, 'not much to talk about. Did you like my thinness enchantment?'

'That was you?' I asked, with some surprise.

'I didn't like the way they kept on taking the sorcerers away,' he said simply, 'so I used that thing that didn't want to be found to increase my power.'

He nodded towards where the terracotta pot and ring were located in my desk, and I took them out and stared at them. It still didn't make any sense.

'How is this working?'

'I have no idea,' replied the Moose. 'It's suffused with emotional power. Loss, hatred, betrayal – you name it. I can almost hear the screams.'

'Negative emotional energy? A curse?'

The Moose gave another toss of its antlers.

'Sort of. But good or bad, I can tap into it and draw as much power as I want. It's like having a sorcerer, sitting right there in that pot.'

I had an idea. It was a long shot, admittedly.

'What are you like at building bridges?'

'Well,' said the Moose after some reflection, 'we weren't talking to the Siberian elk for a while after the whole cash-for-wolves scandal, and I was instrumental in bringing them to the negotiating table. I was alive then, of course, and real.'

'I didn't mean building bridges as in "making people talk to one another", I meant building bridges as in "actually building bridges".'

'Ah,' said the Moose, 'you meant *literally*, rather than *metaphorically*.'

I nodded, and the Moose gave out a short whinnying noise.

'What a suggestion,' it said. 'A moose, building a bridge?'

It paused for a moment, then asked why I wanted it to build a bridge, so I told it all about the contest and it said that it *thought* something odd was going on, but wasn't sure, and I said that it could be sure that something *was*, and asked it if it thought it might be able to help.

'There's a lot of power coming out of that terracotta pot,' said the Moose thoughtfully, 'probably enough to build a bridge.'

I stood up. Perhaps all was not lost.

'You need to come and see the remains of the bridge. The contest starts in half an hour.'

'Leave the building?' said the Moose in a horrified tone. 'Out of the question. I haven't been outside since it first opened as the Majestic Hotel in 1815.'

'Have you tried?'

'Yes.'

'Are you sure?'

'No. And that's not the point,' said the Moose in the manner of a moose that had realised it was very much the point. 'I'm not leaving the hotel and that's final.'

'Agoraphobic?'*

---

*It's the fear of open spaces. Jennifer never did find out what the Moose thought she meant.

223

'No thanks, I've already eaten.'

'I heard,' I began slowly, 'that there is some snow outside – and a female moose. Not to mention some sodium. And most of the town centre is pedestrianised so you won't have to worry about being run over by a car.'

'I'm only a spell,' said the Moose wistfully, 'I only *think* those things are important. It's the Mandrake Sentience Protocols. I know I'm not real, but I think I am. In any event, I'm not going outside.'

'Final?'

'Final.'

And it vanished.

I sighed. It was worth a try, but we were back to square one again. No sorcerers to do the contest. Not one.

'So let's talk about something else,' continued the Moose, reappearing as suddenly as it had left. 'Are you going to go out on a date with the young wizard with the tufty hair?'

'How do you know about me and Perkins?'

'It's all they talk about,' he said, looking upwards, presumably at the retired ex-sorcerers in the building. This was news to me, and I wasn't sure I wanted to be the subject of bored sorcerer tittle-tattle.

'It's complicated.'

'Love always is,' said the Moose, sighing forlornly. 'I'm only a vague facsimile of a moose once living, but I share some of his emotions. Ach, how I miss Liesl and the calves.'

'Who are you talking to?' asked Tiger, who had just appeared at the door.

'The Moose.'

I pointed at the Moose, who simply stared at me, then at Tiger.

'You were saying . . . .?' I said to the Moose, but it just looked at me blankly, and then slowly faded from view.

'Are you okay?' Tiger asked.

'I've been better. Come on, let's go and show some dignity before we get trashed. How do I look?'

I had put on my best dress for the event, and Tiger was wearing a tie and had combed his hair. We would at least make an appearance at the start for good form's sake.

We stepped out of the building after making quite sure that Margaret 'The Fib' O'Leary was looking after the front door to enable us to get back in. Margaret was one of our 'hardly mad at all' sorcerers, and also one of the least powerful – she could tell the most whopping great lies and, by skilled distortion of facts and appearances, make you believe them wholeheartedly. As a party trick she would convince guests that *down* was in fact *up*, then laugh as everyone started fretting that they might fall on to the ceiling.

★

Many people had taken a day off work to come and view the contest, and the road leading towards the medieval bridge now resembled something more akin to a fairground. There were barbecues selling roadkill pizzas* and camel's ears in a bun,† and traders selling merchandise such as hats, King Snodd action figures that threatened to execute you when you pulled a string, and T-shirts with unfunny slogans like: 'My dad went to a magic contest and all I got in our damp hovel was bronchitis'. There were tents with Travelling Knee Replacement Surgeons, sideshows where you could gawk at 'Gordon, the amazing two-headed boy' and other 'Quirks of Nature'. There was also a tent where you could pay half a moolah to view parts of a Troll pickled in a large jar.

'Do you have a half-moolah coin?' asked Tiger.

'Don't even think about it.'

As we moved closer to the bridge we could already see the flag-wavers, jugglers, tumblers and ventriloquists performing to entertain the crowds until the warm-up act started, and we overheard in passing that the half-time bear-debating event was cancelled as the bear had come over all mellow and wasn't up for an argument.

'They've got a replacement,' said someone close by.

---

*A Snodd delicacy often served at open-air gatherings. Real 'roadkill pizza' these days is rare as demand far outstrips supply, but the alternative is still baked in the traditional way – on asphalt under a sunlamp.

†These actually are camel's ears. They are considered an 'acquired taste', which is shorthand for 'extremely nasty'.

'Jimmy Nuttjob will be setting himself on fire and then be fired high above the rooftops from an air cannon while yelling "God Save the King".'

'Probably hoping for a knighthood,' said his friend.

'Definitely – but there must be easier ways to do it,' replied the first man.

We worked our way to the front, where the barriers had been erected to keep the crowds from any passive spelling, and Tiger and I showed our IDs to the police on duty. We were permitted to pass, and moved towards a small gaggle of people standing right on the edge of the bridge's north abutment, close to where the royal observation box had been built.

'Ah!' said Blix. 'The defenders approach.'

He was standing with the rest of iMagic's staff: a weaselly character in ill-fitting clothes named Tchango Muttney, the well-dressed Dame Corby, who wore far more jewellery than was good for her, and Samantha Flynt, who was fantastically pretty, but not that bright. I knew this because she had put her pretty floral dress on back to front. Perkins, I noticed, was not with them, but Colonel Bloch-Draine *was*, and he nodded a gruff greeting in my direction.

'No sorcerers to help you?' asked Blix sarcastically.

'Won't be much of a contest, will it?' I said.

'On the contrary,' replied Lord Tenbury, who was hovering close at hand, 'the best contest requires only a winner – not necessarily any competition.'

'And how do you think the crowd will react when they find that the potential winner has no opposition?'

'The people will not riot,' said Tenbury confidently. 'After all, a one-sided contest should be cosily familiar to any resident who has ever voted in a Kingdom of Snodd election.'*

We stopped talking because a colourful parade was approaching from down the street. There was a shiny brass band, several horsemen, and a retinue of hangers-on before the Royal Family arrived in a gilded open-top carriage. Everyone, including me, knelt before our monarch as the carriage stopped and a handy duke offered himself to be used as a step. The King and Queen were accompanied by the two Spoilt Royal Children, His Royal Petulantness the Crown Prince Steve, who was twelve, and Her Royal Odiousness Princess Shazza, who was fifteen. As their accolades suggested, they were horribly spoiled and spent much of their time stamping their feet and wanting things. No governess ever lasted longer than twenty-six and three-quarter minutes.

As soon as they had descended from the carriage, a deafening alarum sounded from thirty buglers all dressed traditionally as badgers, and the royal family

---

*Elections are neither free nor fair in the Kingdom of Snodd. In fact, there is only a yes box to tick against the only two questions: Do you feel King Snodd is doing a swell job? and: Would you like him to continue to do so? Any ballot papers not having both boxes ticked are destroyed as 'spoiled'.

walked slowly up to where we stood, waving at the citizenry while one of their footmen tossed coin vouchers into the crowd. They used to throw coins until the King discovered that his ungrateful subjects were spending the cash in non-Snodd-owned shops. The 'Alms Vouchers' are redeemable only in Snoddco's, the well-known and wholly substandard superstore.

'Ah!' said the King. 'Lord Tenbury and our Court Mystician. Good to see you both. I trust we are to see some sport this morning, hmm? Brave of you to turn up, Miss Strange.'

Since we had been spoken to, protocol dictated we could now stand. I couldn't help noticing that Queen Mimosa was looking around for something. I took a deep breath.

'I would be failing in my duty,' I said nervously, 'if I did not lodge a formal complaint over the fairness of this contest.'

'Your displeasure is noted, Miss Strange,' said the King. 'We will glance at your complaint some time next year. Shall we proceed?'

'Not yet,' said the Queen, staring at me. 'Are you Jennifer Strange?'

'A *foundling*, my dear,' said the King in an unsubtle aside, 'unsuitable for a queen's conversation.'

'Shut up, Frank. Miss Strange, where is the Kazam team?'

There was a deathly hush.

'Let us take our seats, my dear,' said the King, 'I feel the—'

'Your team, Miss Strange?'

'In prison, Your Majesty,' I said, curtsying, 'awaiting a hearing on Monday.'

'I see.'

Queen Mimosa glared at the King, who seemed to shrink under her withering look.

'Are you meaning to tell me that you have imprisoned the entire Kazam team in order to guarantee a victory?'

'Not at all,' said the King, 'it was entirely coincidental. They were all brigands and villains and scallywags and lawbreakers. Is that not so, Court Mystician?'

'Up to a point, Majesty, yes, I think we are agreed on that.'

'One of their number attacked the castle last night,' added Lord Tenbury, 'and caused considerable damage to the palace.'

'Poppycock,' said Queen Mimosa. 'I saw the whole thing. A single unarmed carpet rescued someone from the High North Tower. Any damage was done by your own gunners.'

'And they will be roundly punished, along with the sorcerers we have in custody. I think I have shown considerable restraint – I could have put them all to death, but instead I showed mercy – like you tell me to, pumpkin.'

'The charges are quite serious, my Queen,' said Tenbury, but Queen Mimosa raised a finger and he stopped. I noticed, too, that all the courtiers and hangers-on had taken a pace backwards and were finding something else to do. Queen Mimosa moved closer to her husband and lowered her voice.

'Listen here, you inbred, pompous little twit,' she said. 'I didn't arrange with Mother Zenobia to have the bridge rebuilt in aid of the Troll War Widows' Fund to have you hijack it for your own money-grabbing agenda. Release the Kazam sorcerers immediately, or I will make life so unpleasant that you will wish to have been born a foundling.'

'We will discuss this later, my dear.'

'We are discussing it now,' she said with a look of thunder that would have impressed Lady Mawgon, 'and do you doubt *for even one second* that I would not do as I say?'

The King took a deep breath and puffed out his cheeks. He looked around at the ten thousand or so subjects who were eagerly awaiting the start of the contest. It looked to me as though the King knew only too well that Queen Mimosa could make his life very unpleasant indeed.

'Lord Tenbury,' said the King, 'I think we owe it to the citizenry of Snodd to put on a good show. They have come to see a magical contest, and they shall. Release the wizards. I command it.'

Blix and Tenbury looked shocked at the turn of events, and exchanged desperate glances. There was a very good reason why they had nobbled Kazam. iMagic were rubbish and did not have a hope of winning. In a panic, Lord Tenbury did the first thing he could think of – he started patting his pockets in an absent-minded way.

'If you are going to claim you've lost the keys to the city jail, Lord Chief Adviser,' snarled the King in a low voice while smiling and waving to the crowd, 'I will put your head on a spike and have dogs gnaw at your corpse.'

'Here they are,' said Lord Tenbury, suddenly finding the keys. 'I will see to your instructions this moment.'

'Happy now, pumpkin?' said the King to Queen Mimosa.

'I love it when you do the right thing, bunny-wunny,' she said, tweaking his royal ear affectionately.

Queen Mimosa took her leave with the bickering Spoilt Royal Children while the King hung back for a moment.

'If Kazam win,' he said to both Blix and Tenbury, 'I will have you both stuffed with sawdust while still alive and then use you for bayonet practice. Do you understand?'

He didn't wait for a reply, and turned to me with such a hateful glare that I took an involuntary step backwards. But he made no comment, and turned to join his family, who were all present to view the contest – even his Useless Brother, the royal hanger-on cousins and his odd-looking mother, the Duck-faced Dowager Duchess of Dinmore.

The King stepped up to the royal microphone and gave a long rambling speech that made reference to how proud he was that the hard toil of a blindly trustful citizenry kept him and his family in the lap of luxury while war widows begged on the street, and how he thanked providence that he had been blessed to rule over a nation whose inexplicable tolerance towards corrupt despots was second to none.

The speech was well received and some citizens were even moved to tears. Once done, he ordered that the contest begin.

'We'll still thrash you,' said Blix to me, 'and if you're worried about your darling boyfriend, he's quite safe for the moment.'

My heart suddenly fell. Perkins had been rumbled.

'I don't know what you mean.'

'No? Here.'

And he passed me the left-handed conch that we'd given Perkins.

'If any harm comes to him,' I said between gritted teeth, 'I will hold you personally responsible.'

'Oh, oh, I'm so frightened,' replied Blix sarcastically.

'Now piss off. Haven't you got some wizards to spring from jail?'

'I'll be back with help,' I said. 'You'll be thrashed. And just for the record, he's not my boyfriend.'

Blix laughed and had his first two stones fitted even before Lord Tenbury's car arrived to take us to fetch Moobin and the others.

Bridge building

'So which two do you want released?' asked Lord Tenbury as soon as we had arrived outside the city jail, a large stone building to the north of the city which was known ironically as the 'Hereford Hilton', much to the annoyance of the *real* Hereford Hilton, which coincidentally was only two doors down, something that worked to the advantage of the prisoners when pizza deliveries were misdirected.

'I was under the impression His Majesty specifically requested *all* were to be released,' I pointed out.

'Then you understand little of the role of Lord Chief Adviser. My duty is to serve my King the best way I can and interpret his orders as I see fit. Two sorcerers. Choose now.'

I could see it was the best deal I was going to get, and every second spent arguing was a second wasted.

'The Wizard Moobin,' I said without hesitation, 'and . . . Patrick of Ludlow.'

Lord Tenbury relayed the orders to the jailer, told us we could make our way back to the bridge and was gone. After waiting half an hour, in which I had

235

serious doubts that Tenbury would keep his word, the pair of them emerged blinking into the daylight. They had their lead finger-cuffs removed and within a few seconds we were in a taxi heading back towards the bridge.

'Well done,' said Moobin, brushing the dirt, earwigs and other prison detritus from his jacket.

'Don't thank me,' I said, annoyed with myself that I had done so little, 'thank Queen Mimosa.'

'She's an ex-sorcerer herself,' he said. 'I think she has a soft spot for us. Who else do we have on the team?'

'You two are it.'

Team Kazam were going be severely underpowered. I told them what had happened since they had been imprisoned. That Mawgon was still stone, her pass-thought unbroken; that Perkins had been captured during an attempt to uncover a missing vision; that the Moose had turned out to be semi-self-aware and was the agent behind the 'infinite thinness' spell, and that Zambini hadn't really been much help – although it had been good to see him.

'The Moose drawing power from a ring?' said Moobin incredulously. 'From a band of *gold*, the single most boringly non-reactive metal on the planet?'

'Zambini was surprised too.'

'Well, it's not important right now,' he said as the taxi dropped us as close as it could to the south bridge abutment. 'We're going to have to wing it a bit and break a few rules. The future of Kazam is in the balance and we have to work together if we're to have any chance of survival. Now listen carefully . . .'

As Tiger took the cab back to Zambini Towers to put the plan in motion, Moobin, myself and Patrick surveyed the wreckage of what had once been a stone bridge with five arches supported by four piers. iMagic had already had an hour's start, and the bridge piers on their side were already cleared of old rubble and three feet above the level of the river. The stones were moving about the site steadily, to many 'oohs' and 'aahs' from the onlookers. It took a moment for us to be seen by the audience, but when they did there was a sudden hush and then a cheer. Blix's past history of hasty, substandard wizidrical building work had spread about the town, and severely dented his popularity. As the cheer echoed around the area, Patrick lifted ten pieces of cut stone from the river bed simultaneously, then moved them in a long procession to be stacked for later insertion in the bridge.

The crowd went wild at this, and the scoreboard, which was offering up-to-the-second live betting odds, had us up from '1000: 1' against to '500:1' against. Not great, but an improvement. I saw Patrick hold on to a crowd barrier for support after his exertions. He would not have attempted such a feat without Moobin requesting it – the purpose was to make the iMagic team nervous. It worked. Two stones that were about to be placed dropped with a heavy splash into the river as the iMagic team momentarily lost concentration.

'Patrick will need continuous food if he does most of the heavy lifting,' said Moobin, exercising each of his index fingers in readiness, 'and check to see how Tiger is getting on.'

I needed no second bidding. I called a street urchin out of the crowd and deputised him on to the Kazam team in order to keep Patrick and Moobin supplied with constant water and food, and told him to find a seamstress to repair their clothes 'on the fly' as continuous heavy spelling unravels stitching.[*]

'To battle,' said Moobin as he walked across the scaffolding footbridge that ran parallel to the stone bridge. He lifted stones from the rubble with a relaxed movement of his hands, and sorted them into categories of dressed, rubble and ornate, ready to be put back into the bridge. It was mostly bravado. As with Patrick, it took a lot more power then he made out. If they tried to keep it up like this they'd be exhausted long before our half of the bridge was finished.

'Surprised to see me, Blix?' said Moobin as they met in the middle.

[*] No one knows why – it just does. Shoelaces untie themselves almost immediately, which explains the almost universal use of loafers among sorcerers. 'Anti-spell' clothing is of man-made cloth with welded seams, and looks terrible. Most sorcerers simply change clothes hourly when working.

'It won't make any difference,' Blix sneered back, 'the team are on a roll.'

It certainly appeared that way. iMagic were now starting on their first arch.

'We'll see.'

They parted to continue their work while I hurried off to see how Tiger was doing.

Zambini Towers is located in the tight network of streets near the cathedral, and was no more than a three-minute jog from the bridge. By the time I got there Tiger was already organising the retired sorcerers, wizards and enchanters into teams to transfer the wizidrical power from the housebound Transient Moose all the way down to the bridge.

To accomplish this we placed two sorcerers at each street corner from the Towers to the bridge. One index finger of a sorcerer would pick up the crackle, and the other would send it on to the next. It was what was known as a daisy-chain, and the residents were all fully aware of how it worked – and were in teams of two only so that they could relieve one another when they got tired, and have someone to remind them what they were meant to be doing.

'How's it going?' I asked.

'Almost done,' replied Tiger, 'but you need to speak to the Moose yourself – he just stares blankly at me.'

I found the Moose in the lobby, gazing at the spreading boughs of the oak tree that was growing there.

'Was this here yesterday?' he asked.

'It's been there for almost twenty years,' I replied.

'Well I never. What can I do for you?'

The thinness enchantment was no longer required as the contest had begun, and it didn't take long to convince the Moose to channel the power from the small terracotta pot towards the bridge – or to be more precise, to Edgar Znorpp at the front entrance, who would then pass it across to Roger Limpet waiting on the street outside – and from him to Julian Shedmaker on the corner.

'Just say when,' replied the Moose with a carefree toss of its antlers, 'and Moobin and Patrick will be able to draw as much power as I can extract from that pot.'

'Will you be all right?' I asked.

'Never better,' he replied, 'and thanks for asking.'

I told Tiger to stand by for my signal, then visited all our retired sorcerers on the way to the bridge to check they were set and ready. It would take only a minor lapse in concentration on the part of one to break the chain. Margaret O'Leary was last in line, and chosen *specifically* because she was the least bonkers and the best liar in case anyone asked what she was up to.

'Don't let it flow to the iMagic team by accident,' I said, and she assured me she would not. I signalled to Moobin and Patrick, who were watching me, then spoke to Tiger through the conch to instruct the Moose to start channelling.

I saw Margaret stiffen slightly as the power started to flow through her. Her plait unravelled, and both earrings fell from her ears. She didn't even notice.

'Wow,' she said with a smile, 'that's good crackle. Can I pinch some to deal with a few grey hairs?'

'At the end, if all goes well.'

I watched Moobin and Patrick as the power flowed through to them, and the effect was almost instantaneous. Moobin lifted two stones from one of the piles in unison and clicked them into place on the far side of the bridge as easily as if it were Lego. There was a gasp from the crowd, a resounding cheer and our odds on the scoreboard rose from 500:1 to 50:1 against. I breathed a small sigh of relief. At least we were now actually in the game, even if far behind. The iMagic team completed their first arch within half an hour and then moved on to the next.

I spent the next hour moving up and down the daisy-chain to ensure all was well and that the areas between the sorcerers remained relatively clear and no one lingered too long within the streams – passive spelling was a very real risk, and it sapped power. There was a minor hiccup when a van parked in the way and we had to interrupt the stream while we moved the sorcerers across to the other side of the road, but it all worked, and within that hour we accelerated to being only one arch behind iMagic.

'Impressive,' said Blix as I walked past him with some chocolate for Patrick, 'but you can't keep up that rate of sustained spelling for ever.'

'We'll see.'

Tiger and I spent our time making sure that the sorcerers were kept cool by drinking gallons – and I mean gallons – of iced water, as simply being a conduit for wizidrical energy without actually using it made one grow hot, as a wire does with an electrical current passing through. We also had to ensure that the changeovers went smoothly when, predictably enough, they needed a visit to the bathroom. And all this subtly, without alerting Blix as to what we were up to. Within another twenty minutes we had drawn level with iMagic, and half an hour after that we had passed them. We were now in the lead, something reflected by the odds on the leader board and much to the delight of the crowd, but not the King, who sat in the royal box, tapping his fingers impatiently on his second-best throne.

Blix paused for a moment and walked over. He looked at us both in turn, then gave a rare smile.

'Where are you getting all this power?'

'Skill, hard work and efficient use of resources,' replied Moobin. 'You should try it some day.'

'Very funny.'

He thought for a moment, then abruptly changed his manner.

'Okay, here it is, with me eating humble pie: congratulations. You've bested me.'

Moobin and I looked at one another.

'A trick of some sort, Blix?' asked Moobin, not pausing for one second in placing a carved piece of stone in place. 'We're barely half an arch ahead.'

'We're almost worn out,' Blix replied. 'Corby and Muttney have been . . . *disappointing*. Perhaps we can negotiate my defeat so I am not utterly humiliated?'

It seemed an astonishing request, given his own deceitful conduct. In answer, Moobin was firm, but clear.

'We will give you the same courtesy and kindness you gave us, Blix.'

'How unpleasant of you,' Blix said after a pause. 'What happened to all the "brother wizard" stuff?'

'It evaporated when you had us all thrown into jail.'

'Really?' Blix asked, as though it had only just occurred to him that we might be annoyed. 'Yes, I suppose it might have. Never mind. I will go and draft a letter conceding my position. But irrespective, we should finish the bridge, yes? A good show for the King and the citizenry?'

'I agree,' said Wizard Moobin suspiciously.

Blix gave us another smile and moved off to speak to the colonel, who had been hovering close at hand.

'I strongly suggest that we don't relax for a moment,' I said as soon as Blix and the colonel had departed, seemingly in some haste. 'I smell a very large Blix-shaped rat that is up to something.'

'I agree,' said Moobin. 'But what?'

I didn't answer, and left them to carry on while the iMagic team, now without their leader, began to fall farther and farther behind. By the time we had the second arch more or less finished, the odds on the scoreboard made us the clear favourites and iMagic merely washed up old has-beens. But just as we were about to start on our final arch, *something happened.*

The surge

_____

It was a surge. A burst of almost unprecedented violence, but oddly, only through Patrick and Moobin – the iMagic sorcerers were unaffected. With the two of them caught unawares, the heavy blocks of masonry that Patrick and Moobin were moving suddenly flew high in the air. One fell on the road bridge two hundred yards away, where we could hear the sound of cars braking and colliding, and another fell into the river. Two others, each a quarter of a ton, were thrown so high in the air that they disappeared from sight.*

Moobin swore as he tried to control the surge. He described it later as like being in a car with no brakes and the throttle jammed full on while trying to negotiate the St Nigel's Day parade without hitting anyone. To absorb the raw energy that was now entering his body, he pointed his fingers at the river and in an

---

*It was found out later that one fell harmlessly to earth in an orchard at Belmont a few miles to the south, while the other landed on the Ross-to-Hereford branch line, derailing a train transporting Hereford Zoo's Tralfamosaur, which was on an exchange trip to Woburn Safari Park. It took three weeks to recapture, with considerable difficulty. For more details see _DS3: The Return of Shandar_.

instant the water had changed to a cheap German white wine and receded in both directions, revealing a lot of mud and more shopping trolleys than I thought existed in the world.

I looked across at Patrick. He, too, was struggling to do something with the massive surge, and had switched his attention to what he usually did – lifting cars for the city's clamping unit. All cars within a 250-yard radius were violently lifted three feet into the air and then, when this wasn't enough to absorb the power, he began moving them all to the car pound[*] two miles away.

I bit my lip. An oversurge of this power generally ended only in one way – when the power overcame the sorcerer completely and caused them to physically burst. It would be painful, and very messy.[†] I watched them with growing concern as random spells began to bubble up from Patrick and Moobin's subconscious as the increased power started to invade their thoughts. There was a brief shower of toads, dogs started barking and everyone in the crowd who had curly hair found it had straightened. The river turned from cheap wine

[*] Later investigations found that he had moved eighty-six cars a combined total of nineteen miles in under twenty-two seconds – a record that would never be surpassed.
[†] The technical term is an 'Accelerated Feedback Oversurge Blowout', when the power you are using is less than the power coming in. The last documented occurrence was fourteen years previously when an unlicensed cadet attempted to direct six MegaShandars of power towards lifting a Buick. He absorbed more than he could safely expel and the resulting imbalance caused him to literally explode. The largest bit of him they found was a small section of bone later identified as a kneecap.

to an expensive 1928 Château La Tour, every watch in the local postal district reset itself to midday and the clouds above the city started to form into farmyard-animal shapes.

Just when I thought our sorcerers could take no more, the surge stopped. The wine river washed back, the cloud shapes and toads vanished, and in the distance we could hear Patrick's cars fall with expensive-sounding crunches. Moobin and Patrick fell to their knees, their index fingers purple with bruises that had spread across their hands to their forearms. It would be painful to spell for weeks.

I ran up to Moobin as the crowd started to murmur in an excited fashion. Blix's team – minus Blix himself, who was nowhere to be seen – were staring at us, open mouthed. They'd never seen anything like it either.

'Check the chain,' muttered Moobin, 'make sure everyone's okay.'

Tiger and I dashed back down the daisy-chain to see whether anyone had burst. The first link was Margaret O'Leary, who was standing on the corner by a sideshow tent, where the Two-Headed Boy had popped his heads out of the tent flap to witness the event.

'What in Shandar's name was *that*?' she said. 'I just channelled more power in thirty seconds than I've expended in a lifetime.'

'Has Blix been past you?'

'No.'

We moved on to the next in the chain, who was Bartleby the Bald. He was in much the same state as O'Leary – in shock, but okay. We worked our way back to Zambini Towers and were relieved to find that although the sorcerers were hot and sweaty and bruised with the effort, none had dared break the chain, and for good reason. If they'd tried, they would have borne the full brunt of the power themselves – the only safe option was to hope those at the end could safely expel the extra power.

'You check the Moose,' I said to Tiger. 'I'll look in on Lady Mawgon.'

I put my head round the door of the Palm Court, but Mawgon was unchanged. Wherever the power was coming from, it wasn't the power stored in the Dibble Coils – they remained as resolutely full and unhacked as before.

'Jenny!' came Tiger's voice. 'In here!'

I dashed through to the lobby, where Tiger was kneeling next to a blackened moose-shaped hole burnt into the carpet. There were similar burned shapes on each of the four walls, too – of neat moosian front, back and side elevations, and a perfect moose-shaped plan view hole burned through the ceiling and three storeys up. It was so neat you could see the delicate splay of his antlers.

'He said it was the only way to stop the surge,' said Ex-Weathermonger Taylor Woodruff IV, who was standing close by, 'by taking the full force internally. He said he was sorry if it messed up your bridge building.'

Tiger and I stood in silence in the empty corridor, musing on the once Transient Moose's passing. He had frazzled every single line of the spell that made up his existence and vanished in a brief blast of energy. I picked up the small pot with the ring in it. It still didn't make any sense. Not to me, not to anyone – certainly not to Tiger, who hated unanswered questions more than anyone.

'Look,' he said, showing me the readout from the Shandargraph. There were multiple peaks from what we had just seen outside, but also *another* drain, sustained over thirty-seven seconds, and peaking at 1.2 GigaShandars. The range and direction were the same as Moobin and Patrick's; up around the old bridge somewhere.

'Was that Blix?' asked Tiger.

'If it was he didn't use it on the bridge,' I said, looking at my watch. It had been reset to midday in the surge, and now read five minutes past.

'1.2 GigaShandars?' queried Tiger. 'Isn't that the power drain requirement of a—'

'It is,' I replied, not far behind him. 'Call 999 and mutter "Quarkbeast" in a panicky voice. I need

Once Magnificent Boo at the bridge as soon as possible.'

'You think—?'

'I do. The Quarkbeast has just divided.'

Risk of confluence

I ran back to the bridge to find Moobin and Patrick sucking on ice cubes and trying to get their breath back. The iMagic team were still working, but without Blix they were a good four hours behind, if they could finish at all.

'The Moose is gone,' I said to Moobin, 'so you're on your own. The surge you felt was a power drain as something latched on to the ambient wizidrical energy and drew what it needed through you. Blix had a plan B in case we were to defeat him. A plan he has hatched with the help of the colonel. This is no longer a magic contest – *it's an assassination attempt!*'

'To what end?'

'To put Blix on the throne. Legally the Court Mystician is eighth in line after the Royal Family and the Lord Chief Adviser. Everyone that stands between him and the Crown is here today, gathered conveniently in one place to suffer . . . death by Quarkbeast!'

'A bit of a long shot,' responded Moobin doubtfully. 'The last incidence of a person savaged by a Quarkbeast was over a decade ago – and he did attack it first with a garden fork. I can't see the King attacking anything with a garden fork.'

'He'd have a footman do it for him,' said Margaret O'Leary, who had joined us, 'but I'm not sure a Quarkbeast would be able to make the distinction between the attacker and the person who ordered it.'

'Not that way,' I replied, still out of breath from the run, 'I mean with a *confluence*. Place a captured Quarkbeast next to a source of heavy spelling and it will draw the vast quantity of power needed to divide. It tried earlier with Patrick when he was moving the oak, but couldn't draw enough. The Moose gave it as much as it needed – and more.'

'But if it is not separated after division,' said Moobin, who knew a bit about Quarkbeasts as well, 'then—'

'Right,' I said, 'if unable to escape itself in a thousand seconds, it will recombine with enough energy to take out a third of the city.'

They stared at me, horrified at the suggestion.

'How long is a thousand seconds?'

'Sixteen minutes and forty seconds.'

I looked at my watch. It was eleven minutes past. If the Quarkbeast divided when the surge ended, we had less than five minutes. We looked around. Most of the south of the city would be taken out and, with it, King Snodd and all his family, half the police, most of the Imperial Guard, all the spectators – and us.

Blix would be taking cover somewhere out of the blast radius.

'No witnesses,' said Moobin, 'and no one to refute whatever version of events King Blix decided on – he could blame it on anything he chose.'

'We need to find a locked room within fifty metres of the royal box,' I muttered. 'Wait here.'

I ran across to where Lord Tenbury was standing, presumably wondering whether the King was serious about stuffing him and Blix with sawdust if they lost. I explained as briefly as I could what was up, and Tenbury, eager to regain the King's trust, immediately ordered the Royal Family's evacuation, then returned to us to see how he could help. He may have been corrupt, but he was no coward.

'Where do we start?' asked Moobin. 'There must be hundreds of rooms big enough to hide two equal but identically opposite Quarkbeasts.'

As we looked about, wasting time, word was getting about that something was up – the hurried way in which the Royal Family were removed most probably, and then the Imperial Guard themselves, who had a reputation for running from danger wherever it presented itself. In any event, the crowd began to grow restless, and when those in the expensive seats started to move away with their jewellery rattling in a panicked fashion, those in the cheaper seats also decided to make a run for it.

I looked around to see where a Quarkbeast might be hidden, but then a notion drifted into my head. I told Moobin straight away.

'Perkins is imprisoned with the Quarkbeast!'

'You *know* this or you *think* this? We don't have time to make a mistake.'

I had to make a swift judgement call. Half of Hereford and thousands of lives depended upon it.

'I *know* this,' I said, taking a deep breath, 'because it's an odd notion that popped uninvited into my head. And if Perkins has any particular skill, it's that of seeding ideas. I think he might be trying to communicate with me.'

I closed my eyes and tried to empty my mind, which was difficult as the mass exit of spectators made something of a noise as the panic increased.

'Moobin,' I said, 'I need you to take out all my senses.'

He pointed his finger at me and in an instant everything went empty. It was as though I had fallen into an empty space within myself that had nothing in it but time, thoughts, smells and the deep red of the sky at dawn. It was extraordinarily peaceful, and without the distraction of overwhelming sensory input I felt unusually clear headed. At first I could sense nothing except the jumble of my own thoughts firing across my mind and the smell of bacon and Irish stew, but after a moment or two I forced these to one side and, all of a sudden, there was a small voice on the very edge of my conscious mind, where the froth of random thoughts meets free will. It was Perkins, and he was sending me ideas. But he wasn't that good at it, and seemed to be coming across like a greetings telegram, and what's more, one that was badly spelled.

. . . WEST OF SNOOD BLVD SELLAR ++
KWARKBEAST DIVIDED ++
EXPLOD EMMENINT ++ THREE STEPS
DOUN ++ STILL WANT DATE? ++
REPEAT SNOOD BLVD SELLAR ++
KWARKBEAST . . .

And so it went on, repeating itself. I listened to it three times, each time spelt differently, until Moobin brought me back to the world of heat, light and sound just as Once Magnificent Boo and Tiger turned up in the Quarkbeast containment vehicle. I related what I'd heard as my watch passed thirteen minutes – three minutes to go.

'Anyone who wants to head for safety has to leave now,' I said. 'No one will think any the worse of you for it.'

No one made a move. Not even Lord Tenbury.

'Right,' I said, 'follow me.'

Snodd Boulevard ran from the cathedral to the

north end of the bridge, and after a hurried search we found a house that had three steps down to a green-painted cellar door. It was locked but Patrick pulled it off its hinges with a powerful flourish of his bruised hands and we hurried in to find ourselves in a long corridor with doors on either side, all locked.

'Where now?' asked Tiger as our final minute began to tick away.

'Doorknobs,' growled Boo, 'find the warm one.'

It was Moobin who found the correct room, and when Patrick had once again torn the door from its hinges we found a small paint store with a vaulted ceiling and a single window high up in the end wall. Perkins was lying cuffed, bound and gagged near the doorway, and at the far end of the chamber were two equal but opposite Quarkbeasts.

One of them was the one I had seen around town earlier, but the other was mine – the one I had lost up on the Dragonlands. Every detail was the same: the sixth thoracic scale slightly askew, the right front dew claw missing, and even the single white foot. My Quarkbeast was back. I took all this in on that first glance, and also noted a high-pitched hum in the air. But another and much more pertinent fact trumped all others for my attention: the Quarkbeasts were almost touching. Our thousand seconds were up.

'Still!' said Boo, and we all froze. The low hum rose in pitch as the Quarkbeasts moved closer to one another, increasing again to a whine as they nearly touched, then dropping again as they moved a few inches apart. This was the Song of the Quarkbeast. Those that have heard it are now little more than dust. But if I was to die, then I was glad to have heard it. It was a lonely song. One of lament, of unknown knowledge, a song of resignation, and of love and poetry given and received. The small movements that the Quarkbeasts made as they padded around one another altered the hum so subtly that it sounded like an alto bassoon, but with one single note, infinitely variable. But it wasn't a song of peace, love or happiness; it was a requiem mass – for all of us.

We all stood stock still. No one dared move in case the Quarks became startled and recombined either through fear, mischief or boredom.

I said the first thing that came into my head.

'Hello, boy.'

The new Quarkbeast turned to look at me and its mauve eyes flashed a sense of recognition. It looked at its partner, then at me again.

'I still have much to do,' I said softly. 'Adventures. *Wonderful* adventures. And I'm not sure I can do them without you.'

It wagged its tail to show it understood, but remained undecided, and the low hum rose again in pitch as the other Quarkbeast paced around it.

'Walkies,' said Tiger, speaking from outside in the

corridor. The Quarkbeast recognised his voice, too, and, eager to drag Tiger around the neighbourhood once again, it gave one final look at its partner and padded past us to where Tiger was waiting.

Almost immediately the low hum in the air stopped, and Once Magnificent Boo moved cautiously forward with some aluminium-coated zinc treats with which to tempt the other Quarkbeast.

'Welcome back,' I said.

'Quark,' said the Quarkbeast.

Within a few short moments Boo had steered the original Quarkbeast from the room and into the riveted titanium crate for onward transportation to Australia.

I untied Perkins, who gave me an awkward hug and thanked me for tuning into his thoughts.

'Hey,' I said with a smile, 'what girl doesn't like being thought about?'

I had a sudden thought.

'By the way, did I detect you thinking about asking me out for a date while you were directing us to you?'

'I couldn't help it,' said Perkins, looking somewhat embarrassed. 'Maybe the idea of sharing a *Potage Jojolie* at the dreary-chic Dungeon Rooms helped me forget that I was about to be annihilated.'

'In that case,' I said, 'I guess you'd better book us a table.'

*

We walked out into the daylight and back the short distance to the north abutment, where the unfinished bridge lay before us. The iMagic team had fled the scene, and of the crowds, only the fearless, stupid and asleep remained. The live leader board still displayed the final odds – 100:1 in favour of Kazam.

We jumped as from behind us there was an explosive report and a flaming figure was shot high in the air. It was Jimmy 'Daredevil' Nuttjob, performing his half-time act. He arced high above our heads trailing smoke as he went, and disappointingly managed only to get as far as 'God save the . . .' before landing with a splash and a hiss in the river. We clapped dutifully as he surfaced, coughing and spluttering.

We sat for a while gathering our thoughts until the Lord Chief Adviser strode up, ten minutes later.

'Recent events have changed His Majesty's mood,' he said. 'Ex-Court Mystician Blix is wanted for high treason along with his accomplice Colonel Bloch-Draine, and I am directed to proclaim in His Majesty's name that you are the winners of the contest.'

We looked at one another. We were all tired and bruised. Somehow jumping around and punching the air seemed inappropriate, given that we had been just ten seconds from dark eternity.

'What about the others?' said Moobin.

The Lord Chief Adviser took a deep breath.

'In addition, I will have the Price brothers released

immediately, and all charges are to be dropped. I will be making a full and truthful account of your exploits to His Majesty forthwith, and will recommend that the position of Court Mystician be transferred from Mr Blix to a sorcerer of Kazam's choosing. In addition, I have known His Majesty a long time, and I foresee medals. Lots of them. Probably big and very shiny.'

'I have a better idea,' said the Wizard Moobin. 'We don't want the the job of Court Mystician and we certainly don't want medals. We want to be left alone to pursue the Great Zambini's stated goal to use magic for the good of mankind. We don't want special favours, we simply want justice.'

'I'll see that you get it.'

'Do that. And remember: we don't respond well to being double-crossed.'

'We also require immunity,' I said, always thinking of my paperwork, 'from prosecution for all spells undertaken today, by whomsoever.'

Lord Tenbury was in no position to do deals. We could have asked for a pink elephant each – and got it.

'Leave it with me,' he said, and bowed low before departing.

We stood there for a moment, wondering what to do next. Blix could be anywhere by now, and although a nationwide arrest warrant would be able to bring him back to Snodd to stand trial, he wouldn't allow himself to be found. When you're a sorcerer of Blix's power, staying hidden is easy.

'How about some lunch?' I announced in a cheery voice. 'Once Magnificent Boo? Will you join us?'

Boo grumbled for a moment, but after I pointed out that she was one Quarkbeast closer to enlightenment thanks to us, she shrugged and agreed to come along – so long as we didn't mention the M-word in her company.

Lunch at last

The surge had not left the sorcerers unharmed. Most had severe bruising to their fingers and an outbreak of warts, but six suffered passive spelling. The mildest was simply a case of migrated ear,[*] while the worst was Francesca Derwent, who spent the next two weeks as a cod. She recovered fully, aside from a tendency to gape a little too much, and have eyes that were just a teeny weeny bit close to the side of her head for comfort.

We could sense the air of excitement long before we walked into the dining room at Zambini Towers, and were met with a roar of applause, and a standing ovation for Patrick and Moobin. By directing the excess energy efficiently, they had done very little damage, and none of it permanent.[†]

---

[*]This was Roger Limpet. The ear drifted down on to the chin, if you're *really* interested. It took two weeks to migrate back. It would have taken less, but he kept on picking at it.

[†]Not quite true. Patrick's dropping of thirty-two cars from three feet when the Moose suffered his fatal blowout caused M29,000 worth of damage. It was fortuitous that Jennifer had asked Tenbury for an amnesty for that day's spelling. The repair bills were eventually paid out of the Minister of Infernal Affairs' rubber-stamp budget, much to the Useless Brother's annoyance.

For all the retired sorcerers it was the first piece of truly practical magic they had committed outside the Towers' walls for several decades. Almost all recognised Once Magnificent Boo, and although sulky and reticent to begin with, she soon moved from utter silence to monosyllables, which was a step forward. I knew I could never persuade her to move to Zambini Towers, but her magicozoology expertise would be invaluable in the future.

The Price brothers turned up in time for pudding, straight out of prison and eager to know how it all turned out. They were almost immediately set upon by Boo, who demanded to know whether any Quarkbeasts were harmed in their Cambrian thermo-wizidrical detonation tests in the eighties, and the Prices, while unwilling to explain their methodology for obvious reasons, were happy to confirm that no Quarkbeasts were harmed in any way.

'Okay,' said Boo.

'Quark,' said the Quarkbeast in a relieved tone.

After that was settled, the Wizard Moobin made a speech, and directed several positive comments towards my conduct which made me blush and stare at the cutlery. Tiger and Perkins were mentioned, and we held a minute's silence for the no longer Transient Moose, and welcomed the Quarkbeast back into the fold.

And that was when Samantha Flynt appeared at the door of the dining room. There was a sudden hush as everyone stared at her. She looked as though she had been crying and was every bit as annoyingly pretty and perfect close up as she was from a distance.

'Are you staring because she's so lovely?' I said to Perkins.

'Not at all,' he replied unconvincingly, 'it's because I didn't expect to see her here.'

She was invited in and offered a seat and some food, which, after we explained was always this bad, she accepted gratefully.

'I'm sorry,' she sniffed, 'but I didn't know where to go.'

'There, there,' said Moobin, offering her his handkerchief.

She explained that Blix had helped snare the Quarkbeast, but didn't know the details of Blix's attempt to seize power, nor where he was now. The colonel, apparently, would have been made Lord Chief Adviser.

'Can I stay?' she said, dabbing her eyes with a handkerchief.

'Absolutely, my dear,' said Moobin.

'Samantha Flynt is very pretty, isn't she?' said Kevin Zipp in a dreamy manner once she had left the table to go to the bathroom.

'I thought that a bit, at *first*,' replied Perkins, glancing at me, 'but not any more.'

We listened for a moment as Moobin tried to

describe what it was like to suddenly be on the receiving end of more crackle than it was safe to handle.

'I was lucky to have Patrick with me,' he said. 'If I'd had to offload all that power on my own I wouldn't be here now.'

We all nodded sagely and I turned back to Perkins.

'Close thing, wasn't it?'

'It was worth it to hear the Song of the Quarkbeast.'

'Quark,' said the Quarkbeast, who was under the table, chewing on a saucepan.

'I don't think we should hear it again,' I mused. 'Twice would be pushing our luck. Listen, I'm sorry for sending you to Blix. I didn't know he'd see through you so easily.'

'That was my fault,' he said cheerily. 'It was all going well until he found me rifling through his filing cabinet. I should have locked the door. I'm new to all this cloak-and-dagger stuff. He realised what I was there for, and in a twinkling reduced all his records to rice pudding to avoid further scrutiny.'

This was disappointing.

'I guess we'll never know about Vision BO55, then.'

'Oh, I found that out,' said Perkins. 'Blix caught me *after* I read it.'

Tiger and I stared at him. Even the Quarkbeast looked interested, and Moobin, whom we had quickly brought up to speed on events while he was away in jail, was keen to know more.

'The vision was nothing specific,' said Perkins. 'It just stated that Blix's wife would be greater and more powerful than he, and ultimately the agent of his downfall.'

'He's not married,' said Full Price. 'Sorcerers rarely are. So what does it relate to?'

We all looked at Kevin Zipp for an answer.

'Search me,' he said. 'It wasn't my vision, anyway – it was Sister Yolanda's. But if she says he's married, then I suppose he will be – or was, or is.'

We mused on this for a moment. Sister Yolanda was usually right, but without Blix here to question, it would have to remain a mystery.

'Look,' I said, 'Dame Corby.'

She was standing at the door as self-conscious as a latecomer to their own party. Standing with her was Tchango Muttney, who was only there because of no better option, and next to them both, Samantha.

'She doesn't *look* as though the ants obey her,' said Tiger, commenting on Dame Corby's appearance, which was that of a rather small, ineffective-looking woman, who didn't like to look anyone in the eye.

'iMagic is finished, the traitor Blix has fled,' announced Dame Corby in a resigned voice. 'We humbly beg to join your establishment in whatever capacity you think fit.'

She looked at Tchango, who nodded, utterly humiliated.

It was embarrassing for us, too, to hear a licensed sorcerer beg in this manner. It also proved what we had thought for some time: that Dame Corby's shares in the family trouser-press business were not doing as well as she had boasted.

'You are welcome here,' said Moobin as he strode forward to greet them in the traditional manner, 'but your status and duties will be decided by a committee led by our acting manager.'

Moobin introduced them and they shook my hand in a doubtful manner. I knew for a fact that Blix had referred to me as 'that upstart foundling' and it looked as if they shared the sentiment.

'I have heard great things about you,' said Dame Corby in a voice taut with forced politeness.

'I too,' said Tchango.

'I'm Samantha Flynt,' said Samantha in a breezy tone, giving me her hand to shake, 'but it's pronounced without the first "A".'

'Smantha?'

'That's it. I don't have my licence yet, but I'm working very hard on my studies. It's tricky because, well,' she tapped her temple with a fingertip, 'I've not much upstairs. Why are you staring at me?'

I took a step back and nudged Moobin.

'What?' he said.

'*Shifter*,' I said out of the corner of my voice.

'You're going to have to speak up. I can't hear you.'

'*SHAPE-SHIFTER!*' I said in a louder voice, and pointed unsubtly at the apparently pretty girl in front of me. Moobin understood what I meant and had a standard Magnaflux Reversal on her in a heartbeat, in order to uncover the Blix hiding within. Surprisingly, there was no effect at all, except her ringlets disappeared, her nose became slightly less cute, her eyes reduced in colour and blueness and her waist size increased by half a size. A Magnaflux Reversal reversed *all* spells, irrespective of who cast them. She had been augmenting herself.

'Whoops,' she said, putting a hand to her nose, 'this is, like, *so* embarrassing.'

But we had more important things to worry about than Samantha's vanity.

'Samantha, were you here ten minutes ago?' I demanded.

'It's without the first "A".'

'*Smantha*, were you here earlier?'

Her now not-so-large eyes opened wide.

'Absolutely not!'

Samantha had remained Samantha for the simple reason that she *was* Samantha. The first one had been the impostor. There was only one person it could be.

'Blix is in the building,' I yelled. 'Containment plan "D"!'

Plan 'D' was one of several we had planned in case of emergencies. In this case, the possibility of something nasty being created that couldn't be allowed to get out of the building. We'd used it on a phantasm a few weeks back who managed to escape from its bell-jar, and it was quite a job to get it back in – especially as a plan D seals the hotel, and there is only about four days' worth of air contained within its walls.

Dame Corby and Tchango Muttney were the first to react by diving under the table with a yelp. They were more frightened of Blix than us, and they were meant to be colleagues. The Prices and Moobin responded more sensibly and steel shutters suddenly appeared across the windows and external doors with a chunk-chunk-chunk that echoed throughout the old building. Perkins dashed to the door to the dining room and peered out.

'All clear out here,' he said.

'Wandering in here is a big risk,' observed Full Price, 'he must want something badly.'

'He knows RUNIX and wants revenge,' I said as a knot began to tighten in my stomach, 'and we have four Gig of raw crackle sitting in the Palm Court.'

We tumbled out of the dining room and headed downstairs to the Palm Court, which predictably enough had a seven-headed dog with flaming eyes standing guard outside. It growled menacingly, the hair on its seven necks bristling aggressively while its fourteen front legs pawed the parquet flooring and drool dripped from its seven tongues and two hundred and ninety-four teeth.

Those less well acquainted with seven-headed dogs gave out a gasp of horror, but Moobin muttered 'Amateur!' and strode through the illusory beast, which evaporated like smoke. Once inside the Palm Court we found the excellent facsimile of Samantha Flynt working at the tear we had last seen open when Monty Vanguard failed so utterly to break the passthought. Next to her were Lady Mawgon and Monty, still stone.

'I lost my way to the bathroom,' said the faux Samantha as she gave a heart-melting smile.

'It's over, Blix,' said Moobin.

'Step away from the Dibble,' ordered Full Price, index finger at the ready. I knew that he'd never newted anyone, but was itching to do so.

'It might have looked like I was frightened by that dog thing,' said Tiger, 'but I wasn't.'

'She looks sort of familiar,' said the real Samantha.

'Quark,' said the Quarkbeast.

'We can negotiate your surrender,' I said, stepping forward, partly to stop him being newted – he currently had eight fingers pointed at him, and while Perkins' skills in these matters were questionable, I knew that the Prices and Moobin could take him in an instant. I think Blix knew this as he melted out of Samantha and back into himself. He made a move to give a slow handclap.

'*DON'T MOVE A MUSCLE!*' I yelled. 'And *very* slowly: fingers toward the floor.'

Blix smiled but didn't comply.

'We can talk about this. All wizards together.'

'Let him make a move on us, Jenny. I so want to take him out.'

'No, Moobin. Blix? Fingers down. *Really* slowly.'

He looked at us all in turn, then slowly swivelled his hands until his index fingers were pointing straight down.

'There is a passage in the *Codex Magicalis*,' said Blix slowly, 'which states that a wizard in trouble should always be afforded every help and assistance by every other wizard, irrespective of the trouble they may find themselves in.'

'Yes,' I said, 'and there is another section in the *Codex* that states that any six wizards may call judgement and punishment upon any other. Tiger, go to the office. In the bottom left drawer you'll find some lead finger-cuffs.'

'Right,' said Tiger and dashed off.

Blix looked momentarily ill at ease.

'Six wizards? You've only got four.'

'Muttney and Corby joined us ten minutes ago.'

'Nonsense. They are loyal only to me.'

'No we're not,' came a voice from the door.

'Traitors!' he spat. 'I'll make you pay for this.'

'You won't get the chance, 'I told him. 'We could turn you over to the King, but he'd only want to pardon you or exile you or something dumb like that. No, I think we should deal with you here and now.'

'What will it be?' he said with a sneer. 'A high tower with no staircase, marooned on an island in the Barents Sea populated only by carnivorous beasts?'

'No.'

'A subterranean cavern with only a misshapen goblin manservant for company?'

'You should be so lucky, 'I replied. 'No, it would be more fitting if you were punished in a manner that would make you better understand the people you almost killed today.'

'Wizards?'

'Ordinary subjects of King Snodd.'

'No,' he said as he realised where this was heading, 'for pity's sake. Don't humiliate me like that—'

'Yes,' I said in as grim a voice as I could muster, 'ordinary incarceration in a common jail, with ordinary criminals. No lonely tower, no force-field, no seven-headed something – just stone walls, gruel, an hour of exercise a day and only the company of thieves and villains.'

'Good call,' smiled Moobin, 'Like it.'

Blix glared at me as Tiger arrived back with the finger-cuffs.

'I should have killed you when I had the chance. And I had so many chances. But you know the reason I didn't kill you? Do you know *why* I put you in the

North Tower rather than simply killing you? Why I allowed you to stay alive?'

'I've no idea,' I replied. 'Stupidity? Some sort of illogical Evil Dark Lord code?'

'No,' he replied. 'Jennifer – *I am your father!*'

There was a deathly hush as I stared at him open mouthed. I had always wanted to know who my parents were, but hadn't pursued it because I was frightened of what I might . . . no, hang on. It was nonsense. For a start, he looked nothing like me, and I was nothing like him.

'You're a liar,' I said, 'you're not my father.'

'No, of course not,' he said with a grin, 'nothing as hideously self-righteous as you could ever spring from a Blix – but it was worth it just to see your stupid hopeful face.'

'You'd pull that sort of joke,' I said coldly, 'on a foundling?'

'I think you're confusing me with someone pleasant, Jennifer.'

'Actually, I don't think so. Full? Cuff him. Moobin, if he even so much as *twitches*, newt him.'

'With pleasure.'

Full Price edged forward, fingers at the ready. It was a tense moment. Until we had the cuffs on him he was still dangerous. His eyes bored into mine with hatred, and as Full Price snapped on the first of the finger-cuffs, Blix shook his head and muttered:

'Bloody foundlings!'

There was a click, a hum and then a rising whine from somewhere deep within the building. We felt the floor flex, and the room suddenly grew lighter and three degrees warmer. The first person to realise what was going on was the most experienced wizard in the room – Blix. The Dibble Storage Coils, brimful with four GigaShandars of wizidrical energy, had just come back online. The passthought had been simpler than we had thought, and reflected Lady Mawgon's feelings for Tiger and myself: *Bloody foundlings* – a feeling shared with Blix with the same deep sense of disdain. Unwittingly, Lady Mawgon had just handed a vast amount of power to the one person who shouldn't have it.

Conrad Blix, formerly 'the Amazing', was now . . . . All Powerful.

The All Powerful Blix

Several things seemed to happen at once. The Prices and Moobin all let fly at the same time, and the room was suddenly filled with spells and counter-spells, weaves, dodges, burns and reversals. So much so that the dust on the floor buzzed with static and the glass in the roof began to cloud. Those of us unversed in the Mystical Arts dived for cover, and when the noise had died down after probably less than half a minute, I looked cautiously from where I had hidden behind the central fountain. Tiger was with me, and Perkins. The Quarkbeast was next to us, but frozen in mid-leap, his mouth gaping wide and now showing us a perfect array of teeth delicately rendered in the finest granite.

'Wow,' I heard Blix say, 'you can do some serious mischief with four Gigs of crackle at your elbow! Jennifer? Are you there?'

'Perhaps,' I said, not revealing myself.

I looked to right and left and noticed that the room had six more figures delicately realised in stone – both of the Prices, Moobin, Corby and even Tchango

275

Muttney, who had been turned to granite just as he reached the door.

'You make a run for it,' said Perkins, 'I'll cover you.'

'And then what?'

He thought for a moment.

'I don't know.'

'We so almost had him,' I murmured. '*Shit.*'

'Language,' said Tiger.

'Sorry.'

I was still trying to think of a plan when I heard a young woman's voice.

'All Powerful Blix,' it went, 'I have always loved and admired you. Take me with you.'

It was Samantha. She had reaugmented herself back to perfect gorgeousness and was approaching Blix, who had improved himself, too. His hair was no longer streaked with grey, he was ten years younger, four inches taller and physically stronger. He was temporarily as powerful as any sorcerer that had ever been. Of course, he'd be back to normal once he'd used up the power in the Dibble, but a clever mage can do a lot with four GigaShandars. A castle, a fast car, a wardrobe full of mouse-fur suits – you name it.

He smiled and put out his hand to take hers.

'Samantha,' he said, 'are you ready and willing to obey my every command?'

'Yes, yes, I shall,' she replied eagerly, 'for every evil

genius there must be a ludicrously beautiful woman apparently doing very little at his side.'

'I see that you and I speak the same language.'

'I hope so,' she said demurely, 'but it's been three years, and you could have made a bit more effort.'

He raised an eyebrow.

'More effort? To do what?'

'To learn my name. *You don't pronounce the first "A"*!'

She attempted to grab his fingers. It was a brave attempt on her behalf, but futile. In an instant there was nothing but a small and very pretty guinea pig scurrying around the floor making loud weep-weep-weep noises.

'What *has* the world come to,' said Blix to the room in general, 'when an evil genius can't even trust pretty girls that throw themselves at him?'

We ducked back down behind the fountain.

'That was brave,' said Perkins.

'Jennifer,' came Blix's voice again, 'it's time to show yourself. It's been fun all this back and forth, but I've got better things to do than monkey around with amateurs.'

'I'll be out in a minute,' I shouted, 'I just have to do something.'

'What's he going to do with us?' whispered Perkins.

'With that amount of power, almost anything he wants. We've not a hope of vanquishing him now.'

Tiger snapped his fingers.

'Unless we can get someone to marry him. Vision BO55, remember? *His wife would be greater and more powerful than he, and ultimately be the agent of his downfall.*'

'Brilliant,' said Perkins. 'What's your plan? Marry him to a dangerously insane sorcerer with ten Gig of crackle on tap?'

'It was just a thought.'

'What if he were already married?' came a voice. 'What if an impressionable young girl had married him in secret against her better judgement and against the advice of her other, better suitor?'

We turned towards the person speaking. It was Once Magnificent Boo. She had taken refuge behind an upturned table. It took a moment to figure it out. Zambini, Blix and Boo had once been close, then fell out. If Boo had chosen Blix over Zambini, it would explain why.

'You're Mrs Blix?' I asked.

'When was this vision?' she asked.

I told her it was just after she had won the seven golds at the Olympics. I saw her jaw tighten and she pulled her gloves off, revealing hands that were missing the index fingers. She looked at them, then at us. Then she stood up.

'Hello, Conrad,' she said, and we peered cautiously over the parapet of the fountain to see what would happen next.

'Ah,' he said, 'Boo. You can leave. My argument is not with you.'

'But mine,' she replied, 'is with you. I just heard that you sought a vision from Sister Yolanda and received one: that your wife — me — would be more powerful than you, and ultimately vanquish you?'

He swallowed nervously.

'I was married. I was young. I was foolish. I was just *checking*.'

'You wanted to check I wouldn't be greater than you?'

'No,' he said in a quiet voice, 'I wanted to check we'd be happy.'

Perkins, Tiger and I exchanged glances. Only a fool or someone in love asks a precog how things will turn out.

'And you couldn't be happy if I was better than you?'

Blix looked sheepish for a moment.

'You had me kidnapped,' she said slowly as she figured it out. '*You did this to me.*'

She showed him her hands and I saw him blanch for a moment as even he realised just how hideously cruel he had been.

'I trusted you,' she said, her voice only rising slightly as she kept herself under control, 'and I could have been someone. We all could have been someone. You, me and Zambini — a force for good in this world.

You didn't just destroy me, you sabotaged a lifetime of research, discovery and the advance of magic as a noble art. *Do you have any idea what you have done?*'

We looked at Blix, waiting for an answer. There wasn't one, of course.

'Yeah, well,' he said with a shrug, 'we've already established I'm unpleasant, untrustworthy and . . . and . . . and—'

'Devious?' I suggested.

'Devious. Right. So what are you going to do about it? You've got *nothing*. Two wizards in a room and only one of them has fingers. Not much of a stand-off, is it?'

'I'll find my fingers,' she said in a low voice, 'and they'll still be as powerful today as when you had them removed in that lay-by. And when I get them, you'll be sorry.'

'You won't find them,' he said with a sneer, 'I made them unfindable. No one can find them. Not even I could find them.'

And that was when *I* stood up, in full view of Blix, who could have turned me into stone in a second. This was the moment to act.

'Lady Mawgon could find them,' I said in a voice cracked with fear, 'with the Wizard Moobin and Tiger with Perkins in reserve.'

'Impossible!' he said.

'We were asked by the Mighty Shandar's agent to

find a ring that was missing. A ring that didn't want to be found. But that wasn't what they were *really* after.'

I paused as this sank in.

'I only looked as far as the ring – *I never checked the small terracotta pot that it came in.*'

I brought the same small pot out of my bag, where it had lain since the Moose had over-surged, and upended it into my hand. The ring fell out first. A large ring, the sort that might fit on an index finger. Then dried dirt, a few scraps of material and finally – several human finger bones. Moobin was right; a ring has no power. The energy the Moose had extracted had come from Boo's missing fingers. Not just her own natural energy, but a power augmented by three decades of loss, hatred, bitterness – and *betrayal*.

I think Blix knew the game was up, and I like to think there was just a small vestige of love in his dark heart that made him pause, lose the speed advantage, and ultimately the battle.

Maybe deep down he knew he had to atone.

Boo grasped my elbow tightly to reconnect once again with her lost fingers, and I felt a pulse of energy shoot down my forearm. My fist shut on the finger-bones so tightly my nails punctured my palm, but I didn't feel the pain. In an instant Boo and Blix were locked in spell, and a wall of blue light welled up between them as they tried to break down each other's defences. They struggled like this for some moments, grappling with one another. The heat and light increased, a heavy wind blew up, and a moment later there was a blinding concussion.

Aftermath

I may have been unconscious for a few moments; I don't know. But when I came to, Boo was brushing herself down and replacing her lost fingers in the small terracotta pot. Blix had come off worse in the encounter and was now himself rendered perfectly in black granite, his last agonising yell of pain preserved for ever. Sister Yolanda's prophecy had come true. They always do.

'Well,' said the the Magnificent Boo in a chirpy voice, 'I think that turned out quite favourably, don't you?'

'Yes,' I said, 'yes, I think it did.'

'Why do you think the Mighty Shandar wanted my fingers?'

'I don't know,' I replied. 'To push destiny? For more power? Maybe Shandar's getting rid of those who might challenge him when he returns. Perhaps we've yet to find out. Magic works in mysterious ways.'

'It certainly does.'

She turned to pick up her gloves and made to walk away.

'Will you be coming back?' I asked.

'I have Quarkbeasts to feed. And they like their walkies.'

She gave me a smile.

'Keep well, Miss Jennifer Strange.'

'I will,' I said, 'thank you.'

She nodded, and walked away.

The formerly stone Kazam staff were stretching themselves after their brief incarceration. A thousand years or eight seconds feels the same when in stone, so I think they were very glad to see Tiger and myself unchanged – and Blix in granite, of course.

'That was very, very brave, Samantha,' I heard Moobin say once Tiger had explained what had happened.

'Thank you,' she said, 'but can I just point out that you don't pronounce the "A" . . .'

'You!' said Lady Mawgon, whose capacity to harangue did not seem to have been diminished by her imprisonment. 'I am hungry. Instruct Cook to make me a cheese sandwich and a cup of tea. I shall be in my room. Don't forget to knock, and if the sandwich is unsatisfactory I will send it back.'

And she glided off out of the Palm Court.

'Back to normal, eh?' said Tiger.

'Back to normal.'

There was a lot of explaining to do to everyone, and word soon came through from Lord Tenbury that the general magic amnesty had been signed by the King. The day's spelling would not require any paperwork at all, for which I was very glad. Everyone in the building of any power, whether licensed or not, took advantage of this and contributed to finishing the bridge – it was completed in twenty-three minutes and was open for traffic by teatime. Now that we knew the passthought, we could use the stored crackle to carry out much-needed repairs to Zambini Towers. By the time the Dibble Storage Coils were once again empty, the old building shone like a new pin under a fresh coat of paint, revarnished wood and polished brass. The Palm Court was once more full of lush tropical vegetation and the central fountain, dry for over six decades, gurgled into life. We even restocked the wine cellar and reinstated the elevators, but kept the service lift empty and free-fall-enabled, just for fun.

Over an extended afternoon tea I had to repeat the story of the trip up to Trollvania about six times as news of Zambini was sparse, and everyone wanted to know how he was.

At five I was in a press conference, and after that I fielded a few work calls from new clients who had seen what we had done that afternoon. If things got busier, we were going to need to license more sorcerers.

'A busy day,' said Perkins, who dropped into the office when things were finally beginning to calm down.

I smiled.

'*Very* busy.'

'Too busy for that date at the Dungeon Rooms?'

I didn't hesitate.

'Not at all – I'd like that very much.'

'Lobby at seven, then – and without Tiger.'

'No Tiger,' I said, 'promise.'

So I went and had a bath and changed into my second-best dress – I didn't wear my very best as I wanted to keep that in reserve.

I wasn't waiting in the lobby for long. Perkins arrived dressed in a suit, and dotted around the lobby were most of the residents, all eager to see us walk out together.

'You're looking very lovely,' he said.

'Thank you.'

He held the door open.

'Wait!'

It was Tiger, running from the direction of the office and holding a sheet of paper.

'I'm off duty,' I told him, 'for the first time in four years.'

'But—'

'No buts. Off duty.'

I smiled at Perkins as he took my arm and escorted me outside to where my Volkswagen was waiting, the Quarkbeast already sitting on the rear seat with a red ribbon tied around its neck in a vain attempt to make it look less fearsome. Perkins opened the driver's door for me, and I paused for a moment.

'Perky, would you excuse me just a moment?'

'Sure.'

I dashed back in and found Tiger walking to the office. A date with Perkins would be fun, but Mystical Arts Management was in my blood, and I needed to know what was going on.

'What's up, Tiger?'

'The Tralfamosaur escaped,' he said, greatly relieved. 'It's loose somewhere between here and Ross.'

'Anyone eaten?'

'Two railway workers and a fisherman.'

I clapped my hands together.

'Okay, we're going to need Lady Mawgon, Full Price and the Magnificent Boo. Have everyone outside in ten minutes ready for the off, and fetch emergency pack Alpha with several sarcastic light globes and a ball of enchanted string. I'm going to go and change.'

I found Perkins waiting for me as I ran towards the elevators.

'I'm sorry,' I said, 'it's the Tralfamosaur. Do you mind if I . . . ?'

He smiled.

'Go. But we'll do this again, yes?'

'We've lots of time,' I replied with a smile, 'a lifetime of times, I hope.'

The end of the story

No need to panic. We caught the Tralfamosaur
– eventually.

Lord Tenbury was as good as his word, and all
charges against the sorcerers were dropped. None of
those in the daisy-chain faced as much as an interview.
The King had learned his lesson by now and for the
most part left us well alone – we didn't really cross
swords again until the Spoilt Royal Princess Episode,
and the 5th Troll War, of course.

The bridge at Hereford stands there still, and looking
at it you would never know that it had ever fallen
down and been rebuilt, a testament to the potential
of Wizidrical Civil Engineering Projects.

The Magnificent Boo never came to live at Zambini
Towers, but we saw much of her in the years that
followed, and she continued her research into the
Quarkbeast with extraordinary results. Tchango
Muttney and Dame Corby became full members of
Kazam and were elevated to 'Amazing' status the
following March, the same time as Lady Mawgon
became 'Astonishing' and Moobin 'Remarkable'.

iMagic was disbanded, and although we did eventually bring the mobile phone network back online, it had to wait until after we had finished reactivating medical scanners, radar and microwave ovens.

Prince Nasil and Owen of Rhayder were grounded for a number of months until we managed to source some angel's feathers to rebuild their rugs – something that became a small adventure in itself. Mother Zenobia was returned from stone just in time for her to go *back* to stone for her 'afternoon nap'. We still see much of her, and value her wise counsel.

Perkins is still learning as he works, and as far as I can see, learning well. For her stalwart yet rash bravery during the final Blix showdown, Smantha Flynt was granted a full cadetship at Kazam, 'no matter how long it took'. She has still to get her magic licence, despite the Useless Brother's insistence that she should have a licence anyway, 'for being so utterly captivating'. She has turned him down for marriage sixty-seven times, proving perhaps that she is not *quite* as stupid as we think.

Tiger is still learning about running the company, and if Zambini does not appear by the time I am eighteen, will take over from me then. He will be good at it, and likely better than I.

As for the once All Powerful Conrad Blix, we donated him to the Hereford Museum, where he can still be seen to this day. His perfidious exploits are outlined for all to read, and his unseeing granite form is insulted and derided by the many schoolchildren who pass him every day. His attempt to murder half the residents of Hereford and seize the throne is often talked about, and his lack of compassion, rampant greed and murderous intent are often compared to those of his mad evil genius grandfather, Blix the Hideously Barbarous.

It's what he would have wanted.

Jennifer Strange will be back in:

The Return of Shandar

About the author

———

Jasper Fforde is the critically acclaimed author of *The Last Dragonslayer*, *Shades of Grey*, the Nursery Crime books: *The Big Over Easy* and *The Fourth Bear* and the Thursday Next novels: *The Eyre Affair*, *Lost in a Good Book*, *The Well of Lost Plots*, *Something Rotten*, *First Among Sequels*, *One of Our Thursdays is Missing* and *The Woman Who Died a Lot*.

After giving up a varied career in the film world, he now lives and writes in Wales, and has a passion for aviation.

You can visit www.jasperfforde.com to find out more.

Last year we ran a Draw a Dragon competition to celebrate the creation of the Last Dragonslayer series. There were lots of wonderful entries for Jasper Fforde to choose from, but the winner is . . .

George Riley from the Central Foundation Boys' School

Jasper says:

'This was a very tricky decision for us as the quality was very high indeed, but after much consideration we decided that George Riley's was the winning entry. We felt that not only was it a very striking image that had been undertaken with much skill and thought, but also captured the spirit of Jennifer's world, with cars and cooling towers. We also liked the dragon with a long, sinuous neck for peering inquisitively at stuff, and quite naturally, a long tail to balance it. It's a lovely picture – thank you!'

The winning picture is displayed on the next page.

George Riley
Central Foundation
Boys' School

The beginning of the adventure – the first
bewitching instalment in

The Last Dragonslayer series

JASPER FFORDE

The Last Dragonslayer

In the good old days, magic was powerful, unregulated by
government, and even the largest spell could be woven
without filling in magic release form B1-7g.

Then the magic started fading away.

Fifteen-year-old Jennifer Strange runs Kazam, an employ-
ment agency for soothsayers and sorcerers. But work is
drying up. Drain cleaner is cheaper than a spell, and even
magic carpets are reduced to pizza delivery.

So it's a surprise when the visions start. Not only do they
predict the death of the Last Dragon at the hands of a
dragonslayer, they also point to Jennifer, and say something
is coming.

Big Magic . . .

NOW AVAILABLE IN PAPERBACK

HODDER

Explore the world of Jasper Fforde's

The Last Dragonslayer

Now available as an App for Apple iPhone and iPad

Discover more about the Ununited Kingdoms,
from the grim wastes of Trollvania to the Corporate Kingdom of Financia.
Become a true Dragonslayer's apprentice by reading
The Dragonslayer's Manual, updated regularly by RSS feed.
Learn about Quarkbeasts and Shridloos, and the other fantastic beasts
that live in the Kingdoms – and of course, the Dragons who once terrorised the land.

You can also read the full text as an Ebook
and listen to the synchronised unabridged audiobook.

Find it online at the iTunes App store
http://itunes.apple.com/gb/artist/hachette-uk/id361205465

HODDER &
STOUGHTON

Enhanced Editions

To find out more about

The Song of the Quarkbeast

keep up to date with Jasper Fforde, or for
fun, forums, merchandise, blogs, photos,
games, the Fforde Ffiesta, book upgrades, newsletters,
questionariums, competitions, Thursday Next X-Treme,
films, special features, free stuff, appearances, signings, tour
details, reader parodies, fan clubs, songbooks, dodo
emporiums, the Toast Marketing Board
and much, much more, go to

www.jasperfforde.com

The sixth book in the Thursday Next series

JASPER FFORDE

One of Our Thursdays is Missing

It is a time of unrest in the BookWorld. Only the diplomatic skills of ace literary detective Thursday Next can avert a devastating genre war. But a week before the peace talks, Thursday vanishes. Has she simply returned home to the RealWorld or is this something more sinister?

All is not yet lost. Living at the quiet end of speculative fiction is the written Thursday Next, eager to prove herself worth of her illustrious namesake.

The written Thursday is soon hot on the trail of her factual alter-ego, and quickly stumbles upon a plot so fiendish that it threatens the very BookWorld itself.

NOW AVAILABLE IN PAPERBACK

HODDER

The latest book in The Thursday Next series

JASPER FFORDE

The Woman Who Died a Lot

'The events described here occurred during a busier-than-usual week in the late Summer of 2004. A week that began with a trip into Swindon in order to find a job, and ended with a pillar of cleansing fire descending from the heavens, a rethink on the Wessex Library Services operating budget and my son shooting Gavin Watkins dead. The last one was a serious downer – especially for Gavin.'

The Bookworld's leading enforcement officer Thursday Next is at a low point in her life: she is four months into an enforced semi-retirement following a near fatal assassination attempt. She is yet to walk without a stick, has double vision more often than she doesn't, and limited mobility in her left arm.

A time, then, for relaxation, recuperation, and rest. A time to spend with her beloved family, avoid stress, take it easy, meet old friends and do very little.

If only life were that simple . . .

NOW AVAILABLE IN HARDBACK

**HODDER &
STOUGHTON**

The first in the Nursery Crime series

JASPER FFORDE

The Big Over Easy

It's Easter in Reading – a bad time for eggs – and no one can remember the last sunny day. Humpty Dumpty, well-known nursery favourite, large egg, ex-convict and former millionaire philanthropist is found shattered beneath a wall in a shabby area of town.

Following the pathologist's careful reconstruction of Humpty's shell, Detective Inspector Jack Spratt and his Sergeant Mary Mary are soon grappling with a sinister plot involving cross-border money laundering, the illegal Béarnaise sauce market, corporate politics and the cut and thrust world of international chiropody.

As Jack and Mary stumble around the streets of Reading in Jack's Lime Green Austin Allegro, the clues pile up, but Jack has his own problems to deal with.

And on top of everything else, the Jellyman is coming to town . . .

NOW AVAILABLE IN PAPERBACK

HODDER

JASPER FFORDE

Shades of Grey

Hundreds of years in the future, after the Something that Happened, the world is an alarmingly different place. Life is lived according to The Rulebook and social hierarchy is determined by your perception of colour.

Eddie Russett is an above average Red who dreams of moving up the ladder by marriage to Constance Oxblood. Until he is sent to the Outer Fringes where he meets Jane – a lowly Grey with an uncontrollable temper and a desire to see him killed.

For Eddie, it's love at first sight. But his infatuation will lead him to discover that all is not as it seems in a world where everything that looks black and white is really shades of grey . . .

NOW AVAILABLE IN PAPERBACK

HODDER